HER
CHILD'S
CRY

BOOKS BY S.A. DUNPHY

BOYLE & KENEALLY SERIES

Bring Her Home

Lost Graves

HER
CHILD'S
CRY

S.A. DUNPHY

bookouture

Published by Bookouture in 2022

An imprint of Storyfire Ltd.
Carmelite House
50 Victoria Embankment
London EC4Y 0DZ

www.bookouture.com

ISBN: 978-1-80314-209-8
eBook ISBN: 978-1-80314-208-1

For Nola, who breathed life into Arizona Rose and gave her not just a heartbeat, but a beautiful soul.

PROLOGUE

SMOKE AND MIRRORS

'Between 2015 and 2019 a total of one hundred children were abducted in Ireland, one third of whom were taken within the Dublin Metropolitan area. Fifty-six of those children have never been found. Their cases remain open.'

Excerpt from Report on Child Abduction, compiled by Ireland's Central Statistics Office, 2019

It happened in the space of five minutes: one moment nine-year-old Arizona Rose Blake (everyone called her Rosie) was in bed in her private room in Beaumont Hospital in Dublin, and the next she wasn't. No one saw her being taken; no one heard her cry out.

In short, no one knew what happened.

But she was gone, of that there could be no doubt.

The oncology nurse rostered to work with Arizona during her stay carried out a routine check on the child at 10 a.m. on the morning she disappeared. She'd been nursing in the paedi-atric cancer ward in Beaumont for twelve years and believed, in the way hardened veterans of tough professions often do, that she'd seen it all.

Yet this was a first, even for her, a patient vanishing as if into thin air. She was wholly unprepared for it. She was used to loss, but this was different.

It was a bitter part of her job that, all too often, she lost children in her care, not through any negligence but simply because the enemy she fought was relentless.

That kind of loss you were trained for. You expected it, saw it coming. It was dreadful, but it was an aspect of what she did for a living. And thankfully, the medical profession was able to keep patients alive much more effectively than they used to.

Yet there were still some who didn't make it.

Medicine had come on in leaps and bounds. While the armies of carcinogenic cells that waged war inside the kids she worked with could be held at bay for much longer than was previously possible – and in some cases the children could go on to lead full and happy lives – in others there was nothing that could be done other than make her small charges as comfortable as possible while they waited for the inevitable.

For an unfortunate few, cancer was probably going to be terminal.

Arizona Rose Blake was one of those children – without constant treatment, she would have been dead more than a year ago.

Peter Blake, Rosie's father, worked for one of Dublin's leading investment firms, so the Blakes were extremely wealthy. Rosie's hospital rooms were always full of every toy and gadget a kid could hope for, and Shauna, her mother, had told the medical staff that her daughter would never want for anything. If Rosie expressed a desire for an item, regardless of cost, she would have it as soon as its procurement was possible.

Yet somehow, such indulgence had not made the child rude

or crass. She remained, in spite of pain and cosseting, sweet and kind and gentle to all.

On the day Rosie disappeared, the rostered nurse called to her room as part of her rounds checked that the machines and pumps were delivering the medication into her system, and asked if the little girl would like anything. The child expressed she would like some water, and Tina went off to get her some.

On her way back to Rosie's room, Belinda, a healthcare assistant, had stopped the nurse to ask about changes to another patient's medication, and they'd had a brief chat about it. The conversation had taken no more than three minutes, after which the nurse returned immediately to Rosie's room, a fresh jug of water in hand.

And when she got there, Rosie was gone.

The nurse stood just inside the door, blinking. Her eyes told her the bed was empty, but this made no sense: how could a terminally ill child, one for whom even sitting upright was a challenge, not be in her bed? She shook her head, closed and unclosed her eyes, and looked again.

The bed was still empty, its blankets pulled back to reveal a rumpled sheet, the intravenous line that had been feeding chemotherapy drugs into the cannula in Rosie's arm slowly dripping its life-saving contents, mingled with a single swirl of blood, into a small puddle on the grey tiled floor.

The paralysis was followed by a burst of motion as the nurse, her heart pounding now, rushed into the room's en-suite bathroom, finding it as empty of Rosie's presence as the bedroom had been.

Still thinking the little girl had, possibly due to a state of chemo-induced psychosis (which is not unheard of), torn out her drip and somehow, in a burst of manically induced strength, wandered off, the nurse ran into the corridor, peering first one way and then the other, looking for the diminutive figure.

'Have you seen Rosie Blake?' she asked, grabbing an orderly

who was coming towards her, rolling another patient on a gurney.

'I'm not supposed to take her anywhere today,' the young man said, trying to pull away.

'You didn't pass her?'

The nurse still had him in a tight grip, her fingers digging into his shoulder, anxiety writ large on her face.

The porter looked confused and just shook his head, finally tearing himself from her and continuing on his way.

'Maybe someone scheduled an emergency procedure and didn't tell you,' he suggested.

It took the nurse a further two minutes to establish this was not the case.

And that was when the panic set in.

'*Rosie! Rosie Blake!*'

Every ward and private room on the cancer wing was checked at a run, nurses barrelling past each other, faces etched with worry, calling the little girl's name. It was a frantic, panicked search that was completed rapidly and yielded nothing.

Five minutes after the child was found to be missing, it was clear something was seriously wrong – no one had seen Rosie leaving her room, no one admitted to taking her anywhere, and when security were called, they observed that the CCTV cameras for the oncology wards had cut out half an hour before Rosie vanished and were still offline.

A brief examination of the system showed that someone had simply removed the relevant fuse.

'Lock the hospital down,' the chief of security said to his head of operations. 'No one comes in and no one goes out until we find her.'

The CO immediately sent a text message he had stored in a folder on his phone to his entire security team as well as the hospital's general manager. It was a message he never thought he would have to send. It read: *All exits and entrances to the hospital buildings and grounds to be sealed forthwith. Every ward, treatment room, waiting area, storage space, elevator, parking garage, car park and vehicle therein to be searched without delay. Every individual: staff, visitor and patient to be accounted for. A patient is missing, and we need them located immediately. More information to follow.*

He rapidly followed this with a photograph of the missing child and a brief message: *This is Rosie Blake. She has cancer and will die if she does not receive regular treatment. This is literally a life-or-death situation. Find her now.*

The process of combing the hospital and its environs was rehearsed several times each year along with the fire drill and other security procedures. Teams of staff broke away from their normal duties and, using a grid system, searched every square inch of the building and the grounds around it. That day it took twenty minutes, which was five minutes longer than hospital policy stated it was supposed to, but as well as rooms and garages, cupboards and kitchen reach-ins were also examined – Rosie was tiny, and anywhere she might have crawled was checked thoroughly. By the time the last section of the medical complex had been searched, there was still no sign of Rosie Blake.

The CO of security called the hospital's chief nursing officer with the news, who in turn contacted the general manager.

'Call the police,' the GM said, an audible tremor in his voice.

But it wasn't the police who found out who had taken Rosie Blake.

It was a hillwalker named Dave Gibb.

Unfortunately, knowing who had taken her did not help anyone to understand why.

That would come a lot later.

PART ONE

AMONG THE HILLS

'One of the oldest human needs is having someone to wonder where you are when you don't come home at night.'

Margaret Mead

An hour later, criminal behaviourist Jessie Boyle and Detective Sergeant Seamus Keneally sat opposite Peter and Shauna Blake in a conference room in Garda HQ in Harcourt Street, close to Dublin's St Stephen's Green. The room was long and narrow, the walls painted a nondescript cream, the only furniture a glass-topped table and eight not very comfortable chairs.

Dawn Wilson, Ireland's Garda commissioner, dressed in a grey trouser suit rather than the blue-and-red uniform of her rank, joined them for the interview, wheeling a trolley laden with pots of both tea and coffee, mugs and a variety of pastries as she arrived. As the highest-ranking officer in the Irish police force, Dawn could easily have asked someone else to do this job for her (there were any number of interns who would have happily obliged) but she wasn't that kind of leader. Jessie knew this was partly because the commissioner was a control freak, but she was also aware her old friend didn't have the patience to wait for anyone else to do the myriad mundane tasks each day presented – so she just did them herself.

The room's final occupant that day was Professor Brandon Cuddihy. The cancer specialist had slate-grey hair and precipitous cheekbones. Jessie found it hard to put an age on him – he could have been anywhere from fifty to seventy.

'I reckoned no one had time for breakfast, so I've come to the rescue,' Dawn said, smiling. Tall and slim, Dawn wore her red hair pulled back in a tight bun. She spoke with a soft Northern Irish accent – the commissioner had grown up in rural County Antrim. 'Don't be shy now – help yourselves.'

Not needing to be told twice, Seamus, his stomach audibly grumbling, rose from his seat and made for the food.

'Nice one, boss. I'm starving!' he whispered to Dawn.

The Blakes remained where they were, looking shell-shocked and pale. Jessie waited for her partner to finish loading up a plate with one of each type of the baked goods his boss had provided before getting a black coffee for herself. Dawn had tea and a Danish. Professor Cuddihy, after some pondering, had the same.

When everyone was back in their seats, the commissioner said: 'Mr and Mrs Blake, I'd like to introduce you to two of my investigators: Jessie Boyle and Seamus Keneally. They're going to be taking the lead on your daughter's case.'

Seamus stood up and extended his hand to shake, but Peter ignored him, nodding at Jessie and Seamus instead, while Shauna gave a half-hearted smile that was more of a grimace. The young detective withdrew his hand, trying not to look insulted.

Jessie and Seamus, along with their colleague Terri Kehoe, made up a task force specially formed by Dawn. They were called in to consult when a case came across the commissioner's desk that seemed unusual or had the Gardaí's rank and file stumped. Each member of the team brought something exceptional to the table: Jessie was a gifted and instinctive profiler with a deep-rooted understanding of human nature; Seamus was a dogged investigator with a laser-like attention to detail and the capacity to make links and see patterns of evidence others would miss; and Terri had an almost mystical ability when it came to research, finding threads of information and following trails through both physical and online sources with incredible skill.

When cases seemed unsolvable or the evidence was just too flimsy to do anything with, Jessie, Seamus and Terri were called in. The abduction of Rosie Blake certainly fit that criteria.

'I hate having to drag you in here during such a stressful time,' Dawn went on, ignoring the rudeness they'd just witnessed from Peter Blake. 'But if you watch television at all, you'll know that the first twenty-four hours are crucial in any abduction.'

'That's hardly our fault, is it?' Peter snapped.

He was a short, stockily built man with sandy-coloured hair and a ruddy complexion. Stress had left dark rings under his close-set eyes, and salt-and-pepper stubble coated the lower half of his pudgy face, which, that morning, wore an expression of barely contained rage.

'No one is insinuating it is,' Dawn said, her tone even. 'I thought it might be worthwhile to ask Professor Cuddihy to come in so we can talk about the reality of Rosie's situation. We can all ask any questions we might have. It's important we all know what we're dealing with.'

'What can you tell us about Rosie's condition, Professor?' Jessie asked.

'Can I just say, Ms Boyle,' the specialist said, 'I find this whole business extremely discomfiting. I don't think I've ever come across anything quite like it. I mean, to have a patient snatched right off the ward, right under everyone's noses... it's simply unprecedented.'

'I can imagine you're very shocked by what's happened,' Jessie said. 'But we need to move away from that for the moment: that a child being taken from a hospital is troubling is a given. Can you tell us what level of risk Rosie has been exposed to?'

'I cannot state in strong enough terms the gravity of the situation Rosie Blake is in if she does not receive treatment,' the professor said sternly. 'Her symptoms are kept in check by a very carefully balanced programme of medication and chemotherapy. Without it, her condition will rapidly deteriorate.'

'Paint a picture for us,' Seamus said. He glanced over at the Blakes. 'I'm sorry if this is upsetting for you, but we need to know what we're dealing with. I hope you understand.'

'Detective, none of this is new information,' Peter Blake said tersely. 'Do you think my wife and I are unaware of the dangers our little girl is facing?'

He looked at Dawn with undisguised anger. 'I do not understand why we're here!'

'You're Rosie's parents,' Dawn said gently. 'Professor Cuddihy knows her medical needs, but you know everything else about her. It's unthinkable we'd have any kind of discussion about managing the case without you present.'

That seemed to mollify Blake, and he sat back, quiet, if still a bit sulky.

'Please go on, Professor,' Dawn said.

'Of course,' Cuddihy said, clearing his throat. 'Rosie has a diagnosis of pancreatoblastoma, a rare form of pancreatic cancer. Without her course of cisplatin and doxorubicin, the mass in Rosie's abdomen will begin to swell within approximately two days.'

'As quickly as that?' Jessie asked.

'I'm afraid so. This will at first be mildly uncomfortable, but you see, the location of Rosie's tumour, right at the head of the pancreas, presents some serious issues. Uncontrolled swelling, over the following three or four days, will compress her duodenum, causing severe pain. This restriction will induce vomiting, fever and anaemia, which will ultimately result in Rosie lapsing into unconsciousness, and finally a coma.'

'In six days,' Jessie said. 'You're telling me she'd be beyond help in six days?'

'I might be able to save her if she's recovered by day seven,' the professor said. 'I'm quite good at what I do. Day ten would be the point of no return.'

'We're quite good at what we do, too,' Jessie said. 'I have no intention of getting anywhere near day seven.'

'Amen to that,' Professor Cuddihy said.

'You've received no ransom demands?' Seamus asked the Blakes around a mouthful of scone.

'We've had no communication regarding Rosie at all,' Peter said.

'Are you sure?' Jessie prompted. 'You haven't had any unusual messages or emails? Something odd in the post perhaps? Criminals are getting much better at covering their tracks. The demand might be coded or encrypted in something else.'

'Why would a kidnapper make their ransom demand difficult to spot?' Shauna asked. 'Maybe I'm being stupid, but that doesn't make sense to me.'

'It would be written in a form that wouldn't be immediately obvious to someone like me or Seamus,' Jessie said, 'but would be completely transparent to you or your husband.'

'I don't follow,' Peter said.

'You're in investment,' Jessie explained. 'I imagine you get all kinds of reports and documents that if I were to read them would make no sense to me at all. It'd be like they were written in a foreign language.'

Peter Blake shrugged.

'Under those circumstances,' Jessie went on, ignoring his scornful stance, 'it wouldn't be difficult to place a sequence of words or symbols into such a document which *you* would immediately understand meant something alarming. That would cause you to sit up straight and pay attention. I don't know stocks and shares, but I bet there's a term that means crisis, or crash or whatever the correct language is.'

'There are several different phrases,' Peter agreed.

Jessie nodded, expecting him to expand. When he didn't, she said: 'Such as?'

There was a flash of irritation again, but he got himself under control quickly this time.

Jessie eyed him with a neutral gaze, but behind it she was taking everything in: his body language, the tone of his voice, the rapid, jerky, nervous movement of his eye, the way his tongue darted out to moisten his dry lips.

He's coming apart, she thought. *And that's totally natural for a parent whose child has been taken. But he's angry too – and defensive. Which could just be his way of coping or might mean he's hiding something.*

This thought was followed with: *Of course, whatever he's hiding may well have nothing to do with his daughter's abduction. How many financiers play hard and fast with the laws governing what they do?*

'Could you give me an indication of what that kind of language might be?' she prompted him again.

Taking a deep breath Peter said: 'The work I do is complex, so the language reflects its subtleties. An issue anyone who works on the markets regularly faces would be the "weekend effect", where Monday often sees a dip in revenue – a severe weekend effect can cause panic though, even among experienced brokers. At the other end of the scale, the more extreme, we speak about the markets going "black", meaning everyone is trying to dump their stocks and get out before things get really bad. Similarly, you might hear someone talking about a "bank run", which is where the financial institutions are attempting to offload debts they've purchased as quickly as possible in the run-up to an anticipated crash.'

He paused, giving Jessie a hard look. 'Do you want me to go on? Is this helping?'

'That'll do for now,' Jessie said patiently. 'The point I'm making is that if you saw mention of something like that in a report, you'd immediately pay attention and really notice whatever follows.'

'I suppose so, yes.'

'That would be the ideal place to embed a demand or a message of intent. Such a communication could be worded so it wouldn't raise the suspicion of anyone other than you.'

Jessie turned to Shauna. 'To answer your question, Mrs Blake, people who commit this type of crime have learned that the police are getting much better at staging stings at the point of exchange, where the victim is handed back after the ransom has been paid. Ransom notes are, of course, a major piece of evidence, so kidnappers will often craft notes they can distance themselves from, something that can be plausibly dismissed as a misinterpretation. If the police happen to be on the scene, the kidnappers can claim they never asked for money, and were simply being good citizens and returning a lost child to their parents.'

'And they get away with that?' Shauna asked incredulously.

'Sometimes,' Dawn said. 'If they cover their tracks well enough. There's no law against bringing a child back to their family.'

Peter looked fit to explode. 'Well, the phrases you're highlighting have not appeared in any document I've received over the past twenty-four hours. Not for the past few months, actually.'

'It doesn't have to have been in a formal document,' Jessie said. 'A personal email? A handwritten note, a memo...'

'Nothing,' Peter said firmly. 'This really is a waste of time. Can we please move to the next item on the agenda?'

'You've looked too?' Seamus asked Shauna, pretending he hadn't heard Peter's attempt to derail the interview.

The woman nodded.

'I mostly talk to friends on social media,' she said. 'Facebook and Instagram. I've been through all my direct messages, and there's nothing sinister or out of the ordinary.'

'Seamus and I have a colleague, Terri, who's really good with technology and can find things most people wouldn't even know are missing,' Jessie said. 'There might not be a message on your emails or your social-media accounts, but it's very possible someone has been watching you, hacking into your system and using the information there to build a picture of your movements, but also of *Rosie's* movements. Shauna, I bet you talk about your daughter's treatment and hospital stays to friends online.'

The woman nodded. 'I know some people who also have kids with cancer diagnoses. They... they understand what we're all going through, so I do chat with them about how her treatment is going. Did... did I cause this to happen?'

'No!' Jessie said, shaking her head vehemently. 'Of course you talk to friends about your life. I'm not saying for a moment you've done anything wrong. How can you possibly know if anyone is watching?'

'Do you use a calendar on your phone or laptop to make a note of Rosie's procedures and appointments?' Seamus asked.

'Yes, I do. I use the calendar attached to my Outlook account.'

Jessie and Seamus exchanged glances.

'I'd like Terri to have a look over your accounts, if that's okay,' Jessie said.

Peter bristled immediately. 'We are not on trial here! I deal with highly sensitive and deeply confidential material on a daily basis, and I do not believe any of my clients would be happy if they knew some tech-head was thumbing their way through private communications!'

Jessie raised her hand, trying to staunch the flow of his ire.

'Mr Blake, we're not trying to catch you out or suggest you've done anything untoward. I assure you, we're not looking for any discrepancies in your work practices or anything of a personal nature that might cause either of you embarrassment. We're searching for clues as to why your little girl has been taken, and who might have her now – that's our purpose in looking, nothing more. Your online activity might hold important information. It's almost impossible to move about online without leaving a trail, and our friend is an expert at finding those digital footprints.'

'I'm sorry, but it's out of the question,' Peter said. 'Precision Investments has a reputation that is unimpeachable. I won't compromise that.'

Dawn sat forward in her chair and said mildly: 'Mr Blake, I'm going to leave room that you're tired and upset. Anyone in your position would be. But let me remind you, we are not some private security firm you've hired to find your wee girl. We're the police. So while Jessie was being courteous asking for access to your emails and accounts, remember that I can go to a judge and secure a warrant that will give us leave to view them, with your cooperation or without it. It'd be nice if you handed over your login details, but believe me, Terri could hack around them without breaking a sweat. She's a very talented lady.'

Peter looked as if he was about to keel over. He turned a frightening shade of puce.

'Do we understand each other, Mr Blake?'

He nodded.

'Good.' Dawn smiled, sitting back and taking a swig of tea. 'Glad we got that out of the way.'

'If you haven't received a ransom by now, I doubt that you

will anyway,' Seamus said, attempting to get the conversation back on track.

'If they don't want money,' Shauna said, looking as if tears were hovering on the edge of her vision, 'what might this be about?'

'That's a hard question to answer,' Jessie said. 'It could be someone who bears a grudge and wants to strike out at you. I'm sure you've made enemies through your work, Mr Blake.'

'None that would do this!' Peter spluttered.

'You move large quantities of money around,' Seamus said. 'I'm guessing some of what you do involves corporate buyouts, closing businesses, people losing their jobs?'

Peter shrugged again. Jessie noted that a shrug seemed to be his response when he didn't approve of the question. She mentally filed it away for future reference.

'Losing a job is a good reason to be angry,' Seamus pointed out. 'It's something that can really mess up a person's life.'

'Would someone like that hurt Rosie?' Shauna asked, and the tears came.

'We have no reason to believe she's been harmed,' Jessie said. 'Another scenario is that she was taken as a result of some kind of rescue fantasy. I worked a case in the UK – a little boy was taken from a children's hospice by a member of staff who had become overly attached and was convinced they could save the kid's life through alternative therapies.'

'Rosie needs her medicine,' Shauna sobbed. 'I don't even want to think about what she'll go through without it.'

'We're going to do our very best to find her,' Jessie said.

Shauna Blake was now sobbing uncontrollably, and Dawn said: 'I think we'll leave it there for now.'

Jessie walked the Blakes back out to their car, a BMW i3 that Peter had parked in a disabled zone just outside Garda HQ's front door.

She noted that the man fumbled for his wife's hand as soon as they were outside the meeting room. Shauna accepted the gesture though seemed unmoved by it. Jessie reminded herself the woman was going through emotional turmoil and decided not to read too much into it.

'Can I ask you both something before you go?' Jessie said as Peter pulled a key fob out of his pocket and unlocked the car.

'We're both very tired, Ms Boyle,' he said. 'Can you make it quick?'

'I was wondering if you might tell me about Rosie.'

Peter looked blankly back at her, and Shauna looked confused.

'What... what do you mean?' she asked.

'I believe that the victim of an abduction can teach you an awful lot about the person who took them. So with that in mind, what is Rosie like? I mean, I know she's sick, but I'm sure that doesn't define her. I want to know if she's funny or quiet or fiery or sensitive? Is she a big fan of a particular TV show or a series of books? What does she like to eat? I want to know as much as you can tell me.'

'That's not a quick conversation,' Peter said, opening the car and getting inside.

Shauna blinked, her hand on the roof of the BMW.

'Rosie is kind,' she said. 'She can get tetchy sometimes when she feels sick or is in pain, but even then she's never mean. She likes a show on Nickelodeon called *Henry Danger*, and she'll listen to a song called "Runaway" by the singer Aurora twenty times in a row and still want to listen to it again. She plays Roblox – there's a game where you trade fish or something like that. I'm not really sure how it works, but I know she's mad about it. She loves comic books of all kinds, and she and I both enjoy David Walliams books.'

Peter beeped the horn impatiently, and Shauna threw an evil look his way but kept talking.

'She doesn't eat very much because the treatment doesn't allow her to. She loves Apache Pizza and Ben and Jerry's Phish Food ice cream, but since getting sick she's likely to throw it right back up after eating it. But sometimes she binges on them anyway, even though it breaks my heart to see her so sick. She'll tell you it was worth it, but when I see the discomfort she's in, I'm not so sure.'

Jessie smiled softly, though she could feel the pain radiating from the woman.

'If you want to win her over, buy her a bag of Sour Patch Kids sweets. She adores them, and they don't seem to sicken her the way a lot of other foods do.'

'I'll remember that,' Jessie said. 'You've been a great help. Is there anyone else I might talk to about her? Just to get a perspective.'

'The hospital has a play therapist who would come in to see

her from time to time,' Shauna said. 'The hospital has her details. I really must go.'

'Of course. Thanks for your time,' Jessie said.

As the BMW pulled out of the hospital car park, Jessie wondered why two parents who were obviously devastated by the loss of their daughter seemed so reluctant to help get her back.

Dawn and Seamus were waiting in the chief inspector's office (which had been loaned to them) when Jessie came back inside.

'What do you think?' Dawn asked as Jessie sat down.

'I think that, despite what I said to Professor Cuddihy, we've got an impossible task,' the behaviourist sighed. 'We're on a countdown to a child's death and don't even have a place to begin looking.'

'We'll go mad if we focus on that,' Dawn replied. 'Let's work with what we do have: what did you make of the parents?'

'There's something not right about them, but it's impossible to tell if it's just how they're coping with the stress of what's happened,' Jessie said. 'I mean, this is any parent's worst nightmare, but you can multiply that tenfold where the child in question is terminally ill.'

'Do you have any sense they're in some way involved?' Dawn asked. It was almost unthinkable, but with any crime you always looked at the immediate family first.

'As I said, their behaviour is odd, but it's not enough to implicate them,' Jessie said. 'They're under unbelievable pressure.'

'It's a fucking awful situation,' Dawn said. 'I mean, if she's not found in time and dies, the charges could justifiably be upgraded to murder, or downgraded... I'm not sure what the correct terminology is. Seamus, help me out.'

'Well if you don't know, I'm damn sure I don't,' Seamus retorted.

'Where are we on this, Dawn?' Jessie asked. 'What's being done to find Rosie right now?'

'Quite a bit, even though it feels like nothing,' the commissioner said. 'Forensics are going over Rosie's room with a fine-toothed comb, so hopefully they'll have something for us. Mostly, though, it's in the hands of the tech people. There's nowhere concrete to look for Rosie until we can get a lead on who took her and which direction they went. So there's a team reviewing all the CCTV footage from inside the hospital before and after the feed went dead. The kidnapper must have been in the building at some point, so I'm hoping they'll look suspicious. We're also looking at traffic cameras on all roads leading to and from Beaumont. It's not much, but we don't have a lot else.'

'I'll get Terri to start digging into the Blakes right away,' Jessie said. 'Hopefully we'll have the logins to their social media and emails before too long, but chances are the key to what's going on is already staring us right in the face. Terri will know how to pare back the white noise and get to the kernel of what Peter and Shauna are all about.'

'And in the meantime, we might as well just go out into the street and start asking people if they've seen Rosie Blake,' Seamus said.

'I have a team interviewing the staff on the paediatric cancer ward,' Dawn said. 'Seamus, do you want to head over there and coordinate things? See if you can't fine-tune what they're doing?'

'I can do that, boss. It sure beats doing nothing.'

'I'm going to speak to Rosie's play therapist,' Jessie said. 'See if she's mentioned anything in her therapy that might help.'

'Will she give you that information?' Seamus asked. 'Isn't there some client confidentiality thing in place?'

'Not where there's a child protection concern,' Jessie said. 'And you won't find a more serious concern than this.'

'True dat,' Seamus said.

Jessie gave him a look. 'Since when did you start saying "true dat"?'

'I've gone very street lately,' Seamus said. 'Since we're back in the big smoke, I thought I should start getting a bit more urban. Hangin' with my Dublin homeboys. You know what I'm sayin'?'

'You were raised in the wilds of Kerry,' Jessie said. 'You play traditional Irish music, you enjoy hurling and you're a native Irish speaker. I don't think it's possible to get any *less* urban than you!'

'I take offence at that,' Seamus said. 'You can play the accordion and still be ghetto.'

'Seamus, I really don't think you can,' Jessie said.

'Boss, you have the casting vote,' Seamus said, looking at Dawn. 'Do you reckon I've earned my street credentials... um... innit?'

Dawn just shook her head and sighed deeply. 'Seamus Keneally, if you want to think you're some kind of gangsta undercover cop, who am I to argue with you? Now would you kindly take your street-speaking ass out of here and do some work? The clock is ticking.'

'I will, boss. Thanks, boss,' Seamus said, grinning triumphantly at Jessie.

'She only said that to shut you up,' the behaviourist said tetchily.

'Doesn't matter. She still said it.'

'Seamus?'
'Yeah?'
'Shut up.'
'Fo' shizzle.'
'Oh for feck's sake.'

4

Marina Halford, Beaumont's play therapist, was a petite blonde in her late thirties with feathered hair, who dressed in a style somewhere between hippy, gypsy chic and a Disney princess. The fact she spoke in a dramatic, self-conscious manner made Jessie think there was something less than transparent about her, which seemed a bit contradictory for a therapist.

They met in the playroom of a community centre in Dún Laoghaire where the therapist had a practice.

'I'm not sure I should be speaking with you, Ms Boyle,' Marina Halford said. 'Even though Rosie is a child, she's still entitled to therapeutic privilege.'

I hate it when Seamus is right, she thought. *He'll gloat for ages about this!*

'I'm not here to ask about your therapy sessions per se,' Jessie said. 'I want to know about her personality. And if she's mentioned anything, directly or through her play, that might give us a clue as to who might have taken her.'

Jessie and the therapist were sitting on child-sized chairs – she knew the correct term was 'small world' furniture – and the behaviourist was fighting not to feel just a little ridiculous.

'You suspect she was taken by someone she knows?' Halford asked.

'There was no disturbance reported,' Jessie said. 'So yes, it seems reasonable to assume Rosie trusted the person who took her and went with them without question.'

'A family member?'

'Maybe,' Jessie said. 'We have very little to go on, so I'll take any information you might be able to offer.'

'Rosie was... *is* a remarkably independent child. Most kids who have experienced childhood illness become clinging and insecurely attached to their parents, but my experience of Rosie is that she has externalised the caring roles in her life.'

'External to her family, you mean?' Jessie asked.

'Yes. It seems to me that Rosie does not see her parents as safe figures, as constants. I've seen it time and again, particularly in her artwork, that there is a clear and defined separation.'

'Do you have any of this artwork?'

'Of course.'

'Can I see it?'

'I'm really unsure how appropriate that is.'

Jessie fought not to lose her temper. Somewhere at the back of her mind she could sense grains of sand slipping through the hole at the centre of an hourglass, and with each one, a moment of Rosie Blake's life was written off.

'Ms Halford, can I suggest you ring Shauna Blake and get her permission to share her daughter's information with me?'

'It's not really about getting Rosie's parents' consent,' the therapist said.

'Then we're at something of an impasse,' Jessie said, 'because Rosie herself is currently uncontactable.'

The two women gazed at once another for a long moment, neither speaking, each sizing the other up. Finally, after what felt like an age, Halford stood and went to a filing cabinet, returning a moment later with a sheaf of paper. Sitting back down, she passed the bundle over to Jessie.

'The top five are all depictions of Rosie's family. It's obvious she sees her parents at a remove from her.'

The pictures could not have told the story more plainly. Jessie had studied art and play therapy at postgraduate level while working for the London Met and believed it could be a powerful tool in understanding aspects of young people's lives that they were either unable or unwilling to verbalise.

Each image was different: one was done in paint, one in crayon, another with felt-tip pens, yet another was a pencil sketch and the final one was a collage. Yet each showed a small, lonely-looking figure set off to the side or in the corner of the page, while two larger figures seemed to be talking or were drinking and eating or in the car – it didn't matter what they were doing, whatever it was, they were clearly doing it far away from their daughter. She was not involved in their lives.

'Have you seen the family together?' Jessie asked.

'On a number of occasions, yes.'

'Did they seem distant?'

'No, but parents are often on their best behaviour when they're under the microscope.'

'So you doubted the... the *realness* of what you saw?'

'I doubted the emotional veracity of it, yes.'

'And you feel the upshot of this is that Rosie Blake has learned to stand on her own two feet and seek caring, stable adult figures elsewhere?'

'Look at the next set of pictures,' Halford said. 'When I asked Rosie to draw what it was like being in hospital, this is what she created.'

The images that followed were full of smiling, happy-looking faces. The same small figure from the previous pictures was here, sometimes in bed, sometimes in a wheelchair, always attached to tubes or drips, but instead of being isolated, in these pictures she was part of a community. There was always someone at her side, always a person caring for her.

'Hospital is where her emotional needs are met,' Jessie said.

'Yes,' Halford said. 'I've never heard Rosie mention any extended family. I'm sure she has them: aunts, uncles, cousins and such. But if she does, she never references them.'

'What are you saying?' Jessie asked.

'The *only* people Rosie Blake really trusted were staff at the hospital.'

Jessie nodded and riffled through the pages. Suddenly she stopped.

'What does this one represent?' she asked, holding up a page that contained what looked to be an oddly shaped stick figure, its elongated limbs multiply jointed, its legs ending in forked feet, its head seemingly narrow and horned.

'Rosie drew that figure a lot,' Halford said. 'She told me an odd man visited her one day and left a figure made of sticks and grass on her windowsill. One of the nurses came and took it away.'

'She didn't know who this man was?' Jessie asked, finding the image unnerving.

'I've never been wholly certain she didn't dream him,' Halford said. 'She said he came in while she was attached to her chemo drip. He was completely bald, she said, and was dressed in what she described as "old-fashioned clothes". I asked her what that meant, and all she would say was that he was wearing an "old suit".'

'Did he talk to her?'

'She said he wanted to pray with her, but that the prayers he said were funny.'

'Funny how?'

'She didn't say any more than that. I think she just meant they weren't prayers she knew.'

Jessie pondered this. Could Rosie have been visited by a

chaplain from one of the lesser-known Christian churches? She
knew many of them congregated around hospitals where people
in crisis were always looking for comfort and salvation.

'What makes you think she dreamed this man?' Jessie asked
suddenly.

'Rosie insisted he had an enormous dog with him,' Halford
said, shaking her head and smiling. 'She described it as being
something like a wolfhound – I mean we're talking about a seriously large dog. There's no way anyone would have snuck an
animal of that size past security, and the only way a dog is going
to be allowed into the hospital at all is as a support animal, and I
have my doubts even one of *those* would be allowed onto the
cancer ward.'

Jessie nodded. 'You're probably right.'

'I think Rosie dreamed up the visitor, and that this figure
represents a depiction of the cancer that is eating her from the
inside. It's a twisted, misshapen thing, turning her own body
against her.'

Jessie looked at the image in front of her and flipped
through to the next one, and the one after that, page after page
of these ugly, slightly creepy creatures.

She wasn't sure she agreed with Halford's interpretation of
the pictures, but she had to agree that it seemed most likely the
bald visitor and his dog had been the products of a fever dream.

5

8.30 A.M. THE FOLLOWING MORNING

Jessie Boyle stood atop Montpelier Hill, a piece of forested earth and stone that rose out of the Irish countryside twelve kilometres south of Dublin city. From where she stood, wrapped in her long grey woollen overcoat, an oversized purple scarf wound about her neck, Jessie could see a gorgeous panorama of Ireland's capital, the lights of thousands of homes and businesses and vehicles twinkling in the darkness of the early January morning.

The sun was beginning to rise to her left, ice motes dancing in the shafts of radiance that cut through the trees that lined the summit of the hill, and around her she could hear the voices of the forensic team as they performed a grid search of the area. Every now and then someone would call out: 'Halt! Object in situ!' and the team, all decked out in protective overalls and foot protectors, would stop moving while a marker was placed on the spot, and the item (whatever it was) was bagged and labelled.

Jessie knew that most of what was picked up would be rubbish left by the hikers and birdwatchers the site attracted, but there was always hope some of it would prove useful. This was a life-or-death situation – every single person on the top of the freezing hill that morning knew a child's life hung in the balance.

Jessie turned away from the sprawling cityscape and gazed at the ancient hunting lodge that stood in the middle of the hilltop clearing.

The structure had been built in 1725 by William Connolly, Ireland's Revenue Commissioner and the richest man in Ireland at the time, as well as a celebrated politician, lawyer and landowner (to be clear, Jessie suspected Connolly had been celebrated by the wealthy elite – his poorer tenants probably had a slightly less tender view of him).

William Connolly had named the building Mount Pelier, and as a result, the hill itself garnered the same moniker, albeit conjoined into one word. But that wasn't the name by which it was known to the locals.

By the 1730s, the farmers and smallholders of the hill country south of the metropolis had started to refer to the building as the Hellfire Club, after a notorious group of occultists who, it was said, rented the lodge from the Connolly family to use as the base of operations for their gatherings; get-togethers which allegedly involved dark rituals and demonic summonings. The name stuck, and myths about supernatural goings-on on the lonely hilltop soon passed into folk memory.

Such ghost stories held little fascination for Jessie though. What interested her was lying under a tarpaulin near the low doorway of the ancient hunting lodge covered by a yellow tarpaulin.

It was the body of a man.

The man the police believed had taken Rosie Blake.

Jessie, forty-five years old and six feet and one half inch tall, short dark hair framing her strong, intelligent face, began to walk across the frost-whitened grass towards the ruined building, silhouetted now in the pale light of the gathering day. She could make out Seamus – seventeen years younger than herself, his auburn hair worn in a crew-cut that, short though it was, always seemed untidy and in need of a trim, this morning wearing an anorak over his rumpled grey suit. He was currently squatting down beside the body, a plastic bag containing what she knew to be a crucial piece of evidence in his hand.

As Jessie approached him, her phone buzzed in her pocket. Pulling it out, she saw it was Terri, the third member of the team, calling from their offices in Cork.

'Hey, Terri. What have you got for me?'

Terri Kehoe was twenty-five and had grown up in care. Jessie knew that, early though it was, Terri would be dressed in her usual style of 'goth light' – a black dress matched, perhaps, with a purple jumper or cardigan. Terri's entire wardrobe was either purple or black, though her hair was dyed a violent shade of blue.

Terri's formative experiences had left her emotionally vulnerable, but she had proven herself to be tough and resilient, and Jessie and Seamus were both protective of her.

'Hey, Jessie. How's it looking up there?'

'Frosty. Cold. Nice sunrise though. What have you got on the vic?'

'The commissioner tells me he is one Richard Roche, forty-three years old, with an address at Father Murphy Road, Tallaght. His driver's licence was in his wallet, and his car – a Toyota Avensis – was left in the car park below the path to the summit. It took me about three minutes to establish he was employed as a porter in Beaumont Hospital.'

'Makes sense,' Jessie said. 'Gave him easy access to Rosie.'

Seamus looked up as she came close.

'I've got Terri on the line,' Jessie said.

'Hey, little sis,' Seamus called in his soft Kerry accent.

'Hey, Seamus!' Terri called back, hearing his greeting. '*Conas atá tú?*' How are you?

'*Go maith, go raibh maith agat!*' I'm good, thanks.

'I'm going to put you on speaker,' Jessie said and crouched down beside the detective. 'What's the status here, Seamus?'

'Richard Roche was shot three times in the chest with a small calibre weapon,' Seamus responded. 'Could be a .22 – the medical examiner will be able to tell us once they've opened him up. He was found last night by a hillwalker named David Gibb, who was up here quite late. He's doing one of those Three Peaks challenges, where he's planning on running up three mountains in a twelve-hour period. As you know, there are two ways to get to the top of Montpelier – a gentle one and a steep one. Mr Gibb has been using the steeper ascent as a form of condition-training to build stamina, and he likes to train at night. He'd come over to the lodge to rest when he almost tripped over Roche's remains.'

'If he wasn't scared of the spooky reputation the place has before, I bet he is now,' Jessie mused.

'He called it in, and the 999 operator sent out the ambulance, the police and mountain rescue,' Seamus said.

'Nothing if not thorough,' Terri said.

'For sure,' Seamus agreed. 'The medics declared Roche dead at the scene, and one of the uniform boys, Harry Jordan, found this just inside the lodge when he was looking for shell casings.'

He stood up and walked a little way into the interior of the old structure, taking a torch from the pocket of his anorak and shining its beam on a forlorn object that was lying on the frost-touched earth floor.

It was a scuffed and almost threadbare stuffed panda.

'Garda Jordan was aware of the amber alert that was out on Rosie Blake, so when he came across the bear, he called it in. The Blake family have confirmed that Rosie had a panda she was particularly attached to. Obviously, they haven't been able to ID it yet, but I think we can be fairly sure it's one and the same.'

'So we can say pretty conclusively that Richard Roche is the person who abducted Rosie from the hospital,' Jessie said. 'He took her up here – I'm guessing to hide out. And at some point during his sojourn here, someone came along and shot him.'

'I can see why they pay you the big bucks as a profiler,' Seamus said, winking mischievously. Jessie flipped him the bird in retaliation.

'Why though?' Terri asked, ignoring Seamus's comment.

'A disagreement over some part of the plan?' Jessie suggested.

'No, you're misunderstanding me,' Terri interrupted. 'I... I get why someone would want to kidnap a child – most parents would sell everything they own to get their kid back. What I don't understand is why someone would choose to kidnap a *sick* child. It just seems far too much trouble. Aren't there lots of healthy ones with wealthy parents?'

Jessie and Seamus thought about that for a moment.

'It's a good question,' Seamus said eventually. 'There must be something very special about Rosie Blake to warrant all the hassle. By which I mean there's something her parents have that Roche wanted.'

'We could be overthinking it,' Jessie said. 'Kidnapping a sick kid does have certain advantages.'

Seamus raised an eyebrow, and Terri said: 'Such as?'

'It speeds the process up,' Jessie explained. 'Parents will want their sick child back as quickly as possible, so ransoms will be paid almost immediately. There'll be no mucking around with negotiators or middlemen. The exchange would be very quick.'

'That's true,' Seamus said. 'So what the hell happened to poor old Richard Roche? What you've described there is a very simple, straightforward business, but there was no ransom demand. He took her and just vanished – until now. This muddies the waters a bit, doesn't it?'

'It does,' Jessie said. 'So what do we think happened here then? Who shot our kidnapper?'

'Probably someone he was working for,' Seamus offered. 'I'd wager he was planning on meeting them here to pass Rosie over to them – kidnap to order, maybe. It's far enough out of the way to be a good hideout, particularly out of season. It's a short enough hike from the car park below – he could carry Rosie up without too much difficulty, and all the ghost stories would keep most people away, particularly at night. I'm prepared to bet good cash money this was a meet, maybe even a handover, that went wrong.'

Jessie thought about that one.

'Not necessarily a handover,' she said. 'I'm more inclined to think it was an accomplice. If the plan was to hold Rosie to ransom, with her being ill and in need of treatment, maybe they wanted to let the Blakes sweat for a while before making contact. Possibly even in an attempt to increase the size of the ransom.'

'That's a possibility,' Seamus mused.

'Well it looks as if this crew weren't in the mood to share,' Jessie concluded.

'I dunno,' Seamus said. 'I'm thinking it's a bit early in the game for that. This is a public enough location, even out of season. They'd have to know Roche's body would be found, and he'd be linked to the abduction in no time. And leaving the bear behind was just plain careless. This doesn't look planned to me.'

Jessie had to admit her partner was right. There was a rushed feel to the scene she didn't like. If a crime was planned and executed well, it was easier to see a pattern, the clear lines of motive. Impulse acts were harder to quantify.

'Is Richard Roche on the system?' she asked Terri. 'Does he have a record?'

'That's a really interesting question,' Terri said. 'As you know, for Roche to have been working as a porter, particularly in a hospital with a children's wing, he'd have to have been Garda vetted.'

Terri was referring to the process of running a full check on the criminal record of anyone employed to work with vulnerable people to ensure they were suitable for such a sensitive and responsible position.

'Mr Roche's record came back clear,' Terri said. 'At least, it did at first glance.'

'What did they miss?' Jessie asked.

'Crimes committed while still a minor don't show up on the checks the traditional Garda vetting system runs,' Terri explained. 'But they do exist on the network if you know where to look.'

'And you know *exactly* where to look, don't you, little sis?' Seamus grinned, his breath coming in plumes as he spoke.

'Of course I do,' Terri said, laughing. 'Richie Roche, as he's more commonly known, spent two years in Hollymount Remand and Assessment Unit for young offenders, from 1991 to 1993.'

'What was he sent there for?' Jessie asked.

'A couple of petty offences, which in and of themselves don't amount to much. But what did catch my attention was a name on Roche's visitation list, someone who came to see him at least once a month while he was a guest of the state.'

'I take it this is the name of someone known to the police,' Seamus observed.

'Very much so,' Terri agreed. 'Richie Roche was regularly visited by one Garth Calhoun.'

Jessie and Seamus locked eyes for a moment.

'The same Garth Calhoun who's the patriarch of the largest gang in Dublin's inner city?' Jessie asked.

'That's him,' Terri said. 'Richie Roche was a soldier for the Calhouns when he was a teenager. To all intents and purposes, he appears to have gone straight after he came out of the remand unit – until now that is. But his having an association with organised crime is... well, I'd say it gives us something to work with, wouldn't you?'

'Have the Calhouns resorted to kidnapping before?' Jessie wanted to know.

'There's not much they haven't resorted to,' Terri said.

'Isn't Rosie's dad a banker?' Seamus asked.

'No. He's an investment advisor,' Terri said. 'What people used to call a stockbroker. But he's worth quite a lot of money. He works for a company called Precision Investment Brokers. They're massively successful. He'd be able to pay a hefty sum.'

'There has to be a connection,' Jessie said. 'I'm not a fan of coincidences. They don't leave us anything to work with. We assume the Calhouns are in this until we have reason not to.'

'Which means we need to pay old Garth Calhoun a visit,' Seamus said.

'All right, guys,' Jessie said, straightening up. 'Let's go to work.'

6

Two hours later, they were back in Harcourt Street, in the same meeting room they'd been in the previous day, with the Blakes sitting in the exact same chairs.

'I've asked you here again because now we know who took your child,' Dawn told them. 'We can begin to try and piece together the why and wherefore of what happened.'

'I don't believe it,' Shauna kept saying, her face pale and her hands visibly shaking as she sipped a mug of sweet tea. 'I just... I *can't* believe it. Richie would never hurt Rosie.'

'You know him then?' Jessie asked.

'Not well... I mean, just from going in and out to the hospital.'

'Well there's no doubt that it was Richard Roche who brought Rosie up Montpelier Hill,' Seamus said. 'Traffic cameras captured his car approaching, and the cameras in the car park showed him taking Rosie from the back seat and carrying her towards the trail. He did this for a reason, and we need to establish what that reason was.'

'As simple as that,' Peter Blake glowered.

'I didn't say it was simple, Mr Blake,' Seamus said patiently.

'But in my experience, most abductions are either about money or love, even if that love can be confused – good if misplaced intentions – or a sicker, more twisted kind of love. Let's try and assume good intentions though, and see where it leads us, okay?'

Seamus spoke mildly, but there was something in his tone that stopped Peter in his tracks, and the older man closed his mouth and shifted uncomfortably on his chair.

'Other than encountering Richard Roche around the hospital, did either of you have any other dealings with him?' Jessie asked. 'Socially, through business, maybe online?'

'No,' Shauna said. She was a thin, angular woman, her dirty-blonde hair tied in a loose ponytail. 'He was always very nice to Rosie whenever he had to bring her anywhere, but other than that I haven't got much to say about him. He seemed a very... unassuming kind of person. Jolly and sweet. I wouldn't have thought him dangerous at all.'

'I wouldn't beat yourself up over that,' Dawn said. 'No one could have foreseen what happened.'

'Do you think he hurt her?' Shauna asked, and her lower lip began to tremble.

'We have no reason to believe that,' Dawn said. 'So there's nothing to be gained by thinking it. For now, let's just focus on getting Rosie back, and the best way to do that is to learn as much as we can about Richard Roche. He's our window into what happened to your daughter.'

'What about you, Mr Blake?' Jessie asked. 'What did you make of him?'

'I don't remember ever seeing the man at all,' Peter said. 'Shauna was in the hospital far more than me. I work very long hours and get in to see Arizona when I can, but I'll admit that isn't as often as it ought to be.'

'So you have no memory of Mr Roche?'

'I doubt I'd be able to pick him out of a line-up.'

There wasn't much to say about that so the investigators let it lie.

'Is there anything you can tell us about either your own or Rosie's interactions with Roche that might help us, Mrs Blake?' Dawn asked. 'Even something small, something that seemed off but you didn't put any pass on at the time?'

'No. No, I'm really sorry. He just seemed like a kind man who was good with children.'

Dawn nodded.

Jessie said: 'Have you given your social media and email login details to Terri yet?'

'We'll do it today,' Peter said.

'See that you do,' Jessie said, less kindly this time. 'The key to this whole thing could be in there.'

'Thanks for your help,' Dawn said, standing. 'We'll be in touch if we need anything else.'

'Just find our daughter,' Peter said, grabbing his wife's hand and stalking towards the door.

'Oh, one last thing,' Seamus said. 'Do you know the Calhouns?'

Peter stopped dead and looked at the detective quizzically. 'The name doesn't ring a bell, no. Are you sure they've gone public?'

Seamus held his gaze for a moment. 'I'll check and get back to you,' he said.

Peter Blake nodded and left with his wife.

ARIZONA ROSE BLAKE

THE PREVIOUS DAY

She liked Richie Roche.

He was always kind to her, and he was big and strong, and when he laughed his whole body shook and his eyes closed and his smile made her feel warm. Rosie knew she was sick, serious sick, and even though she was just a kid, she understood a lot of people felt weird being around her because of it.

Not Richie though. He treated her as if she was normal. He made being in the hospital fun. There was no one big thing he did – it was in lots of small ways. He would come into her room sometimes in the evenings and play games: snakes and ladders and chequers and Kerplunk. He'd watch a TV show with her if one happened to be on when he came in: PJ Masks *or* Spirit: Riding Academy, *and he would laugh and chat with her about what was going on. Rosie liked that he really paid attention to the stories and wanted to chat with her about them.*

Rosie's dad hardly ever came in to see her, and when he did, he mostly talked about whatever procedures she was getting done, and he never laughed or tried to have fun with her. And her mam – well, she tried, but Rosie always thought she seemed so tired and worried and unhappy.

Richie wasn't like that. He was always happy, and the hospital didn't seem to bother him or make him down in the dumps like it did other people. Rosie spotted that he didn't have his blue orderly coat on when he visited in the evenings, so she knew he was coming in his spare time, when he wasn't supposed to be working.

And that made her feel good. He was spending time with her because he just wanted to. And that was nice. It was what friends did. And Rosie didn't have too many of those.

She kind of remembered a time before she got sick, a time of running outside and going to birthday parties and being around other children in the preschool. It seemed so much like another world, she sometimes wondered if she'd imagined it, but when she asked her mam about it, she told her that yes, she had done those things.

And Rosie didn't know if she should be happy or sad about that.

When she thought about it, she decided she was a little bit of both.

And that was okay.

Rosie had learned that life brought darkness and light, and if you wanted to find happiness at all, even a little bit, you had to be prepared to accept both. Every day brought fun and laughter, but it brought pain and nausea too. There didn't seem to be much she could do to change that.

And then, to her surprise, her life changed completely.

Except it wasn't in the way she'd expected.

And what started out as a fun adventure got very scary, very fast.

7

Jessie and Seamus sat opposite Dawn Wilson in an office the chief superintendent had loaned them. Jessie was looking at a photograph of Rosie Blake that she had downloaded from Shauna's Facebook page. The little girl was certainly cute: a shock of dark hair atop a pale, heart-shaped face. Her eyes were large and pale blue, and she was smiling into the camera, as if she was about to burst out laughing.

You'd never know she was sick, Jessie thought. *The poor kid – she's really putting on a brave face.*

'So we're finally at the races,' the commissioner asked, disturbing her from her reverie. 'What's the strategy?'

'Roche's DNA was in Rosie's room,' Seamus said. 'But before you jump to any conclusions, it was on hair follicles. He'd shed a couple. As an employee of the hospital, he had every reason to be there, so in a way his being murdered is terrible for him but good for us, because I don't know that we'd have caught him for this otherwise.'

'Even the Blakes don't like him for it,' Dawn observed.

'They're both really shaken up,' Jessie said. 'He's coping with it by being a bully; she's engulfed in grief. I'm not sure questioning them was even worth our time anyway. Rosie's therapist doesn't believe they had much of a relationship with her. I'm inclined to let them rest and talk to them again in twelve hours. We might learn more.'

'It'd be too late,' Seamus said. 'We need to get out on the street *now* before the trail gets cold.'

'Why doesn't Peter Blake want us to root around in his correspondence?' Dawn asked.

'I'm not sure there's anything more in that than him trying to assert some control over the situation,' Jessie said. 'He wants to be an alpha male, but I'm not at all convinced he is one. I'm guessing that, when we interview his colleagues, we're going to find Peter isn't taken all that seriously.'

'You think he's overcompensating?' Dawn asked.

'Even if he has a poor relationship with his daughter, he's a man who takes his positions in life seriously,' Jessie said. 'They're important to him in that he believes they're how he's perceived. His role as a father has been compromised, and the one thing all fathers want is to be seen as the protector. Peter Blake has already had that status shattered by Rosie's illness. Cancer, an enemy he cannot hope to beat, invaded his home. I'm not surprised he isn't at the hospital as much as he could be; he can't stand to watch his little girl suffer. Now she's been kidnapped, and he's failed all over again. No wonder he's being a bit of a dickhead.'

'I still want to see their online communications,' Dawn said. 'I'm rightly fucking annoyed they're holding out on us about it.'

'Me too,' Jessie agreed. 'I think we've knocked some sense into him though. I'll get Terri to call him later today to get the logins. If he doesn't hand them over, I wouldn't wait around to get a warrant.'

'Do you believe Peter doesn't know the Calhouns?' Dawn asked.

'I do,' Seamus said. 'He seemed genuinely puzzled by the question.'

'He works in finance though,' Dawn said. 'Doesn't that mean he lies for a living?'

Seamus grinned. 'I'm a police detective, in case you'd forgotten, boss,' he said. 'Which means I get lied *to* for a living. I'm pretty good at recognising it when I see it.'

Dawn laughed. 'I'll give you that, young Keneally,' she said. 'Although I've learned over the years never to assume I've seen it all. There's always a better liar than the ones you've encountered.'

'I don't think there's anything to be gained by assuming they're not being truthful,' Jessie said. 'Let's allow Terri to do what she does, and Seamus and I can work with what we've got.'

'Which is?' Dawn asked.

'Richard Roche,' Jessie said. 'We learn everything we can about him and see if that tells us who shot him, and therefore who has Rosie.'

'Terri's already been doing some digging,' Seamus said. 'She's emailed us a list of people to talk to.'

'She's a good girl, is Terri,' Dawn said.

'The other variable we can't ignore is Rosie herself,' Jessie said. 'A criminal's victim always tells you something about the criminal themselves.'

'I'll call Beaumont and see who you can speak to there,' Dawn offered.

'That would be good,' Jessie said.

'It might also be worth checking out where a person who isn't a doctor might get stuff to keep her alive while she's being held captive,' Seamus said thoughtfully. 'It's possible whoever has her knows exactly how sick she is and intends to look after her until they're ready to hand her back. Or pass her on or whatever they plan to do.'

'Yes,' Jessie said. 'I was thinking something similar.'

'I'll have one of the lads from the drugs squad look into it,' Dawn said.

'And we'd best talk to Garth Calhoun,' Seamus added. 'He might have some... some *insights* into the whole thing none of us have thought of.'

'I'll talk to Garth,' Dawn said. 'He and I have a history.'

Jessie raised an eyebrow. 'You do?'

'Let's just say that Garth and I go way back. Right to the start of my time on the force, actually.'

'Old pals?' Seamus asked, surprise evident in his voice.

'I suppose you could call it that,' Dawn said. 'I'm responsible for sending him down for twelve years.'

'Well I'll bet he remembers you fondly,' Jessie said wryly.

'Oh, you have no idea,' Dawn replied, grinning.

They agreed to meet back at Harcourt Street at 5 p.m. and went to see what they could learn.

8

Terri Kehoe sat at the computer lab she'd built in the team's offices on the fourth floor of the Elysian Building on Cork City's waterfront. When she'd been recruited to the commissioner's special investigative task force, Terri had asked – not really believing her wish would be granted – if she might access funding to construct the tech setup of her dreams, and to her great surprise, Dawn had said she could order whatever she needed and send the invoices to her.

So it was that, as Jessie, Seamus and the commissioner each headed out to different Dublin locations to interview suspects, Terri was perched in front of three integrated terminals 260 kilometres away, doing what she did best and hunting down information on the World Wide Web. To the uninitiated, that might not seem like such a remarkable thing to be able to do, but to dismiss Terri Kehoe's skills would be a mistake indeed.

This afternoon, she had her systems running three searches.

The first, and the one she expected would yield the greatest results, was focused on Peter Blake's financial and investment practice. It made sense to Terri that the motive behind Rosie's abduction was in some way linked to what her father did for a living. With the economic recession mostly a thing of the past and the markets buoyant, Peter had, according to the returns he'd filed with the Irish Central Bank in 2017, earned five million euro. As his salary was based on commission (a percentage of the returns on investments he made for his clients), this meant he was working in high-risk/high-yield plans that turned over vast sums of money.

While such work had to be risky – Terri had looked into it, and saw it was tantamount to gambling, just on a very grand scale – there were always methods of minimising that risk, so the search parameters she'd set were designed to scour the financial message boards and Reddits in the hope of picking up even the vaguest hint of insider trading, any rumours of industrial espionage, or suggestions of hostile business practices that might inspire animosity strong enough to induce child abduction.

The second search was rooted in the possibility that Rosie's abduction had nothing to do with her father's job and was instead linked to something even more sinister. Terri had learned during her time working with the National Bureau of Criminal Investigation that if you can imagine a predilection, no matter how seemingly bizarre or twisted, there will be someone out there (usually more than a few someones) who is prepared to pay large amounts of money to indulge it.

A trawl of some select sites and message boards on the deep web informed Terri there was a market for terminally ill children. The reasons people wanted such waifs went from the tragically misguided (one man believed he had the gift of healing and when hospitals wouldn't allow him to just wander in and start laying hands on dying kids, he reckoned he was justified in kidnapping them for their own good) to so dark and unpleasant Terri preferred not to think about it. She wrote an algorithm that would target any online chatter relating to a child who fit Rosie's physical description, and had her particular form of cancer, to see if anything came back.

The final search focused solely on Richard Roche. In Terri's experience, it was unusual for something like a child abduction to be a single, isolated incident. While abductions were often linked to custody disputes within families, those that occurred involving adults outside the child's family were usually due to character defects in the kidnapper. These need not be of a predatory or sexual nature. Rescue fantasy, a desire to be a parent, a need to control something, even a cry for attention – all had been used to justify similar crimes in the past.

Terri knew Roche had never been convicted of any acts against children or vulnerable adults, but she wondered if there might have been any complaints that had never gone beyond the investigatory stage and might still be languishing on the system. She hoped to build a picture of Roche that Jessie might be able to use in her profiling.

And she also hoped that somewhere amid all the information her systems were racing through, there might be a clue as to who had Rosie now.

9

Father Murphy Road, in Tallaght, was a local authority housing estate that had been built in the late 1960s and had matured well. The door of number sixty-seven, the house Richard Roche had lived in with his mother, was open, and forensic investigators were carrying bagged and labelled items out to be loaded into vans for closer inspection. Two more were kneeling on metal platforms on the lawn, carefully examining the grass and earth to see what secrets they might divulge.

The aforementioned Mrs Roche was standing in the porch of number seventy-two, directly across the road, watching the comings and goings with a pained expression. Her first name was Agatha, but the uniformed officer who was leading the onsite investigation told Seamus she would not answer to anything other than her correct title.

'Mrs Roche, my name is Seamus Keneally. Do you mind if I ask you a few questions about your son?'

Richard Roche's mother looked to be slightly under five feet in height and was dressed in a purple overcoat that came to her knees, below which sturdy-looking legs clad in thick brown support tights could be seen, the ensemble completed with black brogues. Her hair was dyed a purple that matched the coat perfectly, a fact Seamus doubted was intentional.

She had a face that was lined and furrowed and two eyes so dark they were almost black peered at the detective with alarming ferocity.

'I've done nothin' but talk about Richard since five o'clock this mornin',' the old woman said in one of the densest Dublin accents Seamus had ever heard. 'What have you got to ask me that the others haven't already grilled me about twenty times? Do yiz think that usin' different words makes it a different question? I'm not stupid, you know. I'm old, but I'm not thick.'

'I never thought you were, Mrs Roche,' Seamus said. 'Can I just say, I'm very sorry for your loss. I don't want to make things any harder for you than they already are, but I'm sure you know a little girl is missing, and we're certain your son took her out of the hospital.'

'So they keep tellin' me. But no one's said one thing that makes me believe it's true.'

'Can we sit down somewhere and have a chat?' Seamus suggested. 'I've been up since the crack of dawn myself, and a cup of tea would be very welcome.'

The old woman snorted. 'You talk nice – I'll give you that.'

'My mother taught me that courtesy costs nothing.'

'Your mother still alive?'

'She was when I talked to her last night on the phone.'

Agatha Roche nodded slowly to herself.

'Mary,' she called into the house behind her, 'I'm bringin' this nice young copper into the kitchen for tea.'

A response that Seamus couldn't understand was bellowed from somewhere inside the bowels of the dwelling, but it was obviously in the affirmative because the little old woman stepped back and motioned for him to come inside. She led Seamus down a narrow hallway into a tiny kitchen.

'Sit yourself down,' Mrs Roche said and busied herself about the space, displaying an economy of movement that told Seamus the kitchen in her own house across the street was a clone of this one.

'So ask me your questions,' the oldster said as she placed mugs, milk and sugar on the small table Seamus was seated at.

'I know your son spent some time in a home for young offenders,' the detective began.

Mrs Roche sighed deeply. 'I wondered when someone would bring that up.'

'I'm not judging you or him,' Seamus said. 'I'm just trying to understand your boy a bit better. He's not around to account for himself, so the people who knew him are going to have to do that on his behalf.'

The old woman put a plate of chocolate digestives in front of the detective who, smiling his gratitude, took one.

Agatha Roche said: 'Richard made some stupid mistakes, but he did his time and learned the error of his ways.'

'What kind of mistakes did he make?'

'Ah. He got in with a bad crowd and they encouraged him to do things he never would have done if he was left to his own devices.'

Mrs Roche poured tea into a mug and pushed it towards Seamus, then filled another for herself and sat down. The detective took a biscuit and dunked it vigorously into his tea. He had a theory about the correct level of saturation a biscuit required to achieve just the right consistency to be truly delicious and had been working on it for some years. Seamus, while not a gastronomist, loved food, and approached everything he ate with relish and enthusiasm.

He was pleased to see Mrs Roche had opted for chocolate digestives, which he believed were the ideal dunker, and his research had shown that a sustained submersion of six seconds melted the chocolate so that it was liquid, but not so much it ran off the biscuit, acting in fact as a kind of glue and holding the structure together.

He took the digestive from his tea, admired his handiwork for a second and then consumed the results in a single bite.

'I know you don't like thinking about it,' he said, pulling his mind back to the interview, 'but can you give me a sense of what got him sent to Hollymount?'

'He got caught stealing stuff from the shops a few times,' she said. 'That was the start of it. There was a bunch of young lads robbing cars. Not big fancy ones – bangers mostly. They'd sell them on for parts and scrap. Richard got mixed up with them.'

'Were these kids working for Garth Calhoun?'

Those black, twinkling eyes bore into Seamus with a frightening intensity as he reached for another biscuit.

'Of course they were working for that evil man,' she said passionately. 'He *owns* this part of Dublin. What chance do poor young lads have when parasites like him are on the prowl?'

'He recruited Richard?'

'He was sixteen, and he'd lost his father to the drink, and I knew he was floundering, but I was so full of grief I wasn't able to stop him getting in deep. By the time your lot arrested him, it was too late.'

'How did he get on in Hollymount? I've heard... well, I've heard mixed reviews of the place.'

'He hated it, but sure, if it was like a holiday camp in there, what would be the point? I told him, I said: "Richard, you're in here for bein' a feckin' thief! The best thing you can do is make damn sure you never end up anywhere like this ever again." And I believe he took that to heart. I really do.'

'You're aware Garth Calhoun visited him while he was a resident at Hollymount?'

'Oh, I know he did. Richard told me.'

'How did you feel about that? Seeing as how Garth is evil and all.'

'Richard didn't believe he was a bad man though. He saw that gangster as some kind of surrogate dad after he lost his own. He always told me there was good in Garth Calhoun.'

'Did they keep in touch after Richard came out?'

'I don't know. I didn't ask him. To be honest, I didn't want to know. When he did come home, Richard trained as a youth leader and got involved in the Order of Malta – you know, the voluntary ambulance and first-aid corps – and he also got a job working with the elderly in a nursing home. And this is the truth: he didn't have time to be involved in anything criminal. He was either working or doing stuff around the community. If he did see Garth Calhoun, it was socially, and for no other reason.'

Seamus sipped some tea and grinned when Mrs Roche pushed the plate with the biscuits towards him.

'I like a man with an appetite,' she said. 'Don't be shy.'

'With the greatest of respect, Mrs Roche,' Seamus said as he took one, 'Garth Calhoun doesn't meet former gang members socially. If he was seeing your son, it *was* for a reason.'

'I don't know anything about that. What I do know is that my Richard was done with the gangs when he left the children's home.'

'Let's leave that aside for a moment,' Seamus said. 'Mrs Roche, there can be no doubt your son was responsible for taking that little girl out of the hospital.'

'Did anyone see him do it?'

'No, but he disappeared at the same time she did, we have CCTV footage of him taking her out of his car in the car park below Montpelier Hill and her favourite toy was found next to his body. If you can come up with another version of events to fit those facts, I'd be very happy to hear it.'

The old woman considered for a moment.

'Richard loved those kids,' she said. 'And before you go looking for something dark or sinister in that, I mean he cared about them. Wanted them to get better. When he got the job in the hospital, I'd never seen him so happy. It was as if all his dreams had come true. He worked hard at it. Put himself forward for every shift that was going. Every course.'

'Were there any new people hanging around lately?' Seamus asked. 'Or did you maybe notice any change in Richard? Has he been worried? Anxious? Moody? Were there any significant alterations to his routine?'

Mrs Roche shook her head. 'No. He was the same as always.'

Seamus drained his mug and set it back on the table. There was nothing more to be learned here. Agatha Roche did not believe her son had committed a crime, despite the evidence otherwise, and he knew from speaking to countless mothers during his career that there was little he could say or do to change that. He decided to approach it from one more angle before he left.

'Thank you for your time, Mrs Roche,' Seamus said. 'Before I go, can you think of any reason your son might have done what he did? I really am open to all suggestions.'

'I'll say this,' the old woman said. 'Richard wouldn't have done *anything* to those kids unless he thought he was helping them. Protecting them. That was the kind of man he was. You've taken one episode in his life, a life where he's done far more good than he's done wrong, and you've used that as a measure of who he is.'

'Mrs Roche, my only wish is to find a little girl and bring her back to the hospital where the staff and her parents can look after her. I'm talking to you because your son is responsible, in part at least, for her being in danger. What he did in the past may or may not be significant, but it's my job to ask about it.'

'Well, you'll pardon me for saying so, but I think you're asking the wrong questions.'

'Maybe I am,' Seamus said with resignation. 'But they're all I've got until the right ones come along.'

10

The staff canteen in Beaumont Hospital was crowded when Jessie met the head of human resources, a fresh-faced blonde woman named Eleanor Saunders, later that afternoon. The HR manager had a frothy cappuccino, while Jessie had black coffee that closely resembled lukewarm brown water.

'I'm not sure how I can help you,' Eleanor said. 'Richard Roche was always reliable, conscientious and punctual.'

'You're aware he had a criminal record?' Jessie asked.

'I am now. We followed the vetting guidelines to the letter – we have to or we'd be shut down. There is room on the form for prospective employees to divulge any information pertinent to their application that might not show up during the screening process.'

Eleanor opened a grey cardboard folder that was lying on the table in front of her and took out a bundle of paper.

'Here's Roche's personnel file,' she said. She leafed through it rapidly. 'This is his Garda vetting form, and as you can see, he left that part – the personal declaration – blank.'

'Do many of your staff volunteer information that could preclude them from getting the job?' Jessie inquired.

Eleanor paused. 'Well... no, not many.'

'Have *any*?'

The HR manager shifted uncomfortably on her chair. 'I'm sure I don't know – I'd have to check.'

'Did you know Richard Roche well?'

'I interviewed him for the position of hospital porter.'

'I thought he was an orderly.'

'The terms are interchangeable. Orderly is probably a bit old-fashioned. Porter is more commonly used now.'

'Thanks for clarifying. When would the interview have been?'

Eleanor checked the bundle of papers, riffling through them until she found the correct page.

'Nearly seven years ago. Third of February 2012.'

'Do you remember the interview?'

'Not particularly. I do quite a few as part of my job.'

'So nothing about Richard Roche stood out?'

'Well, I can see he impressed me enough to come top of the panel.'

Eleanor pushed the page across the desk to Jessie, who turned it around so she could read it. In the top right-hand corner someone had affixed a passport-sized headshot of Roche. Jessie had looked at Roche's lifeless remains briefly that morning, but she knew from experience that a dead body never gave a useful impression of what someone looked like in life. The photo showed a handsome, dark-eyed man with close-cut brown hair that formed a pronounced widow's peak. He was staring straight at the camera, and Jessie thought his expression showed intelligence and no small amount of toughness. This was a face that had seen a lot and had lived through it.

The photograph also showed humour and, Jessie thought, kindness. She'd been around murderers, sociopaths and sadists her entire working life, and she had learned to pick up subtle signs others missed.

The image attached to the form presented her with none of the usual signposts for concern.

Yet this was the face of a man who had taken a sick and vulnerable child from her hospital bed and spirited her away from her family and carers. Jessie searched the image in the hope that the rugged features might offer a clue as to why. But nothing jumped out at her.

'It says here he'd done quite a bit of volunteering,' Jessie said, running her finger down the interview form. 'The Order of Malta, the Irish Wheelchair Association, Meals on Wheels – did you check these out to make sure he wasn't just padding out his CV?'

'We're only obliged to check his references,' Eleanor said.

'And who acted as referees for Mr Roche?'

'His previous two employers – he'd spent a year working in a nursing home in Dún Laoghaire, and before that was with one of those home care companies, you know the ones where a carer comes to the home of an elderly or disabled person?'

'Those are both trustworthy positions,' Jessie observed.

'Yes. If you look at the third page of the interview form, you'll see my notes on the reference checks.'

Jessie did. 'Mr Roche is characterised as "an exemplary employee" by Our Home to Yours Care,' she said. 'And you've noted that Bennett's Nursing Home reported they were sorry to see him leave.'

'As he was going to be working primarily on the children's ward,' Eleanor said, 'we also requested a character reference. I see from Mr Roche's file that it was provided by Garda Frank Russell, at the station in Tallaght.'

'This was seven years ago, too?'

'Of course. All these procedures had to be completed before Mr Roche could start the job.'

'I take it the character reference was as glowing as his employment ones were?'

'See for yourself.'

The reference had been handwritten on paper headed from An Garda Síochána, Tallaght branch, and was dated 5 February 2012.

Sir or Madam,

Richard Roche has been known to me for the past twenty-five years, during which time I have been the community Garda for the Templeshanbo area of Tallaght, County Dublin. Richard Roche came to my attention as a leader of the youth club based in St Logue's church hall, a position in which he excelled, helping many young people to remain in education and diverting them from involvement in local gangs or other criminal endeavours.

As well as the youth club, Richard volunteered for a number of agencies that helped vulnerable people within the local area. He gave generously of his time to individuals with special needs, to the elderly and to the homeless. He is a member of several committees that facilitate important initiatives in Tallaght – Meals on Wheels, Neighbourhood Watch and the local youth information centre.

I am aware he has done several courses in first aid responding and is an active member of the Tallaght branch of the Order of Malta, for whom he is also a trainer.

I have no hesitation in confirming that Richard Roche is a person of excellent character, and I am certain he will be a positive addition to any work environment but particularly one in the caring professions, for which he is ideally suited.

Yours sincerely,

Frank Russell, Community Garda, Tallaght

'It seems that rather than investigating Mr Roche as a potential kidnapper, we should be contacting the Vatican to see about having him canonised,' Jessie said ruefully, handing the report back to Eleanor Saunders.

'As I said, we had no reason to suspect him of being a risk to any of our patients,' the HR manager said.

'And during his entire time here, there were never any red flags?'

'Quite the opposite. The children and their families all loved him. His colleagues had nothing but praise for him. The chap who had been – for want of a better term – senior orderly is due for retirement, and Richard was the main contender for that role. He was a valued member of the staff here.'

Jessie nodded and sipped her coffee, immediately regretting it. She pushed the mug away.

'Would you know if Richard had any personal habits that might cause him to suddenly need a lot of money?'

Eleanor blinked. 'Like what?'

'Gambling. Drug addiction. Alcoholism. Was he in a relationship with someone who was putting pressure on him to buy a fancy car or move to a posher area of Dublin?'

'I wouldn't know that kind of detail about Richard's life. You'd have to talk to his friends and family.'

'He's listed as single on our system,' Jessie said.

'I'm certainly not aware of a wife or girlfriend,' Eleanor said.

'He could have a boyfriend, or a partner who is gender fluid,' Jessie pointed out.

'Oh. Yes. I suppose so.'

'Is there someone here he was very friendly with? A staff member he was particularly close to?'

'I really don't know. Perhaps if you ask down on the children's ward, someone might be able to tell you?'

'Thank you, I will,' Jessie said. 'Can I ask you to have Mr Roche's personnel file scanned and emailed to this address?'

She handed her the team's business card, which had Terri's email address on it.

'Of course. I... I hope I've been some help.'

'Actually, you have,' Jessie said, standing to leave. 'I now know that Richard Roche is the last person in the hospital anyone would have expected to commit this crime.'

'And that helps?' Eleanor asked.

'Well it's more than I knew when I walked in.'

Years of policing had taught Jessie that sometimes, that was as much as you could hope for.

11

Jessie was on her way to the elevator when her phone buzzed: a text message.

Assuming it was Seamus or Terri, she thumbed open the screen without thinking and was immediately stopped in her tracks.

Jessie, it has been too long since we corresponded. I see you are involved in an interesting new case, one that has brought you back to the city of your birth. It has many aspects I find intriguing, but there is one facet in particular I am fascinated by. I simply cannot wait for you to meet the Reavers. That is a treat I am very much looking forward to. In fact, I think this motley crew might just help you find the end I have always wished for you. I shall be watching with rapt interest. Ttfn. ᚾ

Before she had even seen the runic symbol attached to the end of the missive, Jessie knew this was from Uruz, the serial killer who had escaped her during her last case with the London Met.

Somehow, he seemed to know what Jessie was doing before she did.

She gazed at the message, wondering what it might mean. Feelings of anger, grief and resentment threatened to overwhelm her. Uruz, as a parting shot, had abducted and murdered Jessie's partner and lover, Will, and she was still trying to get over that loss. For just a moment, she was afraid the pain would wash over her like a tidal wave and drown her, but just then her phone buzzed aggressively, making her jump, and the avalanche of emotion was gone. This time, thankfully, it was Terri calling her.

'Tell me you have something for me,' Jessie said. 'Because so far, I've got nothing but a headache.'

'You okay?'

'I just got a message from our friend Uruz.'

Terri sighed deeply. 'He's still lurking in the background, is he?'

'I'm sending it to you. Tell me if any of it means anything to you.'

'Okay.'

Jessie forwarded the text to her friend.

'I've got it.'

There was a pause while she read the contents.

'It looks like his usual rubbish,' Terri said. 'I mean, there's nothing here to say he really does know anything about Rosie or Richard Roche.'

'I'd agree, if he hadn't been three steps ahead of us every other time he reached out.'

'True,' Terri said.

'Does the reference to the Reavers mean anything to you?'

'No. I've never heard of any group with that name.'

'Would you run a check and see if anything come up?'

'Of course. I'll do it right away.'

'Thanks, Terri. It could be nothing, but I don't like leaving anything to chance where Uruz is concerned. Now, I presume you were ringing to tell me you've cracked the case and we can all go home.'

Terri laughed. 'Sorry to disappoint you. All the searches I ran on Peter Blake have come up empty. He's not exactly the most ethical operator you'll find, but he's not close enough to the line to warrant any deeper investigation. I'd say he's pretty clean. Or as clean as anyone who does the work he does can be.'

'Not even a hint of dodgy dealings?'

'There's always a hint.'

'I'm listening.'

'He was named in a divorce suit last year.'

That caused Jessie to stop and pay attention. 'He was having an affair?'

'No! The wife, a Ms Sharon Carlisle, claimed Peter sold off her husband's portfolio at a marked loss just so he didn't have to pay her what she was entitled to. Kind of revenge selling.'

Jessie thought about that for a moment. 'Is that legal?'

'Technically, no. But it's impossible to prove it was malicious. The judge threw it out.'

'Okay. Well, it was worth looking anyway.'

'I'm still waiting on an algorithm I'm running on the deep web to come back with results on rumours of child abductions that might fit Rosie's profile. I'll let you know when it completes.'

'Do, please.'

'The only thing I've got that might be useful relates to Richard Roche.'

'I'm listening.'

'I was looking for complaints made against him that might not have amounted to anything but might be enough to show patterns suggestive of a behaviour developing.'

'And did someone make a complaint?'

'That's the thing,' Terri said. 'There are no complaints

against Richard Roche at all. But here's the thing: *he* made a complaint, and it related to Rosie Blake.'

'What?' Jessie asked. 'Could you run that one by me again?'

'Richard Roche made a complaint to the hospital social worker three weeks ago. A child protection referral.'

'Relating to Rosie Blake?'

'Yes.'

'Against whom?' Jessie wanted to know.

'Against Peter and Shauna Blake,' Terri said. 'Richard Roche told the hospital social worker that Rosie's parents were putting her at risk and that she needed to be taken into care.'

'Now I didn't see that coming,' Jessie replied.

12

Hollymount Remand and Assessment Unit had closed in 1997, but Terri learned that Joyce Dobbs, PhD, the psychologist who ran the place while Richard Roche was resident there, was now in private practice and rented offices on D'Olier Street, close to O'Connell Bridge.

Dobbs proved to be a slim woman with long, blue-grey hair, dressed in a black shirt and grey trousers, and she peered at the detective through large-lensed glasses with thick plastic frames. Seamus sat in her client chair, a straight-backed, art nouveau affair that had not been designed for comfort.

'It's been a very long time since I worked with young offenders,' she told Seamus. 'I'm not sure how much help I can be.'

'I wonder, do you remember a Richard Roche? He would have been on your books in the early nineties.'

The psychologist leaned back in her chair, stretching her long legs out before her. Seamus noted that her seat looked like a squashy armchair and seemed a far more restful place to recline than the one he was perched on.

'The name does ring a bell.'

'He was from Tallaght.'

'Was?'

'Richard Roche was shot in the early hours of this morning.'

'I'm sorry to hear that but not wholly surprised. I'd guess a lot of the young men I worked with back then met violent ends.'

'You're not a "glass half-full" kind of person then?' Seamus said.

'I'm a realist. The kids all led hard lives and were deeply entrenched in criminality. Most believed they had no choice but to get involved in organised crime. They perceived the gangs as a rite of passage, a natural progression. If you'd had the opportunity to ask any of the Hollymount boys what their aspirations were as to their life expectancy, they'd have told you they would live hard and die young. In those exact words, in fact. It was a kind of mantra for them.'

'Wasn't it your job to provide those kids with a new set of expectations?'

'My colleagues and I offered them choices, of course. How many of them saw those as viable alternatives, I have no idea. If I had to hazard a guess, I'd say very few did.'

'You're really not an optimist, are you?'

'Not when it comes to this topic, no.'

Seamus sighed and shook his head. 'Do you remember Richard Roche?'

'I think so. Do you have a photograph?'

'I should probably warn you, it's taken post-mortem.'

'I'm not squeamish, Detective,' Professor Dobbs said. 'I've seen human remains before: I have a degree in medicine.'

Seamus produced his phone and found the photograph he'd taken of Roche earlier that morning on Montpelier Hill.

Dobbs looked at it for a long moment before saying: 'Yes, I remember him.'

Seamus took his phone back. 'Professor, we believe that,

before he died, Roche abducted a very sick little girl from the hospital where he was working. She's still missing.'

Dobbs narrowed her eyes. 'Do you have a hypothesis as to why he took her?'

'That's one of the reasons why I'm here. I hoped you might have some insights.'

'My recollection of him is probably full of holes,' Dobbs said, speaking slowly, as if she was picking her way through old, faded memories.

'I'll make a note of that,' Seamus said. 'Anything you can add to the picture we've got will be useful though.'

The psychologist closed her eyes for a moment.

'I would have said,' she began slowly, 'that of all the kids who came through Hollymount, Richard Roche was one of the few I would have expected to make a go of life on the outside.'

'Really?'

'Yes. He seemed genuinely remorseful for the harm he'd caused and appeared dedicated to making positive change in his life. He participated fully in the programmes we ran, engaged with counselling services and availed himself of career guidance. Yes, Detective, I really thought Richard Roche might be one of our success stories.'

'You seemed surprised when I said he abducted a little girl.'

'I wouldn't have thought he had it in him to harm a child. Roche was here due to a "three strikes and you're out" policy the Gardai had initiated at the time. He wasn't exactly a hardened criminal – I'd say he'd been peer-pressured into the gang and was simply unlucky in that he was picked up at one of the Calhouns' breakdown yards during a Garda raid. He was a gentle soul really. I seem to recall his mother being very upset he was sent to Hollymount, but in fairness to her, she attended every single family therapy session and seemed determined to ensure he didn't end up stuck in the revolving door.'

'You didn't have an issue with Garth Calhoun visiting him here?'

'Remember what I said about being a realist?'

'I do.'

'For a lot of these kids, men like Calhoun were family. They looked up to him, and we found it was better to allow him visitation privileges rather than have the boys breaking out to go and see him.'

'You didn't worry about the influence he might be having?'

'Did we think some of the lads might leave and head straight back out into a life of crime? Of course we did, but getting occasional visits from Calhoun made no difference to that eventuality. They'd have gone back anyway.'

'Did Richard have any other friends at Ballymount? Anyone he might have kept in contact with?'

'If he maintained a relationship with the Calhouns, he would have been in contact with some of his peers from the unit. I have no access to files from that time anymore. I'm sorry.'

'If anything else occurs, please contact me,' Seamus said, passing her his card.

'I have to say, this whole thing doesn't fit my sense of Richard,' Dobbs said as she put it into the breast pocket of her shirt.

'His mother said the same thing, but I thought she might be somewhat biased,' Seamus agreed.

'You're saying he not only abducted a child, but a very ill one to boot, which makes the crime doubly heinous.'

'I would say so, yes.'

'I mean, one couldn't pick a more vulnerable victim.'

'He abused a position of trust to do it too.'

'When he was here,' Professor Dobbs said, 'Richard was known as someone who stuck up for the weaker boys. Protected them from bullies. Sometimes at the cost of drawing the ire of some very aggressive individuals upon himself.'

'Did he do that to shorten his stay?' Seamus wanted to know.

'Quite the opposite – if anything, he was at risk of extending it. He was caught fighting more than once, you see, which was frowned upon.'

'Why did he do it then?'

'My, my, Detective,' the psychologist said, shaking her head in mock dismay, 'now who's the "glass half-empty" person?'

'I don't follow,' Seamus said, puzzled.

'It's quite simple really,' Dobbs said. 'I think Richard Roche defended the weak and got beaten up for it because he believed it was the right thing to do.'

Seamus blinked. 'Really?' he asked, looking at the psychologist in disbelief.

'I know it's not what you expected to hear,' Dobbs said, smiling. 'But that doesn't make it any less true.'

ARIZONA ROSE BLAKE

'Rosie, how would you like to go on an adventure?'

She hadn't expected to see Richie that day. Rosie wasn't supposed to be going for any procedures – the drip had been attached to the cannula and it was oozing its medicine into her, and she could feel its coldness working its way up her arm, and Rosie knew well that once that started, there was nothing for her to do except wait for the clear plastic bag that was hanging on its hook above her head to become empty.

So when the big man arrived in his blue coat pushing a trolley (which meant he was working), she was surprised.

'What kind of adventure?'

'I'd like to take you on a journey.'

It was only a little after 10 a.m., and Rosie could see through the window that it was grey and cold-looking outside. She assumed the journey must involve going somewhere inside the hospital, as her doctors would never permit her to be outdoors on a day like this.

But she felt safe with Richie. He would never allow anything bad to happen to her.

'Um... okay.'

'Great. Just give me two seconds.'

Deftly, in a movement so quick she felt neither pain nor discomfort, he removed the drip from her arm.

'I'm supposed to stay on that for the rest of the day,' Rosie said.

'I've got more where we're going.' Richie smiled. 'No need to worry. Being off it for a little while won't hurt you.'

'You sure?'

'Positive. Come on.'

He scooped her up in his arms and gently placed her on the trolley, covering her over with a blanket, pulling it right up to her neck.

'It is a bit chilly out today, even in the corridors, so I'm going to put this on you to keep you snug,' he said, and pulled a big pink-and-blue woollen hat from his back pocket and tugged it down so it covered her ears and almost her eyes.

'Don't forget Panda!' she said urgently, and he grabbed the bear from where he sat on her pillow and handed him to her.

'So are you ready?'

She nodded and smiled at him.

'Off we go then,' he said and whisked her off.

Rosie had noticed ages ago that Richie moved very quickly along the hallways of Beaumont. But he went even faster than usual today.

It was fun going off on an adventure, Rosie thought.

She was to learn that adventures could be great fun.

Until they weren't anymore.

13

The Crossed Guns was a pub situated a quarter of a mile down a narrow tree-lined byroad off the M3 motorway north of Dublin city. Dawn Wilson sat in the black Lexus the Department of Justice provided for her office and gazed at the long, single-storeyed building. The car park was mostly empty, but four cars – one of which was a Mercedes E-Class with blackened windows – were parked in a cluster near a side door.

'I'd say I'll be in there about half an hour,' Dawn said to Detective Garda Todd Murphy, her driver, a thick-necked man with a red face and a mass of greying curly hair.

'Permission to accompany you, boss?'

Todd spoke in a soft, lilting Cork accent, which Dawn always thought sounded incongruous coming out of so large a man.

'Permission denied. I need to talk to someone in there, and he won't be forthcoming if you're standing behind me glowering.'

'That someone being Garth Calhoun, boss?'

Dawn laughed drily. 'I take it you've had dealings with the Calhouns in the past, Todd?'

'I was part of a team that raided this place back in 1996. We recovered half a million quid's worth of cocaine and enough firearms to equip the Irish Armed forces.'

'Sounds like it was a success then?'

'It was in the end. We met with a fair degree of resistance going in though. Two officers were injured – one seriously.'

'I'm sorry to hear that.'

'We all knew the risks. The point I'm making though, boss, is that I'm fucked if I'm going to allow you to go in there on your own, begging your pardon for my language.'

'No pardon required,' Dawn said, 'but I'm afraid you don't have any choice. I'm giving you a direct order to wait in the car.'

'And if you don't come back?'

Dawn opened the door and swung her legs out. 'You can call for backup, but if I'm not out in half an hour, it'll probably be too late.'

'You don't make it easy, boss,' Todd said.

'No, but my sweet nature and jovial tone more than make up for it.'

'They really don't. Try not to get shot. I'll never live it down.'

'I'll do my best.'

And she headed for the side door about which the cars were grouped.

Dawn knocked politely on the door when she got there. She heard the three smart raps echoing through the bar's interior and waited.

And waited. No response was forthcoming.

So she changed tack and hammered on the door with her fist, continuing to strike until her hand hurt, and then kicking it with her booted right foot. After what felt like forever, she heard someone attempting to shout over the noise, and then locks started turning.

'Jaysus, would you stop makin' that racket? Some of us are tryin' to work in here!'

The man who had spoken was as tall as Dawn's six feet two inches but was skeletally thin. He was dressed in an expensive-looking brown three-piece suit, offset by a crisp white shirt and orange tie. The commissioner put him at about thirty years of age, and his dark hair was pulled up in a fashionable topknot, his beard worn long and sculpted into an angular shape. He was, Dawn mused, a hipster. Which was a first in her experience of Dublin street gangs.

'I'm here to see Garth Calhoun,' she said.

'I don't know anyone of that name,' the hipster said. His accent was inner city.

You can dress them up in fine suits and give them fancy haircuts, Dawn thought, *but you can't take the flats out of them. Some things just run too deep.*

'Do you know who I am?' the commissioner asked.

'I can see you're a guard of some kind.'

Dawn laughed. 'It would probably be more accurate to say that I am *the* guard.'

Hipster looked confused. 'You've lost me, love.'

'Tell Garth that Dawn Wilson is here to see him, and that I'm not leaving until he comes out of his cave and talks to me.'

'I already told you—'

'Oh, will you get out of my way?'

Dawn pushed past the young man and, before he had a chance to react, was down the corridor, at the far end of which she knew Calhoun's office was situated. Hipster bellowed after her, a stream of invective in tones so shrill she wouldn't have thought him capable of them.

She hadn't gone more than five yards when a door to her left opened and a burly man in a blue tracksuit, the neck open to show a sprout of chest hair, barged out, clearly roused by Hipster's remonstrations.

'I think my associate is asking you to leave,' Tracksuit said and grabbed Dawn by the arm.

This was a mistake. Most attackers assume when they grab someone that their victim will attempt to pull away and balance themselves accordingly. But Dawn made no effort to extricate herself from the big man's grasp. Instead, she grabbed his hand with her right and, holding it in place, dragged him towards her with her left hand, pulling him with such force he had no option but to go with the movement. Tracksuit was pulled right into a headbutt, which struck him full force on the bridge of the nose and felled him immediately.

'I identified myself as a Garda,' she said to the stunned man. 'You impeded the course of my duties and I responded with reasonable force. If you wish to make a complaint, you'll find the necessary form on the Garda website.'

Straightening her uniform, she continued to the end of the corridor and opened the door opposite her.

'Hey, you can't be goin' in there!' Hipster called, but by then she was in, and there was nothing he could do.

Garth Calhoun was in his late seventies but could have passed for more than a decade younger. When Dawn barged in he was seated behind a large wooden writing desk that looked as if it belonged in the study of an English poet from the nineteenth century rather than in a bar in the Dublin suburbs. The gangster was speaking loudly into the receiver of an old-fashioned rotary telephone. The entire decor of the room was olde worlde: the wall behind Calhoun's head was hung with a collection of framed black-and-white photos of jockeys on horseback, some in the act of leaping fences, others parading about the winner's circle. A stone bust of a stern-looking man sat atop a plinth in the corner, and there was not a computer or smartphone to be seen anywhere.

Dawn might have stepped back in time fifty years.

Calhoun gave the commissioner an evil look and said into the phone: 'Yeah, something's just come up, Derek. I'll call you back.'

He placed the handset back in its cradle before resting his hands flat on the desktop. Hipster arrived in the doorway at that moment and started jabbering an apology. 'I'm sorry, boss – will I chuck her out, like?'

'Don't you think the horse has bolted at this point, Eugene?'

Calhoun's accent was Dublin but much more subtle than the younger man's. Dawn knew he'd been educated in a private school and had never had to claw his way out of poverty the way most of his soldiers had done. Which didn't mean he wasn't tough. It just meant he was a different kind of tough.

'You what, boss?'

It was clear that the hipster, whose name, it seemed, was Eugene, wasn't the sharpest tool in the shed – the reference to horses bolting while stable doors were open seemed to have gone right over his head.

'It doesn't matter, lad,' Calhoun said. 'You can leave us alone. I'll call if I need you.'

'Right you be, boss. I'll just be outside, yeah?'

'Very good, Eugene. Off you go now.'

The bearded man withdrew, and Dawn plonked down in a leather upholstered chair opposite the elderly gangster.

'Hard to get good help these days,' she said.

'You have no idea,' Calhoun said dolefully. 'But to business. To what do I owe this unexpected pleasure, Commissioner? Oh, and in case you didn't pick up on the irony in my voice, I'm joking about it being a pleasure. I'm not happy to see you at all, in fact.'

Calhoun's face was remarkably smooth for someone of his age. He had a healthy tan, and his hair, which was mostly grey, still had strands of dark running through it. Dawn could only see the top part of him above the desk, but it was clad in the jacket of a blue pinstripe suit over a pink shirt and blue-and-white chequered tie.

'Your name has come up in an investigation, Garth. I thought I'd try and avoid the unpleasantness of having my people tear this place apart a brick at a time and do you the courtesy of coming and having a chat. Just like old times, eh?'

Calhoun did nothing to hide his contempt. 'I haven't forgotten where those chats got me. I'm not inclined to repeat the experience.'

'I could bring you down to Harcourt Street so we can have our conversation there.'

'I could refuse to go.'

Dawn chuckled and wagged her finger at him. 'And where would that lead us? I'm sure as hell not going to be pushed around by Eugene the hipster. I've already got around him once – and your other attack dog. Do you *really* want to see Eugene get his arse kicked as an added bonus to the humiliation he's already suffered? Why don't you just answer my questions, and I'll see if I believe you or not, and we'll take it from there?'

Calhoun eyed Dawn with annoyance. 'And what exactly does that arrangement hold for me?'

'I could have got a warrant and arrived with a squad of detectives, every single one of whom would love to haul you in for questioning. With your track record, it would be easy to hold you for forty-eight hours on suspicion alone, and I'll bet if I sent some experienced guys to turn this place over, we'd find something that would give me an excuse to keep you locked up for even longer. Maybe even charged. This way, you've got a chance to stay out of jail. For the moment anyway.'

Dawn saw the gangster bristle, and while her expression remained neutral, inside she was grinning and doing a victory dance.

He's on the ropes already, she thought. *Garth always did have a quick temper.*

'Ask me whatever it is you want and get the fuck out of my bar,' he said through gritted teeth.

'How do you know Peter and Shauna Blake?' Dawn came right in with the question before Calhoun even had time to take a breath.

He blinked for a second but recovered and said: 'I don't. Those names mean nothing to me.'

'Bullshit, Garth. Don't kid a kidder.'

'What the hell is this about, Dawn? I'm a very fucking busy man. Cut to the chase or just arrest me and get it over with.'

'A former soldier of yours was found dead in the early hours of this morning up on Montpelier Hill. He'd just abducted the daughter of a prominent financier. Whoever shot him seems to have taken the kid.'

'You say the dead man is a former employee of mine?'

'Richard Roche.'

Calhoun went noticeably pale below his tan. 'Richie is dead?'

'Taken out with a small-gauge weapon. Three shots to the heart, clustered nice and close together. Looks very much like the work of a professional.'

Calhoun sighed and shook his head. 'Richie worked for me when he was a lad,' he said. 'I liked him. He got sent to that shit-hole of a juvenile lockup, Hollymount, on account of being at one of my garages when they raided it. He was only a couple of days over sixteen, and he'd done a few bits and pieces for me, but – and I'm bein' straight with you – it was all for the legit parts of my organisation. Richie never did anything illegal – not for me anyway. I know he got nicked for shoplifting bars of feckin' chocolate and a six-pack of lager before I took him under my wing, but he was a good lad. When he got sent down, he did his couple of years and he never said a word about me or what he'd seen in my body shops. He could have ratted me out and got time off for it, but he didn't. I tried to keep an eye out for him after that.'

'By bringing him back into your merry band of street thugs as soon as he got out of juvie?'

'No. Him bein' in that place nearly killed his mother. He told me she couldn't take any more stress, so when he got out, I helped him get fixed up in jobs that suited him.'

'And what were those?'

'He was a gentle soul, was Richie. Liked helping people. So I effected some introductions with a company that looked after old people in their homes. A friend of mine got him some work at the local youth centre too.'

'And the hospital? Did you get him the job there?'

'No. That wasn't me. He did that all by himself.'

Dawn eyed the gangster. 'When was the last time you saw Roche?'

'I had lunch with him three weeks ago.'

'Where?'

'Here. He was on the late shift that day, so he got the bus out.'

'What did you talk about?'

'This and that. I've known him since he was a kid, so we had lots to catch up on. His job, his mother, some stuff that was happening in his estate with the community development group... that kind of thing.'

'How did he seem?'

'In good form. I'd say he was really happy. He told me he thought there was a promotion comin' up for him in the hospital. He was chuffed about it. I am... I mean I *was* really proud of him.'

'Did he talk to you about any of the kids he worked with?'

Calhoun shrugged. 'Not by name. He took his job very seriously. When you work somewhere like Beaumont, particularly with sick kiddies, there's... whaddaya call it... *confidentiality*. Richie was always careful about that.'

'So he never mentioned a kid called Arizona Rose Blake? They call her Rosie.'

'That the kid he's meant to have taken?'

'Not meant to. There's no doubt he took her. Absolutely none.'

Calhoun shook his head. 'Not Richie. I'm tellin' you, you've got it wrong. Whatever happened, he wouldn't have kidnapped a kid he was meant to be looking after.'

'You can dress it up any way you like,' Dawn said, standing. 'He took her.'

'That's not the Richie I knew.'

'People change,' Dawn said. 'Why do I think you're lying to me about knowing the Blakes, Garth? Because I strongly believe you are.'

The older man eyed her. Dawn knew the look well. He was deciding how much he wanted to divulge.

'Maybe I've heard of them. Maybe their name came across my desk once or twice. But let me tell you this: I have absolutely nothing to do with any kiddie being taken. That's not my style and you know it.'

'As I said,' Dawn retorted, 'people change.'

'In my experience, they don't change that much,' Calhoun shot back. 'Like, you were a mean-spirited fucking bitch twenty years ago, and you're still one now.'

Dawn paused on her way to the door and turned to look at the old man for a moment.

'Be careful, Garth,' she said. 'I'm prepared to give you a little leeway because of our history. But there's a line I won't let you cross, and you're perilously fucking close to it.'

'Just leave me alone,' Calhoun said and swung his chair around so his back was to her.

'Goodbye, Garth.'

She was almost out the door when he called after her: 'Would you mind calling off whoever that creep is you've got watching the pub? He's not exactly blending into the background, and he's starting to freak me out.'

'I don't know what you're talking about,' Dawn said.

'Bald guy. Brown suit. Sometimes has a dog with him.'

'A dog?' Dawn laughed. 'Do you really think I'd let one of my guys bring his pet around with him on stake-outs?'

'I want him called off, Dawn. He's scaring off my regulars.'

The commissioner shook her head and left, closing the door behind her.

Eugene was sitting on a kitchen chair outside the door when she came out, and he stood rapidly, looking worried.

'You're all right,' the commissioner said. 'I'm leaving.'

Todd could barely contain his relief when she emerged from the bar into the weak winter sunlight.

'Did you get what you came for?' he asked.

'I think so,' Dawn said, sitting back and feeling the tension of the encounter seeping from her as they put distance between themselves and The Crossed Guns. 'Garth knows the Blakes all right. I'm not sure how well or in what capacity. But he was genuinely surprised Richard Roche is mixed up in all of it. It also looks like someone's watching old Garth. It isn't one of ours, as far as I know.'

'So what does that mean?'

'Fucked if I know,' Dawn Wilson said.

PART TWO

OUT OF THE SHADOWS

'We live on a placid island of ignorance in the midst of black seas of infinity, and it was not meant that we should voyage far.'

H.P. Lovecraft, from 'The Call of Cthulhu'

EUGENE DUNLIN

No one had ever taken him seriously.

His father was a brute who beat him for fun, and twice before his twelfth birthday came home drunk and forced him to do things boys should not have to do with their fathers. After that he made it his business to be at home as little as possible.

In school he knew he was academically bright, but coming from the flats, his teachers tended to treat any successes he achieved as flukes or lucky accidents, and while he might garner a patronising pat on the head, he was rarely encouraged to try and replicate the accomplishment. So he drifted in school, doing his best to keep out of trouble in the yard, where the bigger kids (and even some of the not too big) entertained themselves by beating him up.

By the time he was halfway through secondary, barely attending and spending most of his days smoking hand-rolled cigarettes laced with cheap cannabis down by the Royal Canal, he knew the only way he was ever going to have any kind of a life was to rely only on himself. No one else could be trusted to give a shit. He decided, then and there, as he watched a heron fish for chub, that he was going to make a go of it.

Eugene had a notion he might do something with business. His dad, on the rare occasions he spoke to the boy using words rather than his fists, had taken him to Moore Street where there was a market. He had a stall there where he sold knock-off imitation Zippo lighters, flints and lighter fluid, as well as a few hash pipes and some 'legal' highs that were only legally sold in head shops, but which he kept 'under the counter' and sold only to his regular, trusted customers.

Eugene felt he had a talent for sales. He certainly got on well with the people who came to the stall to purchase things, and he usually managed to persuade them to part with a few extra pence, buying something on top of whatever they'd come for and leaving believing they'd got a bargain.

They were happy, and so was he.

He managed to pass an exam that entitled him to a scholarship to study business at the Dublin Institute of Technology. He loved the course at first, throwing himself into it with delight, so proud he was finally something, a third-level student, someone with a future.

It was his dad's idea that he start dealing drugs to the other students. Eugene thought this was a good idea, an attempt to test out his business acumen, make a few euro on the side, and maybe even build up a client base he could use later.

Contacts were contacts, after all.

He was never sure which of his contacts told the college authorities that he was running a veritable pharmacy from the business department canteen. They informed him he was lucky to only get expelled from the college – they could easily have handed him over to the police.

It was his mother who called Garth Calhoun and asked the gangster to give him a job.

He was grateful. He really was.

And this time, he was determined not to screw up.

This time, he was going to be a success. No matter what.

14

Seamus sat in the unmarked Ford Mondeo he'd driven from Harcourt Street, parked now in the multistorey car park on Fleet Street, near Professor Dobbs's office. In the cool echoing shade of the garage, he leafed through the combined file on the Rosie Blake kidnapping and the Richard Roche murder. Something about the whole thing did not sit with him. There was a piece of the puzzle missing, and he couldn't even see what shape the hole was yet.

He'd investigated cases before where the culprit was an unlikely candidate, the last person you'd expect to commit such a crime. There was a murder he'd done some work on early in his career, the death of a twenty-three-year-old burglar named Josh Sliney. Sliney was a nasty character who made his living breaking into the houses of pensioners and pilfering their jewellery and other hard-won treasures, and he wasn't beyond knocking his victims about a bit if they got in his way during the burglary. His body was found in an alley behind a block of flats where many elderly tenants lived. He'd been stabbed through the eye by something long and thin with a rounded, tapering shape.

The lead detective, a man named Grant, suggested the murder weapon was a stiletto, a weapon which did not possess a cutting edge, just a sharp point. Its purpose was to create a deep penetrative wound, and it had been favoured by medieval assassins. No one in Pearse Street, where Seamus was stationed at the time, had ever come across a criminal who used such an archaic weapon.

This fact did not deter Detective Grant, however.

Every known contract killer in the metropolitan area was brought in and questioned, but none of them could be placed around the flats on the night in question. Grant was determined the culprit was Freddy Dunbar, a well-known local enforcer who liked to use blades, but Seamus, who had been interviewing the people of the flats, began to suspect there might be another version of events than Grant envisioned.

Dunbar was six feet four inches and built like a tank, with tattoos of vines snaking upwards from his neck and about his chin and jawline. In other words, he was highly recognisable. No one in the flats had seen anyone who fit the description, and when Seamus began to speak to the tenants, he discovered they were probably some of the most observant people he had ever encountered through an investigation. They spent most of their time watching the world going past through their windows, and most admitted that, if they heard steps passing on the corridor outside, they took a look through the peephole in their doors to see who it was.

If Freddy Dunbar had been about, Seamus was convinced, someone would have spotted him.

Yet no one had.

That said, no one claimed to have seen Josh Sliney either.

And while there were no reports from the occupants of the flats of any break-ins or any valuables being missing, a sprightly sixty-eight-year-old named Mary O'Brien just happened to be sporting a black eye when Seamus called on her. She had tried to cover it over with make-up, but you didn't need to have bionic vision to see that someone had punched her in the face recently. During his interview with Mary, Seamus noted a basket sitting on the floor below the couch. It contained several balls of wool, some kind of half-finished item of knitwear and half a dozen long knitting needles. Far more common than ancient Italian stabbing weapons.

Mary was, according to the local gossip, in a relationship with Bill, a burly, white-haired neighbour from the floor below. Bill was in his seventies, but he looked stronger than many men half his age. Certainly capable of getting a body out of the building and down to the alley outside.

Detective Grant had laughed at Seamus when he'd put his theory to him that two of the aging residents of the flat complex might be behind the murder, insisting that Freddie Dunbar was the only plausible culprit, and that they just needed to keep working the trail of evidence until they could fit him into it. Seamus did what he always did during his time in uniform, and nodded and smiled at his superior officer, giving him a jovial 'yes, boss', and promptly headed back to the flats, where he knocked on Mary O'Brien's door, finding her and the hulking Bill inside.

'Have you come to arrest us?' the old woman asked.

Grant was, unsurprisingly, not terribly happy when Seamus brought the couple into Pearse Street station to be formally charged. Yet despite his displeasure, the arrest was the beginning of Seamus's upward trajectory in the Gardai. And it marked one of the talents he brought to the job: observation. Seamus saw everything, remembered what he saw and was gifted with the intelligence to make connections where others failed to do so.

He continued to leaf through the files in the dim light of the parking garage. Suddenly realising he hadn't eaten since the biscuits he'd consumed in Tallaght earlier that afternoon, he reached into the back seat and produced a bag he'd loaded into the car before dawn containing a thermos of tea and some hastily prepared ham-and-cheese sandwiches. Laying the file out on his lap, he unscrewed the lid of the flask and began to pour himself a cupful.

Just as he did so, the alarm on the car beside him screeched into life. Seamus, who usually had the hands and balance of a surgeon, jumped in spite of himself, spilling tea all over the open pages before they slid off his knees and into the footwell. Swearing loudly, the detective put the thermos's cup on the dashboard and screwed the lid back on, then looked towards the whooping, flashing vehicle to his left to see that a young woman in a blue hoody had bumped it with her shopping trolley. She was hurrying away from the scene of the crime, head bowed, hoping no one had noticed.

Shaking his head in resignation, Seamus leaned down and began to gather up the now slightly damp contents of the file. As he did, his eyes fell on the statement given by Dave Gibb, the hiker who'd discovered Richard Roche's body. And what he saw made him freeze.

Because he spotted a detail everyone else had missed.

15

Rodney Lawler, the hospital's social worker, was an overweight man with thinning dark hair slicked back on his head with some kind of gel. Jessie met him at a café across the street from Beaumont at four thirty that afternoon. The place was packed with nurses, doctors and other employees of the hospital, and the behaviourist and her interviewee just managed to get standing room at a narrow counter to the back of the establishment.

'Yes, Richie did make a complaint against the Blakes,' Lawler said around mouthfuls of burger. 'But I couldn't find any reason to uphold it.'

'What was the nature of the complaint?'

'I'm not at liberty to say.'

'Mr Lawler, I am fully aware you are bound by a code of confidentiality, but this is both a murder investigation and a child abduction case. Do you really want to force me to get a warrant when a child's life is at stake?'

Lawler flicked a look at her from the corner of his eye and continued to work on his food.

'He claimed Rosie needed to be taken into care.'

'Why?'

'He said she was at risk being with her parents.'

Jessie thought about that for a moment. 'He intimated they were abusing her in some way?'

Lawler picked up a napkin and wiped mayonnaise from the corner of his mouth before guzzling about half of a glass of cola.

'He wouldn't specify. He never directly said he thought they were hurting the child.'

'I'm lost, Mr Lawler. What did he say? Precisely please.'

'Richard Roche said that Rosie Blake would be in danger if she remained in the care of her parents.'

Jessie sipped some of her coffee. She'd had far more than she usually did that day and was beginning to get jittery.

'That could mean anything,' she said.

'It could. I suppose him approaching a social worker suggests he thought she was being abused or neglected in some way, but to be fair, Rosie spends more time in hospital than she does in her own home. The fact is, she's not really under her parents' care most of the time.'

'Did you point that out to Roche?'

'I did.'

Jessie waited for him to continue, but Lawler was now cramming a handful of chips into his mouth. She waited while he chewed and swallowed.

'And how did he respond?' Jessie pressed when he still didn't augment his comment.

'Oh,' the social worker said, as if he'd forgotten she was there, 'yes, that was a strange one, now you mention it. Very odd.'

Jessie looked at him expectantly. 'Yes?'

'He said while she was with us, Rosie needed to be placed in a more secure wing of the hospital.'

'Are there secure wings in Beaumont?' Jessie wanted to know.

'There's a small psychiatric ward,' Lawler said, 'which is

locked for obvious reasons. And some of the surgical wards have doors that require fobs to be opened.'

'He wanted her placed on one of those?'

'He seemed to, yes. I told him she was only with us at the moment for chemo, which he knew already, and that those wards have a lot of day patients who come and go as they need treatment, and it just isn't practical to have them sealed.'

'Is it that he was afraid of infection?'

Lawler gave her an *I'm not sure* look and continued to eat his chips.

'Mr Lawler, do you think Roche was questioning the hygiene protocols on the ward she was in?'

The social worker sighed and said: 'I put that to him. I pointed out she's always put up in the same room, and the place is sterilised to a surgical standard. There's no risk to her whatsoever. But I'm not completely sure that's what his issue was.'

'No?'

'I don't think so. He seemed a bit flustered, and his next question was if it would be possible to have her moved abroad for treatment.'

'Out of the country?'

'Yes. He'd done some research, and apparently there's a private hospital in Coventry that specialises in treating children with her condition.'

Jessie made a mental note to get Terri to look the place up.

'So was his issue that he wasn't satisfied with how the Blakes were managing her treatment? He thought there were better hospitals?'

'Beaumont's paediatric cancer wing is acknowledged as one of the best in Europe,' Lawler said. 'I'll be honest, I have no idea why he had a bee in his bonnet.'

'If you had to guess?' Jessie asked.

'It's possible he'd just become overly attached,' the social worker suggested. 'Roche was a middle-aged, childless man and he'd been working with Rosie for about a year. She was cute. A sweet kid. I'd hazard a guess that he simply became fixated on her and felt he could do a better job directing her convalescence than her own family.'

'And when you wouldn't step in, he took things into his own hands.' Jessie completed the train of thought.

'It seems a reasonable premise, wouldn't you say?' Lawler said, pushing his plate aside. 'Now I wonder what kind of desserts they've got on today.'

Jessie made her excuses and left him to his extended lunch. As she exited the café, she noticed a tall, angular man in an old-fashioned brown suit watching her closely from across the street. He had a large, shaggy dog beside him, an animal so tall at the shoulder, its head came up almost to the man's chest. The man gazed at her for a long moment, as if he was about to say something, but then he turned on his heel and strode away down the street. The dog remained in place, also staring intently at the behaviourist. Then all of a sudden, it too spun and followed its master.

Jessie watched the animal disappear into the crowd and then went on her way.

Unless that was one hell of a coincidence, Jessie thought, *I just encountered Rosie Blake's dream.*

16

While Jessie was watching the shaggy dog disappear into the crowd, the computer running the deep-web search in the team's Cork office made a gentle sing-song sound, indicating its work was complete. Terri, who had been making a cappuccino in the office's small kitchen, carried her beverage to the desk and began to scroll through the results.

Although scrolling wasn't really required, as there were only three items on the screen.

What Terri had done to generate the findings was called data mining, going into thousands of different pages and sites on the deep web, looking for a specific set of parameters. Terri had written an algorithm – a beautiful little piece of alphanumeric composition – to lay out the details of the search, setting it to look for any posts – or even comments within posts – relating to requests for or reports (or even rumours) relating to the abduction of a female child, aged eight to ten with dark hair and blue eyes. Refining the search further, Terri had added the child should be Caucasian and English speaking. Finally, she'd factored in that the child's health should either not be a concern or that a child with cancer might actually be a bonus.

She wasn't surprised the process had only brought back three hits – it was an extremely niche search, and she had allowed that she might have to refine the search parameters a few times to generate any results at all.

The first item was an advertisement taken from a page called *Mercs and Men for Hire*. The page was a bulletin board upon which people could post job advertisements looking for individuals who could complete tasks that required a particular set of skills and an ambiguous relationship with the law, an ambiguity that often seemed to blur into outright contempt. The advert Terri's search had unearthed was looking for someone who could locate a woman who could 'pass for eight or nine' and was suitable for 'medical sub-dom role play'. Terri's search program automatically recorded the IP address the advert had been sent from, even though she knew (as this was the deep web) that it would be a remote router station miles from wherever the sender was holed up, and the signal would have bounced around the globe several times more before landing on the message board.

Such details did not present much of an obstacle to Terri, who had several pieces of software (including one she'd designed herself) that could track the pathway the advert had traversed and find the source, regardless of encryption or other digital subterfuge.

That said, she didn't think this ad was what she was looking for.

The second item consisted of a few lines from what looked to be series of direct messages taken from a deep web social-networking site named Galaxy 3.

Tyyyjr$56: *Have you seen the girl?*

*Brandywine*8:* *I've seen pics. She fits the bill perfecto.*

Tyyyjr$56: *I don't blve in perfect. Are you sure she's all he asked for?*

Brandywine*8: *9 yrs old. Skinny. Dark hair pale skin. Got some kind of cancer.*

Tyyyjr$56: *Will anyone be looking for her?*

Brandywine*8: *No one gives a fuck about this kid. Are you ready to commit?*

Tyyyjr$56: *What's the transfer number?*

Terri read the exchange a few times, and while it was compelling and she would certainly look into it further, it didn't fit the bill: no one would believe Rosie would not be missed.

The final item, however, was more interesting. It was an email sent from ProtonMail, a deep-web email provider. It was short but contained enough detail to make Terri sit up and pay attention.

As this was a deep-web communication, the usual details that topped most surface web emails were absent (the date, time and email address of the sender). The lack of such information, however, was not an issue for Terri, who knew ways to retrieve it. The message began without preamble:

> *I have found her. Not yet ten, short dark hair and still physically a kid. She's got a rare form of cancer and her parents, who are not without resources, will go crazy if she's taken. Which means they'll be open to suggestion and coercion. I'm told the child will need medical intervention quickly, so we should plan to conclude the deal as soon as possible. If she dies, it will complicate matters unnecessarily. That said, I would advise you line up some resolute and unemotional men to watch her.*

Some may find the vista of a sickening and pain-wracked young girl distressing to watch. Might I also counsel procuring some opiates to keep her sedated? Something strong, though it should be applied sparingly, as her weakened state would put her at risk of overdosing. The other consideration, of course, will be where to hold her during negotiations. This I will leave in your capable hands – I'm sure there are plenty of places around Dublin and the east coast of Ireland that would make a suitable hideaway.

The message ended there – no sign-off, no farewell, no yours sincerely. But it was enough. If the email's author wasn't talking about Rosie Blake, the similarities were shockingly close.

Terri immediately set up a reverse-tracking search to determine the IP address then picked up her phone and called Jessie without any further delay.

17

Dave Gibb, the man who had discovered Richard Roche's body, was a little under five feet six inches in height and had long grey hair and a red beard peppered with strands of silver that was just the wrong side of untidy. Dressed in a blue windbreaker over green tracksuit pants and walking boots, his blue eyes were pale and moved jerkily here and there, as if he was in a state of constant nervous agitation.

Seamus met him in the car park of Montpelier Hill at a quarter past three while there was still daylight, and they walked towards the summit together. The path wound first through woods, then veered to the right up a steep rocky slope.

'What do you do for a living, Mr Gibb?' Seamus asked.

'I used to be an accountant,' the small man said. 'But I took voluntary redundancy five years ago.'

'So you live on social welfare?' Seamus asked, realising as he said the words that they sounded judgemental. 'Not that there's anything wrong with that.'

'I collect the dole, but I've got savings, and I run crowd-funding for projects and expeditions I want to go on. People love to contribute to things that interest them.'

'Fair play,' Seamus said. 'This Peaks challenge thing is one of those projects?'

'The Three Peaks, yes. I'm going to run up three of the steepest mountains in the Brecon Beacons, in Wales, all in twelve hours.'

Seamus laughed. 'That sounds tiring. I've done a good bit of hillwalking myself, but I've never *run* up any mountains. Fair play to you. You're a hardy man to want to undertake something so strenuous.'

'I'm training for it now. It's all about building up the right kind of stamina. It's not for everyone, but I enjoy it.'

'You're doing some of this training at night?'

'Yes. I'm doing the run on St Patrick's Day, and I'll be beginning at four in the morning, so the first hour or so will be done in the dark. You need to get used to that, or it could be dangerous. Peak running at night is a skill.'

'I'll say,' Seamus said.

They were close to the top of Montpelier now, the old hunting lodge looming above them on the horizon, Dublin opening to their left like a toy town.

'I reread your statement a little while ago, and something you said interested me.'

'Oh yes?' Gibb said. 'I've already been interviewed by guard. Several, in fact.'

'I know you have, but if you'd just bear with me, there's a point I'd like to go over with you.'

'All right.'

They walked across the flat grass expanse towards the ancient building, its windows, long empty of glass and frames, surveying them like hollow eye sockets. Shadows and darkness were within, despite the glow of the setting sun.

'You live near here, don't you?' Seamus asked.

'Yes. I've got the house nearest to the car park on the Dublin city side.'

'What caught my attention was that you told Garda Jordan you'd been seeing lights on the mountain for weeks.'

'I mentioned it when I talked to him, but I don't think he believed me. He certainly never asked me any more about it.'

'I'm taking you very seriously, Mr Gibb. What did you tell Garda Jordan?'

'That I suspected there's someone using the Hellfire Club again.'

'Do you mean historians or archaeologists?'

'No. I do not. I mean the Reavers might have come back. Because I train at night, I've seen the cars coming and going at all hours. And I've seen the lights twinkling on the hilltop and... and I heard their singing. Awful and ungodly it is too. But I've heard it.'

Seamus nodded. The old stone building loomed over them, just a short walk away. It suddenly felt ominous, even though the sun hadn't yet set and birds could be heard singing in the nearby woods.

'How often does this happen, Mr Gibb? Every week?'

'I'd say once a month maybe. Sometimes twice.'

'Yet you still come up here? You use it as part of your training. Aren't you scared?'

'I always told myself the Reavers were harmless. Just nature worshippers. Pagans or whatever. I... I suppose I was wrong about that.'

'Can you remember the last time before last night you heard them or saw lights?'

'It was two weeks ago.'

'Exactly two weeks?'

'It was a Thursday. I remember because I'd watched *Room to Improve* earlier.' Gibb was referring to a TV show in which an architect helped couples with rebuilds and extensions on their homes. Seamus wasn't a fan, but he figured it was on once a week, so was a good way to remember the evening the event had occurred.

'And what time did the noises begin?'

'It was after midnight. Close to one o'clock I'd say. Maybe even later.'

'And you said these people are called the Reavers?'

'My father did a study of them when he was younger. He was fascinated and horrified by their lore, but he wanted to be prepared. He always told me evil things happened on that hill, and we needed to be ready in case they ever came back. Well I'm here to tell you, they've come back to the place where they got their power, just as they promised to do all those years ago.'

'Isn't it much more likely to just be kids messing around?'

'No. Those of us whose families have lived here for generations have been waiting for this. I just wish it hadn't occurred in my lifetime. The Reavers have returned. They've killed a man and taken a child. The final thing to fulfil the prophecy is a human sacrifice. Once that happens, it'll be too late.'

'Why?' Seamus wanted to know.

'Because once they do that, they'll bring about a new age. A new world order, and there'll be no way to save any of us.'

'Oh,' Seamus said. 'That.'

'If you believe in that type of thing. Which I never did before last night.'

'But you're changing your ideas?'

Gibb didn't answer that; he just said: 'Can I help you with anything else, Detective?'

'You told the officer who took your statement that you saw lights in the hunting lodge as you came to the top of the hill,' Seamus said. 'Could you walk me through what happened?'

'The lights... they were... they weren't like anything I'd ever seen before.'

Seamus looked at the man with a puzzled expression. 'What were they like then?'

Gibb seemed to be turning the events of the night over in his head.

'I reached the top of the climbing path at seventeen minutes past two this morning,' he said. 'I know it was that because I'd timed my ascent, and I was three and a half seconds faster than I'd been the previous night.'

'Good for you,' Seamus said. 'That's quite the improvement.'

'Thanks. I was pleased about it. I stopped right over there, more or less at the top of the path, and I took some fluids and opened up a protein bar, and I was only planning on stopping for a couple of minutes before going back down and doing the whole thing again. I usually do it three times two nights a week. I have other, longer routes I do the other nights – this is my lighter routine.'

'So when did you see the lights?'

'I probably wouldn't have seen them at all if I hadn't heard the... well, if I hadn't heard the music.'

Seamus nodded. 'If I heard music and saw lights in a ruined building,' he said, 'I'd have been convinced it was kids drinking or smoking weed.'

'The music wasn't the kind of music kids would listen to.'

'No?'

'Not at all. I started to wonder if I'd really heard it. I'm sure you know how that can happen. You begin to think you imagined certain events.'

Seamus had encountered this phenomenon before – most people went through their lives dealing with the same visual and auditory input day in and day out. When they came across something that didn't compute, or which was completely outside the realm of their experience, they had a kind of sensory overload, and their minds edited out the offending article.

Instances were well recorded. There were countless examples of people being assaulted in broad daylight, sometimes on busy streets, and rather than people interceding to help, they just walked past. It was often written off as fear or callous disregard, but psychologists posited that, in fact, the violence was so shocking, the majority didn't even register it. They blocked it out.

At Garda training college, one of Seamus's lecturers had told the class about the Native Americans who were on the beaches in 1492 when Columbus's ships arrived. Never having seen anything like the *Niña*, the *Pinta* and the *Santa Maria* before, the locals simply behaved as if they weren't there – their perception was unable to process these vast wooden creations, so it just edited them out of the scene. Apparently, the ships were moored offshore, in full view of the populace, for days before landing crafts were launched, and during that time not a single canoe was sent out to investigate. Because the Spanish vessels were effectively invisible.

It appeared something similar had happened to Dave Gibb, except in his case he'd done the editing after the fact, disbelieving what he'd experienced.

'But you believe you heard music now?' Seamus asked.

'It just occurred to me that I *must* have heard it. It's why I turned around.'

'What did it sound like?'

Gibb screwed up his face, as if the act of remembering was a great effort.

'Chanting,' he said at last. 'You know like... like monks do. What do you call it? Gregorian chanting?'

'It was religious music?'

'No. I don't think so. It *sounded* a bit like monks singing, but it was different too. It sounded... well, it sounded horrible.'

'Of course, hearing chanting near a haunted house on top of a hill in the woods in the middle of the night would be horrible,' Seamus said. 'Anyone would be freaked out by it.'

'No. It was more than that. This was different. It sounded... well, it sounded *unnatural*.'

'Unnatural how?'

'It was like it was wrong somehow. It made me feel a bit sick.'

There was nowhere for Seamus to go with that, so he said: 'So you turned when you heard the music, and that was when you saw the lights?'

'Yes.'

'Are we talking torches? Camping lamps?'

'No. Nothing like that.'

'Candles? Firelight maybe?'

'It's hard to describe,' Gibb said, and Seamus could see the man was actually quite distressed. Whatever he'd seen, it had unnerved him.

'It was like a... like a cloud of moving balls of light. I thought my eyes were playing tricks on me at first. I've seen fireflies in other parts of the world, and it was like that, only much bigger. They were... the only word I can use to describe them is *orbs*.'

'You're telling me you heard strange chanting, and then saw a cloud of moving orbs of light, and you still went over to investigate?'

'That's the thing, Detective,' Dave Gibb said, his voice tremulous. 'I have no recollection of walking over to the Hellfire Club. One moment I was here, the next I was standing in that doorway, with the body of a man at my feet.'

'That must have been scary,' Seamus said.

'It was,' Gibb admitted. 'Why am I not a suspect?'

Seamus laughed. 'You were. But during the medical examination you had, your hands were checked for powder residue.'

'Powder?' the peak runner asked.

'*Gun*powder. If you'd shot Roche, your hands would be covered with a very fine coating of it. It'd be under your nails, in the cracks in your skin. Even if you'd washed them with surgical alcohol, it'd still be there in some places. You had none, so you couldn't have done it.'

'That's comforting to know, I suppose.'

And there didn't seem to be much more to say.

18

Gibb made his excuses and went back down the hill, and Seamus went over to the hunting lodge and scanned the area where Roche's body had been found.

His initial idea was that the peak runner had simply hallucinated the whole thing. Seamus had done a couple of boot camps with the Irish Army – it was something the Gardai recommended to encourage fitness levels within the ranks. He remembered a run he and the other participants had completed through the Sally Gap in the Wicklow Mountains, during which they were only permitted a very small ration of water.

Seamus understood the purpose of this exercise had been to demonstrate the real dangers of dehydration during periods of intense strenuous activity, and by the end of the exercise, three of the trainees had passed out and he was seeing lights in front of his eyes and was dizzy and nauseous. He wondered if Gibb might have been experiencing something similar.

The ground around where Roche had fallen, both outside and inside the stone structure, was still cordoned off with crime-scene tape. The grass and earth had been disturbed as little as possible by the forensic team, and he took a small but powerful Maglite torch from his pocket and shone it about the murder zone, first covering the ground and then the walls and high stone ceiling. Would it have been possible to suspend lights from the rough inner structure? He could see no hooks, or even snags or outcroppings that would offer purchase. Could Gibb have seen a number of people holding torches or lamps? And if that was it, why did he believe they were constantly moving? Could the individuals holding the lights have been milling about? Had Roche been killed in some sort of gang fight?

The orderly had been killed cleanly – three gunshots, closely grouped – which made Seamus think this wasn't the case. There had been no bruising, no cuts and abrasions, no defensive injuries or signs of a fight. The murder looked much more like a one-on-one affair. Which still didn't explain the lights.

And the ruined building and the grass and earth outside it told him nothing – there were no scuff marks or trampled areas, nothing to indicate a throng of people.

He switched off his torch and walked to the rear of the building. It struck him that, if there had been a group here (even a levitating one that didn't leave footprints), they would have had to have escaped into the woods behind the Hellfire Club for Gibb not to have seen them. A curved, semicircular window set quite close to the ground offered a path of egress, and from there the treeline was only about ten yards distant.

Seamus squatted down so he was at the level of the narrow gap in the stonework and, using his thumb and forefinger to create a horizon line, slowly surveyed the trees to see if he could spy an obvious entry point where a fleeing killer (or group of them) might plunge under cover and away from prying eyes.

Spying a break in the foliage that would be met by striking a diagonal course from the window, he made his way towards it, rapidly finding a path had already been worn through the grass

– and recently. Someone had passed this way within the past few hours.

Then he was under the trees, and the texture of the light changed and the feel of the air was different, and everything smelled of pine needles, bark and mulch.

The woods that covered the northern edge of Montpelier were ancient but had, for the past two decades, been husbanded by Coillte, the Irish forestry service, and the section Seamus walked through now contained many mature evergreens but also showed signs of having been pruned and thinned – he could pick a path through the cedars easily, and there was plenty of light and air.

As he walked, Seamus kept his eyes on the forest floor, and within fifteen yards of the treeline he'd picked out several clear tracks – one boot print that looked to be a size ten or eleven, beside which he found the tracks of what looked like an enormous dog. A little apart from these he discovered a smaller, more slender indentation that might have belonged to a woman and seemed to Seamus to be a trainer; and a half-track, which appeared to have been made when its owner was running or walking very quickly – only the front part of the foot had left a mark.

This would have excited him had he not also spied some empty beer bottles and a crumpled flagon of Linden Village cider. Had the marks been left by al-fresco drinkers or by whoever had killed Roche and taken Rosie? It was impossible to tell.

He took photos of the tracks on his phone and continued through the trees, casting about here and there for more markings. He was on the verge of giving up when a twig broke loudly behind him, and he spun around, his hand going to the Glock on his hip. The woods seemed to still, as if holding their breath. He took the gun from its holster and held it loosely by his side. Somewhere off to his left, deeper in the trees, another twig broke. He froze, listening intently for more movement, yet reminding himself the woods were full of wildlife, and that a deer, a pine marten or even a blackbird might be making the sounds he was hearing.

Something rustled, this time to his right, and slowly and with purpose, he began to move towards the activity. He'd only gone about five steps when he heard a series of pops and snaps, and then the percussive sound of rapid footsteps, as if someone was running through the woods, having thrown caution to the wind.

Seamus called out as loudly as he could: 'I'm an officer of An Garda Síochána, and I'm requesting you halt and make yourself known to me!'

No response was forthcoming, so Seamus took a deep breath and set off in pursuit.

He could still see no one, but the sounds of the person's trajectory remained audible. Seamus put on a burst of speed but almost immediately regretted it. Not knowing the lay of the land, he was just able to leap over the trunk of a fallen tree to save himself from going head over heels, but he had just articulated that manoeuvre when the ground in front of him vanished and he was sliding down a steep embankment, swearing loudly as a sharp stone tore through the material of his trousers and cut the meat of his thigh beneath, sending a cascade of pain right up into his groin.

His descent came to a concussive halt as his legs hit what felt like hard rock, and another wave of agony enveloped him as a stone was driven into his coccyx. He half lay/half sat, his knees at his chin, feeling sick from the pain and the physical shock.

Seamus remained where he was for a moment, trying to get his breath back. Looking around, he saw that a path had been cleared in front of him, vanishing into trees and scrub that continued into the far distance. Whoever he'd been pursuing had made good their escape into the wilderness beyond, and Seamus ruefully acknowledged it would be foolish for him to continue to give chase.

Pulling himself painfully upright, he looked about for a way back up to the summit. As he did, he noticed that someone – he assumed it was the person he'd just been chasing – had formed some kind of figure from sticks and vines and hung it from a branch above where he'd just landed. The detective could make out two spindly arms and a forked stick that formed what looked like two bowed legs. A strip of bark hung between them – Seamus couldn't work out if it was supposed to be a tail or a penis. The thing had a pine-cone head, and dried grass represented scraggly hair. Despite being made completely from natural materials, the mannequin was utterly grotesque and seemed to be hovering above him accusingly. Taunting him.

Finding a long stick among the detritus on the ground, Seamus made to knock it down.

The first strike connected, and it swayed drunkenly in place. The second caused it to buck a little more aggressively, and the third knocked it free. Seamus made to catch it, but, still holding the stick, he missed, and to his dismay the figure shattered into its component parts as it struck the rocky ground.

He made a half-hearted effort to gather the pieces but realised quickly that he wasn't sure if he was picking up part of the weird figure or just random bits of deadfall. Taking the pine-cone head, the only bit that he could be sure of, he gingerly began to climb back up the embankment down which he'd slid.

ARIZONA ROSE BLAKE

THAT MORNING, VERY EARLY

It was dark, so dark it didn't matter whether or not her eyes were opened or closed – the results were the same either way.

All she could see was a thick, inky blackness.

Far worse than the dark though was the cold. Richie had bundled her up in a coat, hat and scarf as well as putting a thick tracksuit and woollen jumper on over her pyjamas, but the bitter, frigid air still managed to cut through the layers and chill her to the bone. And where was Panda? She seemed to have dropped him somewhere. She wondered if she would ever see him again, and the thought made her panic. She tried not to think about Panda, and her mind automatically went back to her physical discomfort.

Rosie couldn't remember ever being so cold.

She was shivering uncontrollably now as the man who had taken her from Richie trudged through the trees, carrying Rosie over his shoulder. She could feel the rough material of his overcoat beneath her cheek, and it smelled of woodsmoke and fried food. The stench, the irregular motion and the chemotherapy she'd recently had administered (incomplete though it was) caused her stomach to heave, and she threw up a thin stream of green bile down her captor's back.

'For fuck's sake,' she heard him exclaim. 'Did you just do what I think you did?'

He shook her roughly but did not slow his pace, and they moved deeper and deeper into the trees.

Rosie was confused and terrified.

She was unsure what had happened, had only a vague sense of how she'd gone from the ruined old building on the hill, where Richie said they were waiting to meet a friend of his, to being lugged through the night like a sack of potatoes by a man she didn't know (although she was certain she didn't like him, even though they'd just met). One moment she was sitting on Richie's knee while he toasted marshmallows on an old oil burner, the next there was a bright light, as if the sun had come out from behind a particularly dense cloud and was blinding her.

She'd called out to Richie, tried to bury her face in his shoulder, but then strong hands had taken her and she was being lifted, and even though she kept crying for the orderly, the man who had her had ignored her cries, cuffing her roughly about the back of the head, and she didn't know if it was that blow or the shock of it all, but she'd lost consciousness for a time.

When she regained her senses, she had a headache and motion sickness and chemo-induced nausea, and she wished more than anything else to be back in her bed in Beaumont.

It was to be many hours before Arizona Rose Blake saw a bed.

And she never saw Richie Roche again.

At one point during the journey, the moon came out, illuminating the area through which they travelled. Rosie lifted her head and saw row after row of trees, and there, standing several yards away from the man who was carrying her, an enormous, shaggy dog.

Rosie gazed in terror at the scene and then passed out.

19

Jessie learned nothing else in Beaumont, except that Richard Roche was beloved by all, and that no one could envision a scenario where he would kidnap a child in his care. She even spoke (with the child's parents present) to a ten-year-old who was in the room beside the one where Rosie had been receiving treatment. Jessie had been informed by the little girl that Roche was her favourite orderly – in fact, he was probably her favourite person in the hospital.

She'd shown Jessie a stack of comic books on her bedside locker – *Beano*s and *Dandy*s and various other colourful publications, some new and some obviously second-hand.

'Every week, he brought me in a new one,' the kid had informed her. 'I just told him once that I like comics. He didn't have to do it, but he did. He was a awful nice man. *Real* nice. Not fake. He was kind because he wanted to be.'

Jessie pondered this as she drove her MG towards Dame Street and punched in the phone number for the company where Peter Blake worked. It rang out the first time so she dialled it again.

As the ringtone sounded, she continued to ponder Roche and who he had been.

Getting a sick kid comic books could easily be construed as grooming, doing something nice to gain trust and lure the vulnerable child into a false sense of security. Yet she had to admit, it didn't seem like that. Jessie was beginning to think Richard Roche really had been one of the good ones.

Which made the whole thing even more confusing.

The phone was answered and Jessie asked to be put through to the managing director, a man named Robinson.

'How can I help you, Detective?' he asked.

'I'd like to talk to you about Peter Blake.'

'Oh yes. Nasty business. I've told him he can have as much time off as he needs. Peter insists he's fine to work, but I really feel I must insist. What good is he going to be to the clients if his head is elsewhere?'

Jessie ignored the obvious inhumanity in this comment and asked: 'Is Mr Blake involved in any business dealings that might put him in contact with criminals?'

'Ms Boyle, every single one of our clients has criminal leanings. It's our job to skate as close as we can to the line that separates the lawful from the criminal and make as much damn money as we can while we're about it. I'm not going to dress it up, because there isn't a damn thing you or the Criminal Assets Bureau or anyone else can do about it. It's the way business has been done for hundreds – fuck it, for *thousands* – of years. We're not doing anything actionable. We're just playing the game.'

'You're saying *all* of his clients are potential suspects.'

'All of them. None of them. Someone associated with a client perhaps. Or none of the above. What about some of those Occupy fellas? They hate people who make money. Maybe one of them took Peter's sick kid just to piss him off.'

'I'll make a note of it,' Jessie said, refusing to take the bait and lose her temper.

'Do that.'

'Have you ever heard the name Garth Calhoun?'

There was a pause. Then: 'Is he a country music artist?'

Jessie smiled. Robinson had heard of Garth all right.

'I'm going to need copies of all the files Peter Blake was working on. Could you have them sent to me at Harcourt Street?'

'I'll get one of my girls to do it.'

'Do that,' Jessie said.

She hung up. So sleazy was the man, even speaking to him on the phone made her want to take a shower.

EUGENE DUNLIN

Being a gangster wasn't what he'd expected it to be.

He'd thought there would be heists. Hold-ups. High-speed car chases and late nights cutting product and counting money. Instead, Garth Calhoun had put him in a back room in the pub where he did business and given him stacks of ledgers to go through.

'I hear you've some book training in accounts,' the old man had said. 'Well, here's the story of how I make my money, and how I make it look legit. The green books are the ones I show the tax man; the red ones are the real figures. When you understand how it's done, I want you to try and do some for yourself. I'll give you some easy transactions to start off with. If you play your cards right, you could be keeping the whole thing going before too long.'

Calhoun said this as if Eugene should be pleased.

He wasn't.

Yet again, he wasn't being taken seriously.

But he was smart enough to know that what old Garth was doing was opening a window onto his financial world. He really could see how the money was made and, more importantly, how he hid it and where. This he found fascinating.

He also realised that the process of laundering the money Garth earned from his criminal enterprises so it was safe to use was being done in an extremely inefficient way. It was small-time stuff, and it didn't need to be. It could all be done so much more effectively, and Eugene thought he knew how.

He just needed to make a few contacts, set up a few deals.

And he wanted Garth to respect him.

He wanted that very badly.

There were a few guys who worked in the bar whom Garth clearly had a lot of time for. He'd ask their opinions and call them in to advise him on certain issues. When he was going out, he always brought one of them – a big ex-boxer called AJ – with him. Eugene wanted to merit that kind of respect. He craved a place in Garth's inner circle. To get there, he understood that he needed to be more than book smart. He had to be seen as a physical presence too.

Eugene had never punched anyone in his life. When he got beaten up at school, his policy had been to just curl up into a ball and wait for the unpleasantness to stop. When his father attacked him, he took the hiding – or whatever else was involved – silently, and then pretended it hadn't happened. His mother, who was also the victim of his father's mood swings, had never, in all of Eugene's twenty-four years, ever made reference to the fact that the man she married was treating them both worse than junkyard dogs.

As he drew up the plan he hoped would catapult him to the big time, Eugene made the decision to shake up the status quo in all aspects of his life. He wanted to feel that he was a man of destiny, of purpose.

And that meant his father had to go.

20

Terri called just after Jessie had hung up on Robinson.

'I've got something,' she said and told her about the email.

'It sounds conclusive, but it still might not be Rosie,' Jessie said. 'It could be nothing at all. Just someone indulging a sick fantasy.'

'Doesn't it serve us better if we work on the premise that it is her though?' Terri asked.

'Let's use it as a working hypothesis for the moment,' Jessie agreed. 'What can you learn from the email?'

'I've been reverse tracking the IP address. The email was sent from London.'

'Can you tell where exactly?'

'The tracker gives me a radius of a quarter of a square mile. But it's placing it near the Barbican.'

'That's the financial district,' Jessie said.

'Exactly.'

'Which is another coincidence that can't be a coincidence. Can you pinpoint it a bit more than that?'

'It'll take some time, but yes. I should have a precise location within a couple of days.'

'That's great, Terri. This could be what breaks the case.'

'The wording is odd though,' Terri said. 'It's like they've chosen Rosie at random. Like they've found someone to fit a list of criteria.'

'And how would someone in London have located a kid in Dublin? From what you've just read me, the person who wrote the email doesn't know the city, yet he's identified a child here and set her up to be abducted.'

'It's a puzzle all right,' Terri agreed.

'Is there anything else you can pick up from it?'

'The only other obvious line of inquiry would be to ascertain who the message was sent to,' Terri said. 'Which, if we're interpreting it correctly, should be someone in Dublin – or in Ireland at least.'

'I think that would be very useful to know,' Jessie agreed.

'I'll get working on it.'

'Send me the text of the email, will you please? I'm heading back to Harcourt Street so we can compare what few notes we've got.'

'I've already done so. It's in your inbox right now.'

'Thanks, Terri. Keep up the good work.'

'It's not like I've got anything else to do,' Terri said and did as she was asked.

21

Jessie, Seamus and Dawn sat around the table in the meeting room at Harcourt Street, with Terri joining them via Zoom.

'Did Peter Blake hand over his and Shauna's logins?' Dawn asked the genealogist.

'He did,' Terri told her, 'albeit very begrudgingly. He said he'd sue me if I divulged anything except information directly linked to the case. And he then informed me I wouldn't find any of that in his emails or social media, so he'd be suing me regardless.'

'He is a challenging man, I'll give him that,' Dawn said. 'Is anything jumping out at you yet?'

'Nothing, but I've only just started.'

'That's fine, Terri. Stick with it. So,' the commissioner said, 'I spoke to a friend of mine in the drugs squad earlier, and the cocktail of chemicals Rosie's on has no street value so isn't easily available on the black market. That doesn't mean it can't be got – you can get anything you want if you're prepared to pay for it, but it's not straightforward.'

'I'll run some checks on the medical companies who supply

the specific medication,' Terri said. 'See if any of them have received orders that are out of the ordinary.'

'Worth a try, but I expect this will be an under-the-counter deal, if it happened at all.'

'The email Terri dug up indicates a plan to keep the child sedated,' Jessie said, passing printouts of the message to Dawn and Seamus.

'Which seems far more likely,' Dawn said. 'Cheaper, easier and relatively hassle free.'

'Are we taking this seriously?' Seamus asked, looking up from having read it. 'It could be a complete fantasy.'

'Until we have reason not to, I think we need to assume it's the real deal,' Jessie said. 'It originated in the financial district in London, which is indicative enough, and there aren't obvious signs it's a fiction or a fantasy. It contains quite specific details, none of which are overly lurid, not enough to be titillating at any rate. It seems very business-like, in fact.'

'If we take this as genuine, that opens up the possibility the abduction was planned well in advance,' Seamus said.

'Which offers a different scenario to it being an impulsive act carried out by an emotionally disturbed orderly,' Jessie said. 'Yet he still took her. And that's a question we do need an answer to. Having it might also help us understand who has her now.'

'This seems to be saying it's been done purely for ransom,' Seamus added. 'To extort money from her parents.'

'Which brings us to Garth Calhoun,' Jessie said.

'I spoke to him,' Dawn sighed. 'And he insists Roche wasn't working for him, and hadn't since he was a teen, and then only on the legal side of his business. He got sent down for being in the wrong place at the wrong time.'

'We're sure he took her, aren't we?' Seamus asked. 'I mean, we're not in any doubt about it? From what I've heard today, everyone loved him. He protected weaker kids from bullies, was good to his mother and devoted a lot of his time to charity.'

'I got the same,' Jessie said. 'The entire hospital – patients and staff alike – have only good things to say about the guy.'

'I think we can be certain he did it,' Dawn said. 'The question is why? And who the blazes has her now?'

'I don't know if this is useful to us,' Jessie said, 'but Roche tried to get the hospital social worker to have Rosie either taken into care, placed on a secure ward or moved to a hospital in the UK. He seemed to believe she was at risk.'

'Did he say from what?' Seamus asked. 'Do you think he knew something about the planned abduction?'

'Well, based on what a stand-up guy he's supposed to have been, I have to wonder if he took her because he thought he was protecting her. So maybe.'

'His mother suggested that,' Seamus agreed. 'And Professor Dobbs, who was over Hollymount when he was there, kind of said the same thing too.'

'I couldn't work out what he believed he was protecting her from,' Jessie said. 'I wondered if he thought she wasn't getting the best medical care, but that didn't seem to make any sense. But if he had some clue there was an abduction afoot – that's a scenario that holds together better.'

'Which puts a completely different slant on things,' Seamus said. 'Roche isn't the bad guy – he's the hero. He was trying to stop something bad from happening to one of the kids he was working with in the hospital, kids he was supposed to be taking care of.'

'And he died trying to do it,' Jessie added.

'How do we follow up on it though?' Terri asked. 'I agree the evidence seems to point to that, but where do we go with it next?'

'I'm pretty sure Garth Calhoun knows her parents,' Dawn suggested. 'There was a brief flash of something when I mentioned their names. It was just for a moment, but it was definitely there. If the Blakes were involved in some way with Garth, that would suggest they were mixed up in all kinds of bad behaviour.'

'You think Garth is behind the abduction?' Jessie asked.

'He's a very bad man, Jessie,' Dawn said. 'I find it hard to believe he's not mixed up in it somewhere. Although I have to say, snatching sick kids isn't his style.'

'Would Roche go against his old friend?' Seamus asked. 'I mean, he and Calhoun were tight. Up to recently.'

'I think Richard Roche would put the needs of the vulnerable over friendship,' Jessie said. 'From what I heard, he was all about morality. He was guided by his own sense of what was right.'

'Could it be that Calhoun didn't do it, but he knew the people who did, and Roche somehow got wind of it?' Terri asked.

That made everyone stop and think.

'Were Peter Blake's files sent over?' Jessie asked. 'His boss told me any one of his clients could be behind Rosie's kidnapping.'

'Good to see he has such faith in his customers,' Dawn said. 'Yes, they arrived half an hour ago. I've had them sent down to the forensic accountancy guys and told them to double time it. If he's into something nefarious, they'll hunt it down. That lot can find a dodgy entry in an encyclopaedia.'

'Have you had any luck chasing the email's recipient?' Jessie asked Terri.

'Not yet. It's heavily encrypted. But I will. It'll just take time. Whoever the receiver is, they have someone who knows what they're doing working for them.'

'Lucky you know what you're doing too then,' Dawn said. 'If we can find out who that is, we're a lot closer to getting the child back.'

'It won't necessarily tell us who has her now,' Jessie said. 'I mean, we still don't know what happened on the hill last night. But it's another piece of the puzzle.'

'And here's another piece,' Seamus said. 'I had some strange experiences today on Montpelier. Along with taking a tumble, Dave Gibb told me he heard music and saw strange lights in that old ruin before he found Roche's body, and he claims he kind of... materialised beside it – one moment he was a hundred yards away, the next he was there at the door of the hunting lodge with Richard Roche dead at his feet. In fact, he says there's been activity on that hill at night for weeks now. I went into the woods to look for tracks, and I think I disturbed someone who was skulking about. They knew their way around much better than I did and gave me the slip. I... think they left a calling card – a sort of doll made out of sticks hanging from a high branch. I tried to get it down but it broke apart, and I wasn't sure which bits belonged to it and which were just random ground cover.'

'Did you get a look at the person who left it?' Dawn asked.

'No. But I heard them.'

'What did you hear?'

'Footsteps. Someone running.'

'You're sure it wasn't an animal? A deer maybe?'

'I grew up right under the MacGillycuddy's Reeks, boss,' Seamus said, referring to the mountain range that loomed above the town of Cahersiveen in County Kerry. 'I know what a deer sounds like when it takes off, and this wasn't it. I also know that I wouldn't stand a chance of keeping up with a red deer in the woods. I'd have caught this person if I'd known the terrain better.'

Dawn nodded and smiled at Seamus. 'I daresay you would have too. You didn't hurt yourself too badly?'

'Just a scratch boss.'

'Whoever it was *might* have been connected with the killing and with Rosie, but it could also just be a murder tourist,' Jessie said, referring to people drawn to crime scenes in search of lurid thrills.

'You're sure they left this doll you saw?' Terri asked.

'No,' Seamus admitted. 'But it seems the most likely scenario. The place I found it – it was way off the beaten track. I think they wanted me to know they knew who I was. And that they were involved in the crimes.'

'Rosie had been drawing pictures of a figure made of sticks,' Jessie said. 'She said a man in strange clothes with a dog brought it to her.'

That made Dawn sit up. 'Garth told me a man with a dog had been watching his pub,' she said. 'He thought he was one of ours.'

'I saw a man like that today in the city, just outside Beaumont,' Jessie said. 'He and the dog had been watching me, I think.'

'What the sweet fuck does *this* mean?' Dawn asked.

'I've no clue,' Seamus admitted. 'Unless it's some reference to Rosie: a doll, a little girl... I don't know – I'm grasping at straws here.'

'It's all gone a bit weird with strange dolls and moving lights and unearthly music,' Dawn said.

'Dave Gibb seems to think the Reavers – the group who used to do strange things in the Hellfire Club – has reformed and moved back in to the hunting lodge.'

'Aren't they an eighteenth-century thing?' Dawn asked. 'I mean, they don't exist anymore, do they? If they ever really did.'

'Oh, they existed all right,' Terri said. 'I have an article open here, if you don't mind my referring to it. The first incarnation of the club – which is what the Reavers called their meeting place – occurred in England, in 1719. You need to remember that this is the era of the age of enlightenment. The intelligentsia were moving away from blind faith in the Church, and replacing the hole it left with science and a new philosophy based on logic. Most scholars see the Hellfire Club as a rebellion against that, and an attempt to return to the love of chaos and misrule of the late Middle Ages.'

'So these guys were like a protest movement?' Jessie asked.

'In a way. Ireland wasn't a good place to be in the eighteenth century unless you were rich, and very few were. The vast majority of the Irish populace was desperately poor: most were subsistence farmers, living hand-to-mouth on a diet of potatoes and nothing else. Those so poverty-stricken they didn't even have a patch of land to grow spuds on poured into cities like Dublin and made a crust through begging and petty theft. Even before the Famine, many starved. Bodies were often left in the gutters to rot.'

'So is that what the Irish Hellfire Club was protesting against?' Jessie asked. 'The class system?'

'In a twisted kind of a way, perhaps they were,' Terri said. 'The Reavers – which, just as in England, were made up of the idle rich – preyed on the lumpen masses of destitute beggars that filled Dublin's alleys and side streets. There are reports of the "sacrifice of maidens" and of cannibalism. One eyewitness, who fled Montpelier in terror, told the authorities that the Reavers were trying to summon demons, and how the mutilation of a victim was used in these ceremonies.'

'And this didn't ring any alarm bells?' Dawn asked.

'These guys had no fear of the law. They courted publicity, engaging in public displays of obscenity and aggression, arriving in randomly chosen public houses and causing mayhem, drinking to excess, sexually assaulting other patrons and engaging in violent outbursts, which on at least one occasion resulted in deaths.'

'They sound like a bunch of rowdy teenagers,' Dawn said. 'They should have just been arrested and have done with it.'

'They were all from landed, titled families,' Terri said. 'No one was prepared to take on the aristocracy. Which gave them a licence to behave abominably.'

'So what happened to the Irish version of the club?' Dawn asked. 'Could they still be around?'

'The police of the day, along with some of the locals, ran them from Montpelier in 1741, but the club revived in the 1770s and was apparently even worse. There are stories of people being burned alive in ceremonies, and of a farmer's wife from the area being abducted, murdered and then eaten. Once again, the authorities were forced to assert pressure to prevent the activities of the group continuing. But there have been rumours for years that they didn't disband but went into hiding.'

'Gibb told me his father believed they've been waiting,' Seamus said. 'Biding their time while watching for the portents to be right.'

'What portents?' Dawn asked.

'He said something about how certain things need to happen on top of the hill, on the site where they work their magic: the death of a man, the taking of a child and a ritual sacrifice.'

'And this will make something happen, will it?' Jessie asked.

'According to Gibb, it will bring about a new world order. A new age. Or something.'

'The Reavers maintained that hell was already here,' Terri said. 'That the way had already been paved for Satan himself to come and rule the physical plane. That's absolutely what they were trying to accomplish – to open a portal to hell and let all the bad things through.'

'Excellent,' Dawn said. 'And we have to accept that this isn't the first time the Reavers have come up in this investigation. Uruz mentioned them too.'

'Which is a fact, though not one I'm happy about,' Jessie added.

'It's no great surprise he's interested in them,' Terri said.

'The Reavers are known killers. Their group was linked to a series of murders on Dublin's docks in the late 1920s. The allegation was that they were targeting the destitute as sacrifices for occult ceremonies. Éamon de Valera, who was President of the Executive Council in 1932, which basically made him Prime Minister, formed a squad of what were, for want of a better word, assassins to wipe them out. He's reported to have said he considered the Reavers "the most dangerous group in all of Ireland, morally corrupt and an insidious blight on the spiritual lives of the citizens of the fair city".'

'Were the assassins successful?' Jessie asked.

'There was a gunfight on Marshall Dock on the fourteenth of November 1932. Five men were shot and killed, but a sixth escaped, throwing himself into the Liffey and letting the current, which was very fast due to a spring tide, take him out to sea. The assault team reported him as missing, probably drowned, but his body was never recovered.'

'Do we have a name?' Dawn asked. 'Not that it's important, I suppose, but no information is wasted.'

'We do,' Terri said. 'And that's maybe the most interesting thing about all of this. And... well... maybe the weirdest too. The man who escaped was the leader of the Reavers, the Superior Mage of the Order, and was known under several aliases, but he was baptised Algernon Patrick Parsons. He was a well-known character in Dublin in the early part of the twentieth century, regarded as a volatile, violent man. And he was rarely seen without a dog: a deerhound, a Scottish breed of hunting dog not unlike the Irish wolfhound.'

Dawn and Jessie exchanged glances.

'Brilliant,' Jessie said. 'Just brilliant.'

22

'Okay,' Dawn said. 'Let's take a breath. Even if this Parsons guy did survive being washed out to sea, he'd still have died fifty odd years ago.'

'I agree it's batshit crazy,' Seamus said, 'but Uruz doesn't mess about. I say if he's pointing us at something, we pay attention to it. Judging on past experience, whatever it is, it's likely to try to bite us on the arse sooner or later anyway.'

'I agree,' Terri said. 'I'll see what I can learn about Algernon Parsons. Maybe there are surviving family members.'

'All right,' Dawn agreed. 'But let's not go down too many rabbit holes on this one. We have a sick kiddie to find, one who's already been missing for over twenty-four hours. That's where I want us focused. I would like to come back to Uruz, but let's finish the briefing first.'

'So do we have a plan going forward?' Seamus asked. 'That's what this meeting was meant to be about, and I'm none the wiser.'

'Well, we have a report of lights and strange sounds on Montpelier, one such incident on the night we believe Rosie was there,' Jessie said. 'I think that warrants following up. It might just be some kind of weather disturbance, but it could be significant. The place is run by Coillte, so perhaps someone with them might be able to help us.'

'A door-to-door needs to be done on all the other nearby houses too,' Seamus said.

The commissioner nodded and said: 'I'd like to look into the connections between Garth Calhoun and the Blakes. There's something there – I just know there is.'

'I'll continue to work on the email's recipient, and I'll do some more digging on the Reavers,' Terri said. 'Maybe there's a version of them that's still operational but so far underground they haven't raised any red flags yet.'

'It might be worth talking to someone who knows about cults and that kind of thing,' Seamus said.

'I know a guy,' Terri said. 'I'll give him a call and arrange to meet.'

'Good stuff,' Dawn said. 'Now, I've a bit of news I need to share. We've had a request from outside the department.'

'What kind of request?' Jessie asked.

'For us to consult on a case.'

'How are we going to do that?' Jessie asked. 'We don't have the time.'

'They assure me the experience will be mutually beneficial.'

'How exactly?' Seamus asked.

'A new guy has just started in J2, the intelligence service,' Dawn said. 'He's Irish, but he's been working in the United States. He's done a lot of analytical work, particularly with the National Security Agency. I'm told he's working a case that intersects with this one.'

'With the abduction of Rosie Blake?'

'So I'm told.'

'Didn't they give you any more information than that?'

'This is J2,' Dawn said ruefully. 'We aren't even supposed to know they exist, for fuck's sake.'

'Okay,' Jessie sighed. 'But if this proves to be a waste of our time, I'll send them packing sharpish.'

'Good. I'll set it up.'

'J2 musta heard of our bangin' skills, y'know what I'm sayin'?' Seamus said.

'I don't know how to even respond to that,' Dawn said. 'So I'm just going to nod and smile.'

'Wicked,' Seamus retorted. 'Just trying to keep it real, ya feel me?'

'The whole urban thing really isn't working, Seamus,' Jessie said, grimacing.

'I quite like it,' Terri said.

'For the love of God would you not encourage him,' Dawn said in exasperation.

'Dope,' Seamus said.

Jessie just put her head in her hands.

ARIZONA ROSE BLAKE

NOW

She slept a lot.

This was unusual for Rosie, because the chemotherapy drugs made it hard for her to sleep, and she was used to being awake long into the night. Her mam had given her an iPad with lots of games and some nice movies on it, and she watched that when sleep wouldn't come. She liked some YouTube shows too: the Norris Nuts were her favourite, and she'd watch their channel for hours and escape into the lives they led and the fun they always seemed to have.

And Panda always helped. She knew he wasn't real, was just some soft material with sponge stuffing inside. But he'd been with her since she was a baby, and she'd given him a personality and she talked to him, and in her head, he talked back. So it was like he was alive.

Rosie knew that at times she was very lonely, but there wasn't much she could do about that. She'd asked her mam once if there was any hope she would one day have a little brother or sister, and her mam had given her a strange look and told her she was a special child, one that had been gifted to her for a special purpose, and that she wanted to devote all her time to caring for her.

Rosie took this to be about her being sick and tried not to be sad that here was another thing she'd been robbed of by this awful illness. So she'd watch the Norris family and wish her world was like theirs.

Now, as everything spiralled out of control and she found herself trapped in a nightmare, Rosie retreated into a place in her mind, somewhere the strange people couldn't reach. She wasn't harmed – they didn't beat her or even say hurtful things. Mostly she was treated with benign apathy. But she was cold and hungry a lot of the time, and she wasn't sure the medicine they were giving her was the right one.

And no one would tell her what was going on.

Why did they have her? Where was she going? What had happened to Richie?

When sleep came, she plunged into it gratefully. It was a release from the awfulness that she could now see no escape from. Rosie hadn't been to school much, but she was a clever girl. She read whatever she could lay her hands on, and she understood far more than her mother would probably be happy about.

Rosie knew about bad people. And she had an idea what sort of things bad people might do to a kid.

She was pretty sure the bald man and his friends were bad people.

And just because really awful things hadn't been done to her yet didn't mean they couldn't still be.

So she slept.

And prayed that someone would come to rescue her.

23

Jessie was almost back at her hotel when her mobile phone rang. Using the hands-free, she answered.

'Jessie Boyle?' a voice at the other end asked. It was an educated Dublin accent, but she noticed a slight American twang in the background.

'Yes. Who am I speaking to please?'

'My name is Donal Glynn. I believe my friend Dawn Wilson mentioned me to you.'

'She did, but I wasn't expecting to hear from you so soon.'

'This couldn't wait,' Donal Glynn said. 'I'm sending you Google Map coordinates. Can you come directly over please?'

'Why?'

Her phone buzzed.

'Come now. You'll be glad you did.'

And he hung up.

Jessie opened the link and saw that it was for a housing estate in Donaghmede. Sighing in resignation, she executed an illegal U-turn and went to meet the intelligence officer.

. . .

It was ten minutes after eight when she got to the location – which was in the middle of a large, local authority area – to find four police cars parked outside, as well as an ambulance. She showed her ID as she approached the door, and the uniformed officer on guard there peered at it.

'The brass are inside,' he said in an Offaly accent.

'I'm here to see Donal Glynn?'

The uniformed Garda shrugged. 'I've just been told to send you through,' he said. 'They're in the living room.'

Jessie nodded and went in.

She found a cluster of cops, uniformed and detective, most with cups of takeout coffee in their hands, just where the Garda on the door had said she would.

When she entered, there was a conversation going between two young men in plain clothes.

'Why exactly are Organised Crime involved in this one?'

'It's a rental property. The dude who owns it is linked to some gangsters.'

'Is he implicated in some way?'

'Not that I know of.'

'I still don't get it.'

'It isn't your job to get it, Joe. You get paid to show up, is all.'

'Excuse me,' she said. 'I'm looking for Donal Glynn.'

The two looked at her, puzzled, but just then she heard: 'I'm right here, Jessie – thanks for coming.'

Glynn was probably ten years older than the behaviourist and of average height, a pale man with a lean frame and a complexion that bore the scars of acne. He was wearing a well-tailored three-piece suit, on the lapel of which was a pin in the shape of a rifle – Jessie knew it meant he'd been a sniper in a former life. Her deceased partner, Will, had worn a similar one. The sight gave her a momentary flash of grief, which she pushed aside immediately.

The intelligence officer extended his hand, and she shook.

'I'm here, Agent Glynn, though I'm not sure why.'

'Donal is fine, Jessie. Let's not stand on ceremony. Now come, come. I want to show you something you might find interesting.'

He led her out into the hallway towards what she assumed was the kitchen. There was crime-scene tape across the door as they approached, and a rolling clothes rack with protective crime-scene full-body overalls.

'Suit up,' Glynn said, grabbing one for himself.

Jessie did and they ducked underneath the tape, Glynn calling: 'Hello, the house! Officers approaching.'

Jessie could smell the scents that had, over all the years she'd been working as an investigator, become irrevocably linked to crime scenes in her mind: fingerprint powder, takeout coffee and, underneath it all, the coppery, metallic stench of dried blood.

There were two detectives inside crouched down on their haunches scribbling in notebooks, and in front of them the body of a man lay spreadeagled on the floor. He'd been pinned to the tiles with metal rebars, one through each wrist and one through both his feet. Whoever had done it had stripped him naked and then cut his throat. Jessie had seen a lot of violence in her time, but this stopped her in her tracks.

What also stopped her in her tracks was that she knew this man. She had, in fact, interviewed him only a matter of hours ago.

This doesn't make sense, Jessie thought. *Killing him doesn't make sense – particularly like this. This isn't a crime of expediency. Whoever did this wanted to hurt him.*

Glynn seemed unaffected by the scene. One of the detectives, a skinny young man with a stubbled chin showing under his face mask stood up and turned to them. His partner, still scribbling something in his notebook, muttered something to the other man and left the room.

'Jim Marsh. I'm with the Donaghmede station,' he said. 'You the two from the NBCI?'

'Yes. We have a special interest in this case,' Glynn said after introducing himself and Jessie, who wondered exactly what interest she was supposed to have.

'Well, it's all yours,' Marsh said. 'The medical examiner will be here in an hour, but you can look him over if you like.'

'Why don't you indulge me and walk us through it?' Glynn said expansively. 'You local boys were first on the scene. Tell us what you know.'

'Happy to oblige,' Marsh said, his chest swelling with pride. 'The vic is Rodney Lawler – he's a social worker in Beaumont Hospital. He was found by his boyfriend – they were supposed to be going out for dinner this evening.'

'He was in work today,' Jessie pointed out. 'When does he usually get home?'

'One of the neighbours saw him arrive at 5.30 p.m. But apparently that's early. He's usually not here before six.'

'So this is very recent?' Glynn asked.

'Killer was here within the last two hours,' Marsh agreed.

'This is a built-up neighbourhood,' Jessie said. 'There are neighbours on both sides and across the street. Anyone see anyone else coming to the house?'

'We've canvassed everyone up and down the street,' Marsh said. 'There are cameras on the street lamps at fixed points up and down the block, and we've requisitioned the footage. That'll take a while to go through, but if it brings up anything, we'll let you know.'

'You said he was going out with a boyfriend,' Glynn said. 'Do you mean in a romantic sense?'

'Is there any other meaning? He was gay.'

'And you're certain the boyfriend didn't do it?'

'He's five foot five inches in his stockinged feet,' Marsh said. 'As an enlightened modern man, I'm not going to suggest that means he couldn't have overpowered his partner before hammering four solid metal bars through his hands and feet and then slicing his neck wide open. But judging from the physical strength required, I'd say it's unlikely. Also, he became hysterical on finding the body and had to be sedated.'

'Did he have anything to say we might be able to use?' Jessie asked.

'He was fucking incoherent,' Marsh said. 'We'll talk to him again when he's calmed down.'

Glynn nodded. 'What does your instinct tell you, Detective Marsh?'

'There's no reserved parking on the street outside, and I'm told that people around here are free and easy about where they leave their vehicles. A car parked right outside the house don't mean it belongs to the person inside the house, if you get my drift. Also, the yard outside to the rear of the property backs out onto a drainage ditch which in turn links in with one of the city sewage systems. If a person had a mind to, it would make a pretty good access route and just as good an escape path.'

'Any cameras or security on it?'

'I've called the council, but no one's working at this hour.'

'And why would they be?' Glynn sighed. 'He got any other family other than the hysterical partner?'

'The hospital CEO says he has a father in a nursing home. Mother's dead. No siblings.'

Something caught her eye and Jessie walked over to the window that overlooked the yard.

'What is this?' she asked.

Glynn looked across at Marsh. 'Could you leave us for a moment, Detective?'

Marsh nodded and ducked out. Glynn waited until he was sure the young man was gone before saying: 'I apologise for the small talk – I wanted to see if he'd noticed what you just did.'

'This is why you brought me here?'

'What do you make of it?'

Hanging by a piece of what looked to be rough baling twine and suspended from a nail someone had hammered into the wooden frame of the window was a figure made of sticks and twigs. It was crudely human-shaped, but horns seemed to be coming from what might have been the head, and a twig that protruded from the V that denoted the legs made it look as if the creature had a prominent erection.

'Well it's pretty damned creepy,' Jessie said. 'A child who was abducted and who I'm trying to find had been drawing something like it, and I think my partner, Seamus, came across one in the woods near Montpelier Hill earlier today.'

'It's not the first time I've seen one of them either,' Glynn said.

Jessie gave him a hard look. 'What's going on?'

'Dawn forwarded me a copy of the message Uruz sent you today,' the thin man said.

'Dawn pulled me aside earlier this evening after we'd had our team meeting and told me you were going to help get him off my back.'

'I intend to. This is all connected. I think Uruz is in communication with the people who left that figure here. And in Rosie Blake's room too. And in the woods for your partner to find.'

'Is Uruz manipulating them?'

'All in good time. Tell me what you think of the figure there.'

Jessie looked at it. 'It looks like some kind of pagan fertility symbol. I'm reminded of *The Blair Witch Project*, but this is even creepier.'

'The Blair Witch didn't exist. This is very real, and it's the fourth one I've found in Ireland in the past seven months.'

'All at homicide scenes?'

'Yes.'

'Why haven't I heard about it?' Jessie demanded. 'There's

been nothing in the papers, and I would have thought Dawn would have mentioned a series of murders where the killer left a calling card.'

'It's out of her jurisdiction,' Glynn said. 'My people were investigating it.'

'J2?' Jessie asked. 'That means you're taking this as a threat to national security?'

'Maybe.'

Jessie looked at the effigy, and then at the dead man pinned to the floor. 'Is the MO the same in the other cases?'

'The scenes are all violent but the cause of death differs. The cruelty, though, that's the same. And he – or they – leave one of these awful things behind in each case.'

'You said this is the fourth one you've seen *in Ireland*.'

'I did say that, didn't I?'

'You've seen similar figures elsewhere? In the States?'

'I have.'

'How are the killings connected with Uruz's message?'

'I bet if you asked your Ms Kehoe about the murders the Reavers committed in the 1920s, she'd tell you they left behind a figure just like this one at the scenes.'

'How do you know Terri has been looking into them?'

'Dawn sent me the text message he sent you. I assumed your Terri would be on the case, and the 1920s murder and Éamon de Valera's attempt to wipe the Reavers out would be the first thing she'd find.'

'Seamus mentioned he came across a figure, and I spoke about one being given to Rosie, but she never mentioned it as an aspect to the deaths in the twenties,' Jessie said.

'Do you think she'd give much thought to the MO of murders that are almost one hundred years old? Maybe she didn't take note of it herself.'

'Terri is very thorough. I'll give her a call.'

'Do whatever you feel is necessary to corroborate. But I assure you, the information I'm giving you is accurate.'

'It's obviously a copycat,' Jessie said.

'I wouldn't say that was an obvious conclusion at all,' Glynn said. 'One of several possible hypotheses perhaps.'

'I can't understand why Rodney Lawler was killed,' Jessie said. 'He wouldn't take on Rosie Blake as a case and barely knew Richard Roche, and I'm not aware of him having any connection with the Hellfire Club or Montpelier.'

'Which doesn't mean he didn't, or that there aren't links and actions you know nothing about.'

'That's what's annoying me,' Jessie agreed. 'What did I miss?'

'There are more things in heaven and earth,' Glynn said, 'than are dreamed of in any of our philosophies, if you don't mind my butchering the Bard.'

'Can I look at the files on the other cases?' Jessie asked.

'I'd be obliged if you did.'

And that was how the stick men came into Jessie's life.

24

Jessie and Glynn stood outside the terraced house, watching Rodney Lawler's body being loaded into the coroner's minivan.

'Have you had dinner yet?' Glynn asked.

'I was on my way when you called.'

'Do you still have an appetite after seeing the unfortunate Mr Lawler's remains?'

'I've been doing this for a long time, Donal. I could eat.'

'There's a decent pub about ten minutes from here that does good food and serves till late. Shall we retire to it and have a chat?'

'Why not?' Jessie said.

The Donaghmede Inn was exactly as Glynn had described – a large gastropub that had an expansive menu of pub-grub favourites and friendly staff who, at Glynn's request, seated them in a corner, a little bit away from the rest of the clientele.

'You're telling me that man was murdered by a group of pagan extremists who were believed to have been wiped out in the 1930s?' Jessie said when their waitress had taken their orders.

'That is precisely what I'm telling you. And if your Mr Keneally came across one of their *púca* men, then it seems you and your team are on their radar. And that, Jessie, is not a good thing.'

'I could have worked that out for myself. The *púca* men are what you're calling the stick figures?'

'It's a Celtic reference. The *púca* is a Celtic spirit that can change shape at will – sometimes it's a horse, sometimes a dog, sometimes a seal. But it's said that its natural shape is that of a man made of the very fabric of the landscape, which in Celtic times would have been trees and grasses and reeds and pine cones. I always feel that's what these stick figures are – reflections of Ireland's dark past. They're rudimentary and they only vaguely resemble people, but you still know what they're supposed to be: cruel, misshapen images of humanity at its worst. All hunger and lust and rage. Some said it was this primordial form of the *púca* that used to steal children for the fairy folk. Which is kind of ironic under the current circumstances.'

'You're inferring a lot from a tangle of sticks and ivy,' Jessie said.

'You'd interpret it differently?'

'Serial killers are usually pretty simple creatures in my experience. When they start to get flamboyant, signing their work and leaving little messages, it means they're getting bored and want to up the stakes. It's the equivalent of calling out the police. Of throwing down, challenging us to a duel.'

'The Reavers are not ordinary serial killers though,' Glynn said. 'They're zealots. They do not kill simply to kill but as a vehicle to bring about metaphysical changes to the world around them. You cannot apply the same logic to them as you do with standard sociopaths.'

'I disagree,' Jessie retorted. 'Every single murderer I've tracked has believed they were different, that they somehow existed on a plane that others don't. Many seemed to think they were acting on some kind of divine, or more usually diabolic, inspiration. It's never the case. Drill down into their psyche and you've still got a socially inadequate incel with mother issues and a persecution complex.'

'I'm telling you these are different.'

'How can you say that?' Jessie asked. 'Unless you had a Reaver in custody and got the chance to analyse them, there's no way of establishing a motivational profile.'

Glynn smiled. 'Exactly.'

Jessie threw him a look. 'You've got one?'

'I *had* one,' the intelligence officer said. 'I've been chasing these people for the past ten years.'

'In the United States?'

'That's where I first came across the Reavers. And they're why I've come to Ireland. Them and Uruz.'

Jessie tried not to look shocked at this statement, but her jaw still dropped open for a moment.

'Brilliant,' she said, almost to herself. 'Just brilliant.'

25

'I encountered the Reavers first when I was a field agent with the National Security Agency,' Glynn began.

The waitress brought their food – a smoked salmon salad for Glynn and pasta napolitana for Jessie – and as soon as she had disappeared back behind the bar, he continued.

'I don't know if you're aware, but the NSA is primarily an information-gathering organisation. The vast bulk of what it does it electronic surveillance. Of course, the data accrued sometimes needs to be confirmed – every now and again a message is decoded and the results don't make a lot of sense, and when that occurs, someone needs to be sent out to check its veracity. I was one of the agents whose job it was to do those checks.'

'Interesting, I'm sure,' Jessie said.

'Usually not,' Glynn said, laughing drily. 'A lot of what I did was seeing if an address was correct, or that a particular individual did, indeed, work at a specific location. So not very interesting at all.'

'I take it your first encounter with the Reavers was the exception to that rule.'

'You would be correct in that assertion,' Glynn said, delicately placing a sliver of smoked salmon on some soda bread and taking a bite. 'My associates had intercepted a series of telephone conversations emanating from what we thought was a toy factory in east Detroit. The analysts were convinced from the tenor of the communications that they were dealing with some kind of terrorist cell, probably formed along religious grounds. I regret to say that working for an employer like the NSA, one is only told what is deemed absolutely necessary, so that's the only information I was given. My partner Floyd and I were tasked to surveille the place and confirm how many individuals were operating there and assess the threat.'

'What did you find?'

'A building that was virtually derelict but had regular visits from five individuals – four men and one woman – who arrived, usually in the evening, though sometimes briefly during the day, and stayed often until the wee hours of the morning. We were using long-range microphones, but a lot of what they spoke about made little sense. They made reference to rituals with odd names, they spoke about the "approaching sacrifice", but at the time, my partner and I assumed they were building up to a suicide-bomb attack or driving a van into a crowded street. Possibly a mass shooting.'

'Which you had every intention of thwarting,' Jessie said.

'Well, not us personally,' Glynn said, dipping a bunch of leaves on the end of his fork into some dressing. 'Our role was to monitor and report back. But yes, we would not have permitted such an event to pass.'

'So what did happen?'

'On the third night we were there, something out of the ordinary occurred. A van we hadn't seen before arrived, and two men who were new to the group emerged and took a figure from the back, a man whose hands were bound behind him. It became clear from the chatter inside that *this* was the sacrifice, but we didn't know if that meant this was the person who was to be the suicide bomber, or who would pilot the van or whatever their plan was. We didn't know how to ascertain these details remotely, so there was only one thing for it – one of us needed to get closer.'

'You mean you needed to take a peek.'

'Precisely. We tossed a coin, and Floyd lost.'

'So he went to see if he could find a window to peer through, to see what was going on inside?'

'We weren't quite as primitive as that. He had a mirrored periscope, fibre-optic cameras, a camera with a telescopic lens. He was well equipped.'

'How'd he get on?'

'He disappeared around the back of the building, and I waited.'

'For how long?'

'The rule on field investigations is that, if separated, one checks in every three minutes. It's a simple thing – you just radio "red team, all's well" or something to that effect.'

'How many check-ins before he went silent?'

'Two.'

'What did you do?'

'I called for backup and I went after him.'

'Were you armed?'

'This was America, Jessie. Of course I was armed. They were waiting for me as I rounded the corner of the old building. Luckily I was prepared, and I went to the ground when they opened fire. There were two of them, and I was able to take them both out with expediency.'

'You shot low, didn't you?' Jessie asked, identifying an old marksman's trick every armed officer was taught.

'No one ever expects you to shoot the legs from under them,' Glynn agreed. 'They went down and then it was simple to deliver the kill shots.'

'In Ireland, they wouldn't do that,' Jessie said. 'It would be considered unreasonable force.'

'As I said, this was America. They had forfeited their lives the moment they discharged their weapons at an agent of the federal government.'

'Did you identify yourself?'

'That's hardly relevant now, is it? There was a door to my left, and I pushed it open. A narrow hallway led to another door that had those thick plastic curtains you see on freezers – you know the ones in strips? They're heavy and act as good insulators, which is their purpose. They didn't quite block out the sound of someone screaming on the other side of them though.'

Jessie, who had a forkful of pasta ready to consume, paused with her food halfway to her mouth for a moment before putting it down.

'You could have waited for backup,' she said. 'You'd taken out two, but by my count, that still left you to deal with five, plus the guy they'd brought in in cuffs, who might or might not be on their side.'

'I knew the man who was screaming was Floyd,' Glynn said, his voice deadpan. 'We'd been partners for almost two years by then. You know what that bond is like. If your partner was taken, what would you do to get him back?'

Jessie had been in that situation – it had happened during the first case she, Seamus and Terri had worked together. Jessie had put herself at incredible risk to get him back. And she had done so willingly and would again in a heartbeat.

'I'd say there's nothing I wouldn't do for either Seamus or Terri.'

'Exactly. I gave myself a count of three and went through the curtains shooting.'

Glynn stopped talking for a moment and pushed his plate away.

'You've seen action and you know what it's like. I had a

momentary glimpse of the room while I identified the visible threat. It was a wide concrete room which probably originally held a production line but was now empty of all equipment. I noticed there were odd clusters of sticks and what I took to be dry leaves hanging all about, but at that moment I didn't have a chance to pay them any heed.'

'Stick men.'

'Yes. *Púca* men. Of course, I had more immediate problems to address. I took out two of them with my opening shots – two men were directly in my line of vision when I entered, and I don't think they were expecting me. The soundproofing had blocked out the noise from outside as much as in, so they had no warning the guards they'd posted had been subdued. I took them very much by surprise.'

'There's still three, maybe four unaccounted for,' Jessie said.

'Indeed. Well, I'd lost the element of surprise, once those first two shots were fired, and before I had the chance to turn, I was hit from behind. A shotgun blast right to the middle of my back. The Kevlar took the brunt of it, but it still put me flat on my face and took the wind out of me. I managed to roll over and put one in his throat before he had a chance to reload. A woman came at me with what looked like a cleaver and I managed to shoot her before she was able to split my skull – that was touch and go; I don't think I've ever seen someone move so fast. I was able to get to my knees, and shot the other as he ran for the door.'

'We're down to one,' Jessie said.

'One and poor old Floyd,' Glynn said sadly. 'The person we'd watched them take in from the van was shackled to an overhead pipe, suspended so his toes just touched the ground. It looked to me as if they'd been bleeding him – there were a couple of long incisions cut into his arms, and blood had pooled on the concrete floor. He was alive but seemed semi-conscious.'

'And your partner?'

'They'd...' Glynn paused for a moment as if considering how to continue. 'They'd carved him up pretty badly. He died in the ambulance on the way to the hospital.'

'And the guy who'd been chained up?'

'At that stage, I was working under the assumption he had been abducted and was a prisoner. It wasn't until he'd been medically treated and I had the chance to interview him that I realised he'd been there voluntarily. He was one of them.'

'A willing sacrifice,' Jessie said. 'I've come across people like that before. It's a rare form of psychosis – individuals who give themselves over to be tortured or even killed. It's an extreme form of self-harming. His being bound didn't mean he was a prisoner. It was part of the ritual.'

'Yet again, I would cast that as an oversimplification,' Glynn said. 'This man, who told us his name was Cain, was a Reaver. Neither I nor anyone at my organisation knew what that meant – there was nothing on our records about them. What made me begin to wonder was the fact that Cain's fingerprints had been partially removed. I'd seen this done before to try and protect the identity of agents going under deep cover – it's effective for a short time, but then the skin regenerates and the prints return. We were able to take a partial from the man's left index finger and it was enough to identify him. He'd worked for an aid agency that used to go out to regions embedded with the US Marine Corps, and his real name was Charles Boothroy Parsons.'

'Parsons, did you say?' Jessie asked, remembering the surname of the Reavers' leader in the 1920s.

'Yes. I take it the name means something to you.'

Jessie narrowed her eyes. 'You know it does.'

'Interesting, isn't it? That familial connection?'

'Was he Irish?'

'Born in Dublin, according to his paperwork. Held a dual passport.'

'Any criminal history before this?'

'Well, Jessie, can we affirmatively say Mr Parsons, aka Cain, actually committed a crime? I found him bound and showing clear signs of having been physically assaulted.'

'He admitted to being a member of their sect or cult or whatever they are.'

'He rambled about bringing about the "black dawn of a new age". Of how his brotherhood had sought out sites of spiritual significance upon which to perform the correct rituals. He gave me some rubbish about how his blood was intended to be the conduit by which some demonic force would be brought forth.'

'Is that really what they're about? This idea of turning earth into a living hell?'

'It's hard to be certain,' Glynn said. 'I've been chasing them ever since, and from what I can gather there are those among them who believe all the occult nonsense, and others who see the Reavers' mission as more political, to effect a new world order.'

'So they're terrorists? I thought you said they were religious nuts?'

'You're not listening to me, Jessie. Who or what the Reavers are is far from simple. Yes, they very closely resemble terrorists. Why do you think they fall under the remit of the NSA in the United States and J2 in Ireland? They organise themselves very much along the lines of terrorist cells we've seen aligned to the likes of Islamic extremists, or some groups within the incel movement. With the Reavers, there's usually no more than five to a cell, which is designed to reflect a patriarchal family structure. The leader tends to be a more mature male, and often is the son or nephew of a previous leader. There's a female member who organises ceremonies and rituals and hierarchically is second in command. There's a younger male who is given responsibility and authority as if he were the oldest son, and then there are two soldiers who act as enforcers and security.'

'They sound a bit like gangsters too. I've known some fraternal organisations who organise as if they're all related, even if they're actually not.'

'Quite. Now, I do accept that there is a pagan and occult element. I think Charles Parsons, Cain, does truly believe he's bringing about some kind of spiritual weapon of mass destruction. But I have evidence that he is not beyond hiring out his group's services as contract killers, that he has dabbled in people-trafficking, and all Reaver cells – and I mean *all of them* – are associated with the far right, even if just by extension.'

'So this Cain person was one of the religious zealots?'

'He gave himself over to be ritually bled, so yes, I think it's fair to say he was a fanatic.'

'And you don't feel he was complicit in the death of your partner?'

'Oh, I wouldn't dispute his complicity, but whether one could say he was of sound enough mind to make an informed choice about it is another argument.'

Jessie sat back, thinking about everything Glynn had just told her.

'This is all fascinating,' she said. 'But I have to tell you, my focus is really on two things right now: number one, how does all of this help me to find Rosie Blake, and two, how do we know Uruz is really involved in it, and what does his involvement mean? And how can we stop him, of course.'

'I'm getting to that,' Glynn said. 'Will I continue?'

'I'm listening.'

'The decision was made to send Parsons to a black site based on a certain island nation with whom the United States government has had a somewhat tenuous relationship.'

'Which indicates the NSA believed the cell he belonged to

was one of a larger network,' Jessie said. 'That he might have information about them.'

'Almost certainly. As a low-ranking field agent, I wasn't privy to their deliberations, but it follows, yes.'

'Is that why you said you *had* him in custody?'

'Oh no. Charles Parsons never made it to Guantanamo Bay.'

Jessie looked at the intelligence officer, incredulous. 'What happened?'

'The prison convoy was hit en route. Every officer killed.'

'The Reavers broke him out?'

'Maybe.'

'Who else would have done it?'

'I think you should see this,' Glynn said and took out his phone, fiddling with it for a second before passing it over.

On the screen was a photograph of a van with strong wire mesh covering the windows. It was sitting diagonally in the middle of the road, and Jessie could see what looked to be a military Humvee parked just behind it. The rear doors of the van were crumpled and blackened, as if explosives had been used to open them.

None of that was what drew Jessie's attention though. Her eyes immediately fixed on a symbol that had been spray-painted on the side of the damaged vehicle. It was an old Nordic rune. The mark of the auroch. Uruz – ᚢ.

'Fuck,' Jessie Boyle said.

'I think that about sums it up,' Donal Glynn agreed.

26

Jessie rang Seamus once she was back at her car.

'Can you come out and meet me? I've got a break in the case and with the clock ticking, we'd best act on it now.'

'What's happened?'

She told him.

'Where are you? I'm on my way.'

He met her at the end of the road where Rodney Lawler lived. The sky was a river of stars, and frost was already forming on the kerbs of the pavements, sparkling in the electric glow of the street lamps.

'This is a turnup for the books,' the young detective said. 'How the feck is the social worker involved?'

'That's what I'm hoping to find out.'

'What's your feeling about this Glynn fella?'

'I'm reserving judgement. One thing I do know though: Uruz is in it up to his neck. We're going to need to be very careful.'

'Well we're used to doing that.'

.   .   .

Lawler's partner was named Barry Madigan, and he was pale
and trembling, perhaps thirty-five years old with curly red hair.

'Why did this happen?' he asked, when Jessie and Seamus
introduced themselves.

The small man was in a private room in the hospital where
his deceased partner had worked. The space was in semi-dark-
ness, and in the pale halo of light that shone from a bulb just
above his head, Jessie thought the man looked tiny, his slim
frame barely noticeable under the sheet.

'That's what we're trying to find out,' the behaviourist
responded. 'Did Rodney seem worried about anything? Was he
in any trouble?'

'No. Nothing.'

'He hadn't mentioned any rows at work?' Seamus
suggested.

An odd look came over Barry's face. 'A man he worked with
did call over the other evening,' he said. 'Rodney took him into
the living room, and I think they had a fight.'

'Do you know what about?' Jessie asked.

'No. I just heard raised voices. Mostly his, but Rodney did
get angry too.'

'You didn't try to ask him about it? What might have
happened?' Seamus pressed. 'That'd be normal for a partner to
do, wouldn't it? Check in to see if the other is okay?'

'I asked him if he was okay,' Barry said. 'When he said he
was, I let it go. I suspected he was lying to me, but I wasn't going
to make a song and dance out of it. Rodney is a social worker, so
his work is confidential.'

'The man who visited,' Jessie said. 'Was it this man?'

She held up her phone – she'd taken a shot of the photograph of Richard Roche from his personnel file; she didn't think
it appropriate to continue using the post-mortem one.

'Yes. That was him.'

'And he'd never called before?' Seamus asked him. 'This was a first?'

'I'd never seen him before,' Barry said. 'Do you... do you think he might have done this?'

'We're in the very early stages of the investigation,' Jessie said.

But as they were leaving, she looked at Seamus and whispered: 'He might not have done it personally, but I have a feeling that visit brought Rodney into something he was very ill-equipped to deal with.'

'I think you might be right,' Seamus agreed.

EUGENE DUNLIN

He decided that he wanted it to be as intimate as possible. He wanted it to be up close and personal, no shortcuts and no chickening out. If he was going to make it in the world of organised crime, he would need to be able to say he'd had blood on his hands, and he felt that this needed to be literally.

He told AJ he wanted to arm himself and asked for his opinion on the best tools for the job.

'You can't go wrong with a Glock 17 9mm,' the big man said. 'The great thing about Glocks is that they're built to be as simple as possible – there isn't much to think about with them. You make sure the load is in, you point and squeeze the trigger.'

'Should I have a knife as well?'

AJ snorted. 'If you've used up all the bullets in your Glock and he's still coming at you, a knife would be useful, yeah. I'd hope you wouldn't need to cut him that much after emptying your gun into him, but I suppose he might be hopped up on a load of coke or whatever.'

'What's the best knife to use?'

'Get one where the tang – that's the piece of metal attached to the blade that goes down into the handle – goes right down to

the end of the handle. That keeps the structure of the knife strong, and you don't need to worry about the blade breaking off.'

'Is there a style of knife I should be looking for?'

'What, like a fucking Bowie knife or something? Eugene, you've been watching the Discovery Channel again, haven't you? This is Ireland, so you can't be going around with a knife in a fucking sheath on your belt – you'll be arrested for carrying a concealed weapon. Get one small enough you can put it in your pocket, but with a long-enough blade that'll do some lasting damage if you stick it in someone.'

Eugene nodded. He'd been taking notes as Calhoun's bodyguard was speaking, scribbling details into a leather-bound notebook, which the big man seemed mildly amused by.

'If I give you the money, can you get me a Glock 17 and the kind of knife you just described?'

'Do I look like your messenger, boy?'

'I don't mean it like that, AJ. How about this: I want to learn all I can about the business, and right now everything is new to me. Could I go with you to buy them then? You could show me exactly what you're talking about with all the features and the tang and the right load and all of that?'

AJ sighed but nodded his big, slightly misshapen head. 'All right. I can take you. But you're buying me a pint on the way home, all right?'

'Done.'

And that was when he crossed the red line. He hadn't done it yet, but as soon as he got those tools of death, he became a killer.

The night after he and AJ bought them, he crept into his father's bedroom and cut the old man's throat while he slept. He didn't want to have to kill his mother as well. But she became quite hysterical.

Now there was no going back.

27

They went back to Harcourt Street. The nightshift desk sergeant informed Jessie a bundle of files had been delivered by a military policeman and had been left in the conference room.

'You two look like death warmed up,' the sarge said as the pair trudged past him.

'We've been on for close to twenty-four hours, and it'll be a few more before we get to clock off,' Jessie said.

She was dead on her feet, and Seamus looked as if he was ready to curl up in a corner and pass out.

'Tough case, I take it,' the sarge commiserated.

'The toughest,' Seamus said.

'These will be the files from Glynn,' Jessie said as she unpacked them and laid them out on the table.

'I have to tell you, Jessie, this case is driving me a bit crazy,' Seamus said as he pulled up a chair.

'I hear you. It's always awful when kids are involved.'

'Did I tell you I'm seeing someone?'

Jessie threw him a look. 'You're like... dating?'

'I don't know if I'd call it that.'

Jessie put the last file on the desk and sat down opposite her partner. 'Well let's take a moment and turn this over – you've met a person you like.'

'It's a girl, yes.'

'Okay. So you've met a girl you like. You've been out with her more than once?'

'We've been out three times.'

'This is where – in Cork?'

'No. She's based here in Dublin.'

'And you like her?'

'She's great, yeah. I really like her.'

'Have you told her you like her?'

'Well I... well not in so many words.'

'How many words did you use?'

Seamus looked a bit perplexed at that. 'We haven't really talked about that side of things at all.'

'Do you think she likes you?'

'I think so. Like I mean, the third time we went out, she kind of asked me.'

'Probably a good sign,' Jessie agreed. 'I'm going to surmise from the fact you're telling me about her that you're planning on making it a long-term arrangement?'

'I'd like to, yeah.'

'Do then. You don't need my blessing.'

'I know but... well we're in each other's lives so much. I spend more time with you than I do anyone else.'

Jessie grinned. 'I'm your partner. That's a relationship only another cop would understand. What does this young lady do?'

'She's a schoolteacher. Senior infants – so like six, seven years old.'

'Your mum was a teacher, wasn't she?'

'Yes.'

'And does Katie Keneally know about this girl who's turned her son's head?'

'Not yet, no.'

'I'd love to be a fly on the wall during that conversation.'

Seamus and his mother had a very close relationship. Jessie often thought that a woman had not yet been born who would meet the standards Katie would set for a mate for her beloved only son.

'The thing is, Jessie, Christina, she has a little girl. She's younger than Rosie by three years, but it really hit me the other day that if anything was to happen to Steffie, Christina would be inconsolable. I mean, I think it'd kill her. And I've only just met the wee thing, but I already care about her. Don't get me wrong, I know I'm not her dad or anything, but... it's gotten in on me, this case.'

Jessie narrowed her eyes. 'What are you getting at, Seamus? I know you're building up to something.'

'Christina would be destroyed if Steffie was taken. *I'd* need to be scraped up off the ground if anything was to happen to that little girl. But the Blakes... they seem upset all right, stressed and anxious, but they're not *that* upset. They just aren't overly affected by what happened. And it's annoying me. It's bugging me a lot, in fact.'

'Which is perfectly understandable,' Jessie said. 'If you need to take some time, I can ask Terri to come up and work from here. She likes doing fieldwork from time to time, and she's good at it too.'

'I'm all right,' Seamus said. 'I just wanted to let you know. It's important we talk about these things, isn't it?'

'It is. Will we order some pizza and have a look at these files?'

Jessie had already eaten, but she knew her partner would be hungry.

'We'd be fools not to,' he grinned.

. . .

The paperwork relating to the three other deaths in which stick men, or *púca* men, as Glynn insisted on calling them, was impeccable. Every page was signatured and the information was clearly and concisely laid out.

And it was obvious once they started reading through them that there was nothing obvious to link the victims.

'There's nothing to connect any of the four,' Seamus said, tossing the file he'd been reading down onto the table. 'There's no pattern when it comes to geography, social class, education, profession, religion or ethnicity. We're looking at an irregular pattern on the map and a broad spread of ages. One was a retail assistant, one an administrator, one a homemaker and one a college student.'

'What about sexuality?'

'Rodney Lawler was the only gay victim.'

'There's usually a connection except in rare circumstances,' Jessie said. 'It just isn't always an obvious one. And the really serious question here is what links him to the Rosie Blake abduction to the degree he needed to die. Why kill him? He must have been a danger to the people who have Rosie. He must have known something, even if he didn't know he knew it, that may put them at risk.'

'What though?'

'What was Roche rowing with him about when he called over to the house? What might that have been?'

'We know he was on a mission to take the child out of circulation in some way,' Seamus said. 'I think he had to know there was an abduction planned. He was trying to get her safe before it happened. It's the only thing that makes sense. And by trying to save her, he got himself killed and Rodney too.'

Jessie pulled a map over and spread it out on the floor between them.

'Here's where Rodney was killed in Donaghmede,' she said,

circling the street with a sharpie. 'And here's the location of each of the deaths.' She circled them all too. 'Coolock, Fairview and Rathmines. Notice anything?'

Seamus leaned over and looked at the map closely. Finally he said: 'Help me out here, Jessie. I'm not seeing it.'

'They're all on the number fifteen bus route. It struck me when I was talking to Glynn. Whoever is doing the killing is using the bus.'

'But that would mean Rodney's death occurred because it fit the profile? I can't accept that.'

'I don't believe it either,' Jessie said. 'I think Richard Roche drew something down on him. Poor chap hadn't a clue what he was getting pulled into.'

'I'm not sure,' Seamus said. 'It's a leap to suggest the presence of a bus route connects these killings.'

'Maybe,' Jessie agreed. 'I think we need to get Terri's view. I have a feeling she'll already have something for us on the Reavers.'

Jessie opened the room's laptop and called Terri on Zoom. As Jessie knew she would, given the urgency of the case, she answered right away, despite the late hour, the darkened expanse of their Cork offices visible behind her.

'Hi, Terri, we're going through some files related to the Rosie Blake case, and the Reavers specifically,' Jessie said.

'Before you get into that, I've got a location for the person who sent that email.'

'Okay,' Jessie said. 'We're on tenterhooks.'

'It was sent from a terminal in a corporate law firm: Brooks, Hadlington, Bennet and Associates.'

'Do we know anything about them?' Seamus asked.

'They're big,' Terri said. 'And they're international. And they work with Peter Blake's firm a lot.'

'Any names we might begin looking into?' Jessie asked.

'Oh yes. Peter has had a lot of dealings with a lawyer at Brooks, Hadlington and Bennet named Harold Asquith. Now, I did some digging and Asquith has been linked to some very shady people. He was one of a team who worked on investments and deals for Jeffrey Epstein when he was in the UK, and more than one person has suggested he had a hand in hiding monies earned from people-trafficking and other awful transactions.'

'So this is a bad man with a track record that would put him right in the frame for planning Rosie's abduction,' Seamus said.

'I would say so, yes,' Terri agreed.

'I'll call some of my colleagues in the Met, see if they can bring him in for questioning,' Jessie said.

'Excellent. Now, what did you want to talk to me about?'

Jessie and Seamus told her everything they'd found out in the few hours since they'd last talked, and Jessie's theory regarding the placement of the other murder victims.

'Bus route fifteen runs in a north-easterly direction from Ballycullen Road to Clongriffin Station. It takes in Knocklyon, Templeogue, Rathmines, the North Strand... it's a vast area, Jessie.'

'So you think I'm grasping at straws here?'

'I would, except for this,' Terri said. 'I'm sharing a screen with you.'

A black-and-white image of a stick figure, hanging in a window, filled the screen. It was almost identical to the one Seamus had seen on Montpelier that afternoon, and Jessie only a few hours ago.

'Just as you asked, Jessie, I checked and the murders attributed to the Reavers in the 1930s were all marked with a stick figure. This photo was taken at a crime scene fifteen years ago,' Terri said. 'On the North Strand.'

Seamus gazed at the photo. 'So this person has killed before?'

'There were six deaths across a period of eight months. All of which were marked by these figures.'

'And all along that route?'

'All except one,' Terri said. 'And that's the frustrating part: it occurred miles away.'

'Where?' Jessie asked.

'Tory Island. It's a small island community fourteen miles off the coast of Donegal.'

'Shit,' Jessie said. 'What are we supposed to do with that?'

'My thoughts exactly,' Seamus agreed.

'Why didn't Marsh and local homicide find the connection?'

'There was nothing in the media about these deaths, and you won't find them mentioned on Pulse,' Terri said. 'Intelligence picked up on them right away. I suspect the fact that de Valera took such an interest resulted in the Reavers being seen as a threat to national security. This won't have appeared on any files civilian law enforcement would have had access to.'

Jessie sat back, shaking her head. 'How'd you get them then, Terri, or shouldn't I ask?'

'Your Agent Glynn emailed me with some passcodes which allowed me to access files with a certain level of clearance,' Terri said. 'I'm not getting everything, but the chronologies and basic information is here.'

'Was anyone arrested for those deaths?'

'There's no mention of it in the files, so I'm guessing not.'

'Tory Island is a small community, isn't it?' Jessie said. 'So someone coming and going would be noticed.'

'They would. But settlements like that often value privacy and are loath to speak to the police.'

'I bet they'd talk to a very un-cop like person like you though,' Jessie said, winking.

'You want me to head out there and take a look?'

'I do. First thing in the morning.'

'I'll go home and pack right away.'

'Pack for a long stay,' Jessie said. 'I think you'd best come to Dublin after that.'

'Yay!' Terri said.

And she meant it.

PART THREE

AN ISLAND PEOPLE

'I feel we are all islands – in a common sea.'

Anne Morrow Lindbergh

HAROLD ASQUITH

He'd worked for Brooks, Hadlington and Bennet for ten years and had made the firm more money than he cared to keep track of. They did business with people from all over the world, and the majority of those they represented were at the narrower end of the legal wedge, plying their trade in shallow waters where it was possible to step on something dangerous that was hidden in the sand unless you knew how to tread very carefully indeed.

When Asquith had been contacted by someone from Ireland, looking to exert pressure on a broker over there, he knew what to do right away. This was something he had seen done countless times (there was a media mogul he'd worked for in the 1990s who used kidnapping as a standard form of practice, and that man actually preferred to take children – 'Easier to store,' he'd always said – and of course, families fell over themselves to get them back).

The youngster in Dublin – Asquith insisted he did not want to know names and instructed him to only communicate using the deep web going forward – seemed utterly gormless, so the English lawyer had done the legwork for him. The man he was looking to leverage had a kid, and as luck would have it, the kid *was sick and would need treatment quickly, and it struck him that the family would pretty much give him whatever he asked for to have her back.*

For Asquith, this was business as usual.

So when the police arrived and took him away for questioning, he wasn't that concerned.

He told them nothing. Had an email been traced back to him from the deep web? Obviously this was the result of a faulty router. He'd never used the deep web in his life. Go and check his computers – they'd find no Tor browsers or encryption software. Brooks, Hadlington and Bennet were ethical operators.

He'd been in the interview room for forty minutes when his own lawyer arrived. He was on the street an hour later.

What he hadn't told them, and what had not been included in the snippet of email they'd retrieved, was that he had advised the Dublin gangster not to give the child back. In another email he had written:

Take the money by all means, but my advice to you is to keep the child, find a buyer and sell her on. In my experience, a child is worth more money than most people realise – a good specimen can fetch hundreds of thousands, in some cases more than one million pounds, if you know where to look. If you have gone to the trouble of abducting her, why not take the next step and sell her to the highest bidder? She's dying anyway. Why not invest her young life with some meaning and make yourself rich?

The young Dubliner had assured him that he would do just that.

Asquith was glad he'd been able to help.

And only for a small percentage of the profits.

28

Terri arrived on Tory Island at noon the following day on one of the regular ferries that left Magheroarty Pier in County Donegal to bring passengers and supplies to Ireland's most remote island community. The sea was choppy and grey, white-topped waves crashing against the side of the small boat and herring gulls swooping down on the air thermals. Terri was nauseous and miserable by the time they were ten minutes into the forty-five-minute voyage.

Tory was an anglicised version of the Irish Toraigh, which meant 'the place of the steep rocky heights', and Terri could see why as they approached the island. Five kilometres long and one kilometre wide (at its widest point), the chunk of rock in the middle of the Atlantic looked as if it had been carved into jagged edges and shaved slivers by an enormous hammer and chisel.

She was glad to be back on solid ground and made her way to Tory Island Harbour View Hotel, a long, low building that overlooked the North Atlantic. She left her bags and went in search of An Club, the island's main bar, where she was to meet Detective Inspector Sean O'Dubhaill, who had been involved in the investigation into the murder in 2004. The detective had business on the island that morning and had travelled on the earlier ferry.

An Club (*The* Club in English) was another single-storeyed, white-painted building, about a five-minute walk from the hotel. Terri made the trip with her hands deep in the pockets of her long, black trench coat, her collar turned up against the wind that whipped in from the sea. Tory offered no shelter – no trees grew there because of the relentless gale, and all the buildings were low-slung and solid to withstand the storms that occasionally struck and threatened to rip them from the earth and suck them out into the maelstrom.

She paused outside the pub for a moment, looking with amusement at the mural of a puffin serving a tiny auk a pint – Tory was a bird sanctuary, she knew, and home to vast colonies of sea birds – and then went inside.

The bar looked like it had been adapted into a drinking establishment from a community hall: the place had a wooden floor, a tiny makeshift bar from which the drinks were served, a stage for music at one end, and simple tables and chairs set at even intervals. A piece of traditional Irish music – Terri thought it might be a jig – was being piped over a couple of speakers hung from the wall behind the bar, at a volume that would not interfere with conversation.

Other than the middle-aged woman serving behind the bar, there were only two customers. One was an old man with a cloth cap, nodding gently over a large bottle of Guinness. The other, who was at a table at the very end of the room, next to the tiny stage, was a tall, lean man with a thick head of greying hair and a heavy moustache.

'DI O'Dubhaill?' Terri asked.

'You must be Terri,' he said, smiling and standing. '*Conas atá tú?*' How are you?

'*Tá mé go maith, go raibh maith agat.*' I'm good, thank you.

'*Iontach.*' Excellent. 'So you're here to talk about that weird murder back in '04. I don't know how much I can help you. I was only starting out as a detective and just did a few interviews on the case. It was mostly investigated by John Joe MacSwain, but he died last year. Cancer got him.'

'I've read the file, such as I can access, on the case,' Terri said. 'No one was arrested?'

'No. And the investigation was taken out of our hands after we did all the initial groundwork. John Joe was livid.'

'Who took it over?'

'Two men in suits. They said they were from the Department.'

'The Department of what?'

'That was never expanded upon. I always assumed they were some government investigators. Made me think the whole thing was connected – someone knew someone else who knew someone else.'

'Can you tell me about the person who was killed here?'

'A fisherman named Póilín Duggan. Not a popular man, by all accounts. He'd made a lot of enemies, hereabouts and in Donegal. I mean, there were probably half a dozen reasons to kill him, if you really wanted to turn over all the stones, and God knows, we did. But I have to tell you, none of us who worked that case had ever seen anything the like of how that poor man went to his death.'

'The file I read didn't have full crime-scene photos. I saw the stick man, of course.'

'Some sort of pagan thing. John Joe suspected witchcraft or a satanic cult. But there's never been anything like that on Tory. Not for hundreds of years anyway.'

'This island is said to have been one of the strongholds of Balor, during the Celtic era.'

Balor was allegedly a warrior king, chief of the Fomorians, a small army of fighters who came to Ireland from over the sea and took over most of the Celtic kingdoms, particularly in the west of the country. Terri, Seamus and Jessie had encountered a killer who believed he was the reincarnation of this Celtic demon some time ago, and the fact she was now in a place that was rumoured to be one of his keeps didn't make her feel particularly comfortable.

'So they say. There's stories about him keeping a girl prisoner in a tower here. But that was two thousand years ago. They talk about witch burnings on the island too. And not all of them were burned. One poor woman was tied to a post out on the Anvil, a promontory of rock that goes right out into the ocean. They tied her up out there as a storm was coming and let the sea take her.'

'I've read about that,' Terri said. 'That was in 1653.'

'And is generally believed to be the last instance of witchcraft on the island,' O'Dubhaill said. 'I cannot believe we're talking about this. It's feckin' ridiculous.'

'I know it's frustrating,' Terri said. 'But please bear with me. As I explained, we're looking for a little girl who's in grave danger, so any information you can give me is critical. Would you say the killing showed signs of ritualistic violence?'

'He'd been nailed to his living-room door,' the detective said. 'Then whoever did it hammered more nails into his head, until he died. So it was messed up. I don't know if you'd call that ritualistic. Whoever did it really didn't like Póilín, that's for sure.'

'Did you have any suspects?'

'Only one serious one.'

Terri sat up at that. 'Can you give me a name?'

'I would if I had it to give.'

'You never identified the individual?'

'No. And we did try. But we drew a blank at every turn.'

'Do you have a description at least?'

'I've got better than that,' O'Dubhaill said.

He took an envelope from the inside pocket of his leather jacket and passed it to her.

Terri opened it and took out a grainy photograph.

'That's all we have,' O'Dubhaill said. 'It was taken from security-camera footage and I know it's a bit blurry. But they say a picture speaks a thousand words.'

The image was of a man and had clearly been blown up from video footage shot at a distance. It was difficult to put an age on him, as his facial features were blurred from the enlarging process. What Terri could tell was that he was power-fully built and dressed in an old-fashioned brown suit. His head was completely bald, and his forehead had wide furrows in it, as if he spent a lot of time frowning. She sensed he had a heavy brow, and his eyebrows looked to be quite bushy, but again, it was hard to be completely certain due to the quality of the image.

Beside the man was an enormous dog, which Terri thought first was an Irish wolfhound, but then she paused.

It's a deerhound, she thought. *This can't be Algernon Parsons. He'd be long dead – but I think it's someone attempting to emulate him.*

'He arrived on Tory the afternoon of the murder,' O'Dub-haill said. 'The following day he was gone. We don't know how, as no ferries operate during the night, but that said, boats can be chartered. In these hard times, fishermen will rent out their vessels if you can pay for the privilege.'

'No one came forward to say they'd taken him back to the mainland?'

'They did not.'

'And then the Department came in and took over the inves-tigation,' Terri said. 'Did they tell you why?'

'Of course they didn't. I did get a call about a year ago from someone called Glynn, said he was with the NSA. Said he was following up on the case, but that was all I ever heard about it after I handed it over.'

'So there wasn't much follow-up at all?'

'It would be more accurate to say they came in and shut the investigation down. They removed any and all evidence – the door he was nailed to was even taken away. No one here talks about it anymore. Póilín had no family, so it's as if he was never here. He was a miserable bastard, but he deserves to be remembered, don't you think?'

'I do,' Terri said. 'I think everyone's stories should be heard.'

'His is not a pretty one,' O'Dubhaill said. 'But as Gardai, it's our job to tell the grim stories, the ones without happy endings.'

'The ones where no one lived happily ever after,' Terri agreed.

29

The forensics report on the Montpelier killing was due at 11 a.m. on the day Terri interviewed DI O'Dubhaill on Tory Island, and at nine that morning – after grabbing a scant few hours' sleep – Jessie and Seamus were back in the conference room, comparing the files on the 2004 deaths with the most recent spate.

'Looks like we're back to the drawing board,' Seamus said after an hour had passed.

'I'm not sure why you'd say that,' Jessie said. She was furiously scribbling notes on a yellow legal pad.

'Okay, there are similarities to the deaths,' Seamus said. 'They've all been pinned to something using some sort of metal spike: nails, rebar, railway pins, tent pegs. There's a stick figure at each crime scene and I agree they're all on the number fifteen bus route. The problem is, I don't think the bus route offers us anything useful. It's too big an area – it cuts right through Dublin and there are poor areas and posh areas and industrial estates and beauty spots and all sorts along it, and from what I can see, victims can be found in all those areas. I think them all being on the bus route is a coincidence,

Jessie. And we're no closer to finding Rosie! I'm freaking out here!'

'I don't like coincidences,' Jessie said flatly. 'We keep on digging. There has to be something we've missed.'

They took each of the deaths, the four that had occurred in the past seven months and the six murders from the noughties, and spent the next hour examining each detail, no matter how insignificant. It was slow and frustrating and got them nowhere. Jessie thought she would jump up and down in delight when the time came to make their way to the Phoenix Park to talk to the state pathologist.

Professor Julia Banks was a short, broadly built woman with close-cut grey hair and a business-like manner that, Jessie knew, hid a funereally dark sense of humour. She met them in her lab on the second floor of the Forensic Science Ireland building. The fierce electric light illuminated a tiled floor, dissected here and there by gutters to catch the various fluids Julia and her colleagues' work caused to fall. On a table in the middle of the wide room was a mound covered in a sheet. From out of one corner of this mound, a foot protruded.

'Cause of death was shooting,' Julia said, beginning without saying hello, as was her custom (one that annoyed Seamus no end – the young detective believed courtesy cost nothing and was irritated when he encountered people who behaved contrary to this).

'We'd worked that out for ourselves,' Jessie said. 'Can you give us a little bit more detail?'

Julia pulled back the sheet to reveal Richard Roche's remains. The Y incision, red with black stitches holding it closed, stood out, livid against the man's pale flesh.

'Three bullet wounds directly to the heart. Closely grouped and, I would say, fired in rapid succession. He died almost instantaneously. I would imagine he felt the first one, but if you've been shot, you'll know it's more like a punch initially. The pain doesn't come for a little while. I'd say Mr Roche here suffered little.'

'Do his remains tell us anything else?' Seamus asked. 'Other than he was shot to death?'

'I can tell you he was shot with a .22 gauge handgun.'

'Once again, we'd pretty much worked that out for ourselves,' Seamus said.

'Well aren't you two the gifted amateurs? What do you need me for at all?'

'Prof, will you stop messing around and tell us what you've got?' Jessie asked. 'We're both finding this case a bit draining.'

For a moment she thought about Rosie, and wondered where she might be, and if she was afraid, or in pain, or missing her parents. She felt her mental clock counting down the hours the child had been missing and prayed they would find her before it was too late.

'All right, all right,' Julia retorted. 'The body itself doesn't tell us anything other than he was in good physical shape for a man of his age and that he died as a result of rapid blood loss as the bullets effectively shredded his heart, stopping the oxygenated blood from reaching the brain. There are no other wounds – no bruising, no scrapes or tears. His shoes showed he'd walked up the mountain – we found grasses and earth that all belonged to various points on the ascent from the car park.'

'Anything else on his clothes that helps us?' Seamus asked.

'Some saline solution was soaked into his sleeve. I'm guessing that came from the hospital. There were traces of carboplatin, which is a drug used in chemotherapy treatments, on his hands. Once again, I think we can surmise where that came from. The only other thing we found was some liquid paraffin. There was a small quantity on his jeans, and a few drops on the rear of his jacket.'

'Liquid paraffin?' Jessie said. 'Like heating oil?'

'No. This stuff was much more refined than that. I would say you're looking at a very high-end lamp oil. This one had a vaguely herbal scent to it. Sage, I think.'

'Gibb talked about lights on the mountaintop,' Seamus said. 'This might be the source of it.'

'You said it's high end,' Jessie said. 'So you're talking about expensive stuff?'

'I'm not an expert in it, but I would say what we found on Richard Roche's clothes was made by an artisan company. The oil, when we extracted it from the material, was almost smokeless, and the only odour it contained was from the herbal extract that had been added. Sage is supposed to be a purifier, if I remember the few classes I took on plant fibres in college. Maybe he'd been visiting with some hippy friends recently.'

'Anything else from the site?' Jessie asked.

'There were virtually no markings or tracks about the inside of the building,' Julia said. 'It's dry earth inside, so there should have been. I think some kind of surface cover was put down to protect the floor. The crime-scene boyos found some filaments of coarse fibres made of a canvas and polyethylene mix.'

'Which suggests?' Jessie asked.

'A tarpaulin was put over the ground inside the hunting lodge. It prevented anything being detected on the floor. Except for the traces the tarpaulin left.'

'Pity tarps are so common,' Seamus groaned. 'That doesn't tell us a whole lot.'

'Don't be so hasty, young man,' Julia said. 'Fibres can tell you an awful lot. Especially when they have traces of other things attached to them.'

Jessie, who'd been looking a bit down in the mouth, suddenly looked up. 'What was attached to them?'

'Kaolin.'

Jessie and Seamus looked at Julia blankly.

'What's that?' Jessie wanted to know.

'It's a type of clay used by potters,' the pathologist said. 'And a bit like with the lamp oil, this looks to be a very fine example of the stuff. Whoever Mr Roche met on that mountain is not short of a few quid. And isn't afraid to splash it around.'

Back in the car park, Jessie and Seamus sat in the MG with their phones out, googling the information Julia had just given them.

'We usually get Terri to do this stuff,' Seamus said. 'I never realised how tedious it was before.'

'I know,' Jessie said. 'Remind me of that before I send her off to do fieldwork again. Okay, I've got two producers of "bespoke lamp oil" in the vicinity of Dublin.'

'Jessie, there are about forty places to buy that type of clay in and around the city.'

'The prof seems to think the one on the fibres is a really expensive one,' Jessie said.

'Right. I'll google the most high-end version, contact the suppliers and find out who sells it in Dublin. I'd imagine it's probably going to be a speciality item.'

'More than likely.'

'Let's split up on this for speed. I'll take the clay, you do the lamp oil.'

'Done. I'll drop you off in town. You okay to pick up a car at HQ?'

'I can do that. The sooner we get onto this, the sooner we get that wee girl back.'

'Agreed.'

Jessie had just started the engine when her phone rang.

'Hey, Dawn. Seamus is in the car with me.'

'Hiya, boss.'

'I need you both to meet me on Parnell Street,' the commissioner said. 'Peter Blake has been found dead.'

'On our way,' Jessie said.

'I'll see you in there,' Dawn said and hung up.

'I did not see this coming,' Seamus said.

'That makes two of us,' Jessie agreed. 'That makes two of us.'

30

O'Dubhaill brought Terri to the house on Tory where Póilín Duggan had lived and died.

'Can I leave you to it?' he asked, wrapping his leather jacket about himself against the wind. 'I need to get back to Letterkenny. No one has lived here since the death, so you can spend as long as you like.'

'What will I do with the keys when I'm finished?' Terri asked.

'Just leave them with Grainne in the hotel reception. She'll hold on to them until I'm back on the island.'

'Thank you, Detective. I appreciate all your help. And the photograph you gave me will be very useful.'

'I hope you find more success with it than I've had,' he said, shaking her hand before he walked back towards the pier.

Terri opened the front door and went inside.

The house, which was an old fisherman's cottage, had that anxious, nervy feeling houses do when there's one home. The living room, where Póilín had found his awful end, was to the right off the hall. It was still missing a door, and inside Terri found a crumbling fireplace and a single overturned armchair with the stuffing, now grey and grimy and alive with spiders and other bugs, spewing out of it.

Terri didn't know what she expected to find and stood for a moment, leaning against the mantelpiece and just taking in the wrecked, dust-addled space, trying to get a sense of the pain and horror that had unfolded here. The house was set a little apart from the others in this part of the island, Baile Thiar, West Town. It was in a slight dip, with a wall partly shielding it from the prying eyes of anyone coming down the path. Terri also thought that, with the crashing of the waves, the cries of seabirds and the ever-present wind, screams and cries of agony wouldn't be heard. It was a well-chosen kill site.

She walked to the window and gazed out. The sea was high outside, waves rising and falling to such magnitudes, she wondered the island itself wasn't swallowed completely. This was a harsh place. A difficult spot to scrape a living from and a hard place to die.

Shaking herself from her reverie, Terri decided to take a quick look about the house then head back to her hotel. It was moving on towards two in the afternoon and the sky was darkening as a weather front came in. Terri didn't want to be caught in a rain squall on the walk back to the comfort of her room so decided to quicken her efforts.

The kitchen yielded nothing except more large spiders. There was a door leading off it, Terri presumed to a shed or storage room out the back, but none of the keys in the bundle O'Dubhaill had given her opened it. She decided to check the remaining rooms and return and try one more time. If she couldn't get it open, she could always get one of the men from the hotel to break it open for her in the morning.

There were two tiny rooms, empty of everything but foul carpets and a dusty crucifix (which Terri noted was hanging upside down, but she wrote it off as just an unfortunate accident that had happened over time) and a bathroom with a cracked sink and a toilet with no water in the bowl or cistern. The only sense she was getting from the house was sadness and loneliness. There was, hanging in the air, the feeling that a sad and angry man had met a death he didn't deserve here.

Because, Terri thought, *no one deserves a death like that. No matter what they've done.*

She tried the keys again, and now, taking her time, found that one of them came close to turning, and she wondered if the mechanism was just a bit stiff, or if the key had just become slightly distorted over time. She jiggled it a bit this way and that, pulled the handle of the door towards her then pushed it back, and suddenly the tumblers turned and the key twisted.

Terri stepped back and opened the door.

Inside was a mattress, upon which a blanket had been neatly folded. The blanket was pink and had light blue unicorns on it. The type a little girl might like. The room had no window, and Terri switched on the torch on her phone and shone it about the space. There, in the corner just beside the top of the mattress, was a clear plastic pouch. Terri went over and, using the sleeve of her jacket, picked up the item. Written on a label on the front it said: *Doxorubicin.* Terri didn't know what that was, but she was prepared to bet a whole month's salary that when she googled it, she would find it was some kind of chemo-therapy drug.

They'd had her here. Rosie had been on Tory Island.

And perhaps she still was.

Terri was about to call Jessie when she heard a strange sound behind her. At first she thought it was the sound of thunder and wondered if the storm that had been threatening the island all day had finally arrived.

But then she realised what it was. Terri was hearing the low, rumbling growl of an enormous dog.

31

Peter Blake was lying face down on the filthy, frozen ground in an alleyway near the intersection of Parnell Street and O'Connell Street. He was wearing an expensive-looking blue suit, the trousers of which had been pulled down to reveal his pale posterior. Jessie hadn't liked the man, but she felt a flash of anger at the indignity that had been visited upon him.

'He was found at 1.15 p.m. by a kitchen porter from one of the restaurants next door to the alleyway,' Dawn explained. 'He's Korean and doesn't speak much English. We've sent for an interpreter, but from what I can gather, he's saying he has to come out to the alley regularly to put stuff in the bins. Mr Blake wasn't there the last time he was out, which means he was either killed within the last sixty minutes, or at the very least his body was dumped here within that timeframe. The medical examiner can tell us if the times match up. If he's been dead longer, we'll know he was moved here.'

'Cause of death?' Jessie asked.

'He's a mess,' Dawn said. 'Beaten to death, by the looks of it.'

'Has he been... interfered with?' Seamus asked tentatively.

'You mean due to the fact his trousers are down around his knees?' Dawn asked. 'The short answer is I don't know. I haven't looked closely enough to tell, and I've no intention of doing so. I've known criminals who do that to their victims so their families think they have been – adds to the pain and the grief, which is just fucking awful. It could also have been done to suggest he was here looking for rough trade. Or who knows, maybe he got caught short and came down the alley to relieve himself, and someone attacked him. He's wearing a suit that screams out that he's got money. There are a lot of very poor and very desperate people on the streets this winter. Anything could have happened.'

'And yet we had a death linked to this case yesterday,' Jessie said. 'Which could also be disconnected but probably isn't.'

'My thoughts exactly. There's something going on here that none of us has gotten a handle on yet, and it's starting to really bother me. Too many people are turning up dead or missing these past few days, and I want some answers.'

'We're all working flat out, boss,' Seamus said. 'It's wrecking my head as well.'

'Well we need to work harder,' Dawn said through gritted teeth. 'Before anyone else meets their maker.'

'Has anyone spoken to Shauna?' Jessie asked.

'Not yet,' Dawn sighed. 'He's just been found.'

'I'll do it,' Jessie said.

'I'll follow up on the leads from this morning,' Seamus said. 'The clay and whatnot.'

'I'll be in touch soon, Seamus,' Jessie said.

He nodded and turned to walk back up the alley to the street.

Terri turned slowly, placing her hand into the tote bag she had slung about her shoulder.

The dog was as tall as her shoulder, its head almost level with her own. She had never seen a deerhound up close before, and it was a beautiful, powerful and terrifying beast. And she had no idea how it had got inside. She knew she'd closed the front door behind her, and as far as she knew, there was only one key to the house, which she had in her pocket at that very moment.

'Good dog,' she said. 'Good boy.'

The words caused the dog's growling to alter its cadence. It became shriller, more electric. And the animal, which was standing in the middle of the kitchen, took a step towards her. It was just one, but to Terri it spoke of an immediate threat, one she knew she had to extricate herself from immediately.

The genealogist had not been around dogs much. She had never been afraid of them, but neither did she have any great fondness for them. To Terri, dogs were a feature of the world around her, but one she paid little heed to. They simply didn't blip on her radar very often, so there was never any cause for her to study them in any great depth.

'Who's a pretty boy then?' she asked, keeping her tone calm and measured, and maintaining eye contact with the beast.

That's not for dogs, it's for parrots, she thought, almost hysterically. *Maybe I should give him a cracker!*

This thought was followed by an almost overwhelming desire to laugh, but she pushed it deep down inside her, and did something that scared her so much she almost wet herself.

She took a firm and deliberate step towards the snarling creature.

She had hoped this would cause the animal to take a step back. But it didn't. It stood very firm, and its snarling rose in pitch again.

The dog was grey/brown in colour, its coat thick and long. Terri could see pieces of grass and some sand clinging to the fur on its legs and the lower part of its body. She could smell it too: a scent that was all at once wild and heady and angry. It told her that this dog was very far away from the fat, lazy, hand-fed animals she saw people walking on the waterfront in Cork. This was a creature that was not used to petting or spending time on a leash. She saw that its collar was a short length of rope, knotted in place, a nod to the social convention and no more than that.

What stood before Terri was a wild thing.

She knew she had very few options.

Slowly, with painstaking movements, she searched through her bag with the tips of her fingers until she found what she was looking for: half a ham sandwich she'd packed for the boat trip but then abandoned when she'd started feeling nauseous. She'd discarded the plastic container in a bin on the boat and the sandwich was wrapped in a napkin now.

She very gently drew her hand from her bag and held the sandwich aloft for a moment, letting the tissue paper fall open so the food was revealed. Keeping her movements slow and languid, she waved the bread and meat about in the air, so she was sure the scent would reach the dog.

The animal's eyes followed the path of the sandwich. For a second, just a second, the growling stopped. It was only a moment, but something in Terri whooped in jubilation.

Throwing caution to the wind, she tossed the sandwich over the animal's head and into the corner behind it. The dog watched the food passing over, even turned for a second to see where it had gone, but instead of rushing to gorge on the offering, it remained firmly in place, and the growling rose to a crescendo. Terri watched in horror as the animal then lowered itself so its chin was almost touching the ground, and she knew it was going to spring any second.

I really didn't want to do this, she thought, *but it's not giving me any other option.*

Not bothering to go slowly, Terri plunged her hand back into her bag. She didn't have to root around this time. She knew exactly what she was looking for and precisely where it was – she'd rehearsed the movement a thousand times and had it down so it was second nature, a muscle memory that she could rely on without having to think.

The dog barked once and then made a noise like a roar and rushed her. As it did, Terri whipped the can of pepper spray from her bag and delivered a blast right into the animal's face, filling its eyes and snout with the noxious mist.

The effect was instantaneous. The dog made a sound that, to Terri's surprise, was very like screaming, and careered past her and into the room with the mattress, thudding into the wall and rebounding, coming to rest on the mattress itself, rubbing at its eyes with its paws and squealing miserably.

'I'm so, so sorry,' Terri said, 'that's the last thing I wanted to do to you, but you would have hurt me, and I won't allow anything to do that. Never again.'

And she closed the door of the room, leaving the wailing deerhound to its suffering, then ran from the house into the storm outside.

If she hadn't been so focused on keeping to the narrow path and not losing her footing, Terri might have seen the tall man in the brown suit standing in the shadows by the old house. The rain was beading on his head and his dark eyes were glistening with rage at the pained sounds his beloved dog was making.

33

Dawn Wilson sat in a small café near the O2 arena. It was dark outside, and while she knew the Liffey was rolling past beyond the windows, all she could see were the blurred lights of cars as they went past slowly, their speed low because it was rush hour, and blackness beyond them.

The place she was in consisted of four tables and a narrow counter, and it had been there for as long as Dawn had been in Dublin. Its clientele were originally dock workers, but as the area gentrified, the café (which was just called The Caff) went upscale too, and the old lady who had once been the proprietor retired and brought in two kids in their twenties who called themselves 'baristas' (whatever the fuck that meant) and served coffees made out of milks that came from nuts and beans, something that made no sense to Dawn but which Terri told her were much healthier for you.

'How do you milk a fucking oat?' Dawn had retorted. 'I mean, how is that even possible?'

Terri had shaken her head dolefully, patted her friend on the shoulder and gone about her business.

The commissioner had a cup of tea in front of her (she had

brought her own Barry's teabag with her, knowing they'd only sell organic, gluten-free bags here) and was nibbling a fruit scone when the door opened and Garth Calhoun came in.

'It's a while since we met here,' he said, shaking raindrops off his coat and placing it carefully on the back of a chair.

'Used to be our spot, didn't it?' Dawn responded, smiling.

'I remember it fondly.'

'Would you believe I do too?'

The gangster laughed and shook his head. 'Dawn, I have to tell you, I do not believe that.'

He was a tough man, was Garth Calhoun, but Dawn could see he was still hurting, all these years later. Their affair had been short but intense, and despite the fact they came from separate worlds, and she'd been forced to betray him, she knew that when she'd told him she loved him, she'd meant it.

She'd loved her job more though. And the oaths she'd taken were sacred to her. Which meant she'd had no option, when the moment came that she had to choose.

'I actually did care for you, Garth,' she said. 'I could see – and I still do – that you're not all one thing. No more than I am. I've asked you here this evening to appeal to the side of you I know is good. There's a child who will die if we can't find her and get her back to her mother and her doctors. I think you know what happened. Some of it at least. Anything you tell me will be off the record. I will walk away and bring her back in and I won't mention your name in any report. Only you and me will know, and I'll owe you a favour.'

'Dawn – *Commissioner Wilson* – your word isn't worth shit to me. You made me fall for you, made me trust you, and then you sold me down the river and saw me locked up. By all rights, I should have shot you the moment you set foot in my bar yesterday. Some ridiculous loyalty to what we had stopped me, but I have to tell you, I'm reconsidering my position.'

Dawn heaved a heavy sigh. 'I was a young cop and I was

undercover. My job was to infiltrate your organisation and learn as much as I could. God love me, I had some daddy issues I didn't even know were there and I got my head turned by you. You were quite the man – you still are – and even then I knew you weren't the kind of brute a lot of men in your position can be. I mean, which other mobster is going to keep a lad like Eugene around? He's more of an encumbrance to you than a help, but you look after him and pay him a salary because you feel sorry for him or you want to make sure his mother has a few quid extra at the end of the week. That's what I fell for. That goodness.'

'You know I've ordered the deaths of more men than I care to remember,' Calhoun said. 'I've killed with these hands.'

Dawn reached over and took one of those hands and held it. 'And I've killed with these hands too. Help me, Garth. Do you know who took Rosie?'

'I know some of it,' Calhoun said. 'None of it was my idea, and I never ordered it to happen. I tried to stop the whole thing, but by the time I was wise to what was going on, it was too late.'

'Tell me,' Dawn said.

And he did.

34

Shauna Blake was sitting with her head in her hands.

The Blakes' home was in Clontarf, a nineteenth-century townhouse that was opulent to the extreme: deep-pile carpets, original pieces of art, antique furniture (which Jessie thought lacked even the slightest vestige of comfort). What seemed to be missing was any sign a child lived there. It was as if Rosie didn't fit into their lives.

'Are you sure the body was him?' the woman asked, her voice muffled and hoarse from crying.

Jessie noted that, just as the woman's reaction to her daughter's abduction seemed muted, her grief at her husband's death seemed dutiful and proper, yet not exactly overwhelming. It was as if she was going through the motions.

'Yes, it's definitely Peter,' Jessie said, adding: 'I'm so very sorry.'

'He... he was giving them what they wanted. Why did they kill him?'

'I apologise, Mrs Blake, but I'm not sure what you mean. Can you tell me what Peter was doing?'

'The people who have Rosie contacted us. Well, they contacted him at work.'

'We have all your contact details,' Jessie said. 'Your communications are being monitored.'

'There's a phone Peter kept. It's one he uses for some of his business calls. The really confidential ones.'

'Okay,' Jessie said, although she was fuming. 'Can you tell me what they said when they called?'

'That they wanted three million euro. That they'd give Rosie back if we gave it to them.'

'Do you have access to that kind of money?'

'Peter said he could get it.'

'And he was to meet them this morning in town?'

'Yes. They gave him an Eircode and details of what to do when he got there.'

'Mrs Blake, is there anything else you haven't told me? I hate to make you feel worse, but if your husband had told us about that phone, he'd probably still be alive now. I want to bring your daughter home, and you need to help me do it.'

Shauna looked up at Jessie, and the misery was evident in her face.

'Peter got involved with some bad people,' she said. 'He thought he could handle it, but he couldn't. It all started to get scary, and then Richard Roche told us he'd heard they were planning on taking Rosie to put pressure on Peter to do something for them.'

'What?'

'They wanted him to invest some money to... to clean it. Make it usable.'

'Money laundering,' Jessie said. 'They wanted him to process their money so it could be used without being detected.'

'Yes. I don't understand how it works, but that's it, I think.'

'Had your husband been doing other illegal things for them?'

'Only on a small scale. A few thousand here, a few there. This was *millions* they wanted moved about. He was terrified it would be traced back to him. That he'd lose his licence, go to prison. So he politely declined and suggested a safer way to do it. But the person he was dealing with wouldn't take no for an answer.'

'And this person was Garth Calhoun?'

'His organisation. But not Garth himself. Someone else. A man called Eugene.'

'And then Richard Roche contacted you to say he thought Rosie was going to be a target.'

'Yes. He said we needed to put her somewhere secure. The problem is she needs constant chemo and has to be in a sterile environment. So we said no, and that the hospital was safe enough. It was a public place after all. Who could take her from there?'

'But Roche knew the organisation, didn't he?' Jessie said. 'He knew they wouldn't let a little thing like a hospital get in the way of their plans.'

'It was Richard who came up with the plan in the end,' Shauna said. 'It should have worked. How were we to know something so awful would happen?'

35

'It was Eugene who was behind it all,' Calhoun said. 'He's not a bad lad, and he's got ambitions. He just hasn't the cop-on to back it up.'

'What did he do, Garth?' Dawn asked, her voice quiet but a note of steel entering into it. 'What did that lad set in motion?'

'Eugene does have some smarts, but they're book smarts, not street smarts. His mam had notions he'd go to university and make something of himself, and he did a business course at the Dublin Institute of Technology. Accountancy and that. When he was expelled his mam asked me to give him a job, and I figured he might put some of that learning to use and let him at the books. I think it was there he came across Peter Blake and started to take an interest in him.'

'He saw what he did for you, and where he worked, and he thought he'd try and spearhead a little initiative of his own,' Dawn said.

'Cleaning cash is always the biggest problem for someone in my line of business,' Calhoun said. 'I have very large amounts of money coming in from various sources, none of which I can declare to the Revenue Commissioners. I need to find ways of disguising the source of my income, and the reality is, your people are getting better and better at sniffing out the more traditional methods.'

'Well it's no surprise most people in your chosen trade base their operations in pubs, nightclubs or betting offices,' Dawn said. 'They're perfect vehicles for the cleansing of dirty money.'

'Yes, but these days you need to be more high-tech. I'd been looking at investment opportunities, places to put the cash where there are layers of protection even the Criminal Assets Bureau might have trouble getting through. Peter Blake was good at doing that. He had a nose for it. I've the experience behind me to know that when you find a man like that, you treat him well, don't overstretch him. Eugene, the feckin' gobshite, didn't know it. And he took it upon himself to start pushing Peter to move bigger and bigger sums. And it wasn't long before Peter pushed back.'

'What did he do?'

'He came to me. Asked me to call Eugene off. Now, you don't let on to the help that there's any dissent among your family – that wouldn't do – so I told him Eugene was acting on my behalf but that I'd consider lowering the bar. Then I called in Eugene and gave him the bollocking of his life. I hit him a few slaps. Told him to back down and to do it right away.'

'It didn't work though, did it?'

'No. The lad contacted an agency in London, a law firm that specialises in all kinds of nasty stuff. I mean, I use them from time to time because they know what they're doing. After you had me sent away, I realised I needed better representation.'

'Who did you go to?'

'Come on, Dawn. I'm not showing you all the secrets behind the curtain.'

'I can stop this, Garth. Save this kid. Maybe get Eugene off your case too. But I need to know it *all*. Do you understand?'

Calhoun sighed and rubbed his eyes.

'Brooks, Hadlington and Bennett,' he said. 'Those guys can make the most crooked stuff seem absolutely reasonable and completely legal.'

'They sound like lovely people,' Dawn said, and now there was nothing but steel in her voice.

'Eugene asked them how best to leverage someone like Blake. God love the lad, I think he was looking for a business suggestion. Maybe a carrot to dangle in front of the man. But it's not what he got.'

'They suggested taking Rosie.'

'Yes.'

'How did Richard Roche get wind of it?'

Calhoun gazed at her for a long moment. Dawn could see he was ashamed of all of this. That he felt responsible. And she wasn't going to alleviate him of that guilt. In many ways, he *was* responsible.

'Most people think about criminals as people with no moral compass,' the old man said. 'And in some cases, that's true. But a lot of us, as you know damn well, have limits. Lines we won't cross. Hurting kids is one a *whole lot* of guys won't countenance. One of the lads Eugene tried to bring in to take the Blake girl didn't like the plan one bit. Eugene had told them all I'd green-lit the action, so this lad went to Richie.'

'Why did he go to Roche? I thought he wasn't involved in your gang anymore.'

'He's not. But Richie, he's known as a good man. As someone who stands up for people. He got a lot of respect, did Richie.'

'So he tried to have Rosie put somewhere safe,' Dawn said.

'He had to persuade her parents, but they finally got on board with it,' Calhoun said. 'He was to meet Jamesie, the lad who went against Eugene, on Montpelier that night. He wanted to abandon his own car somewhere out of the way, so it looked like he was hiding out in the mountains and the woods. He figured ye'd spend a week at least combing the hillsides looking for him, and by then he'd be somewhere safe. Jamesie has a house in Galway. The idea was to take Rosie down the other side of the hill, where Jamesie had a car waiting, and then make a run for it.'

'But something went wrong,' Dawn said.

'By the time Jamesie got there, the hillside was lit up, and there were cops everywhere.'

Dawn nodded. 'Someone met Richard Roche on the hill that night,' she said. 'Are you engaged in hostilities with any other organisations at the moment?'

'No. There's the usual stuff going on, but nothing out of the ordinary.'

'Could it have been Eugene? Might he have gotten wind of what had happened and retaliated?'

'No. I've had him pretty much on house arrest, and the rest of the crew are treating him like a pariah. He'll be on his best behaviour for the next twenty years or I'll make him sorry he was born.'

'Has Eugene pissed anyone off? Might this be because of something else he's done?'

'No. He's not been at the game long enough to have made any enemies.'

Dawn placed some money on the table and stood up.

'Garth, I'm going to say this to you only once,' she said. 'You've gone soft. The man I fell in love with all those years ago would have dealt with Eugene hard and fast, and he never would have had the opportunity to create the shitstorm he has. I'd do something about him now before he takes the option out of your hands.'

And she walked out into the night, feeling tired and angry.

Seamus spent the rest of the afternoon following up on the clay. After a series of phone calls, he was able to confirm that a place called Sherlock and Toyne, an art shop and gallery that catered for what they described as an 'exclusive' clientele, sold a type of kaolin that was imported from Mexico, and (according to the proprietor, who spoke like he had a bag of marbles in his mouth) offered a texture and finish to pottery products that simply could not be imitated. Seamus asked him for a list of the people he'd sold it to, and the man said he had an exhibition opening that evening, and if Seamus was to pop in then, he would have it for him.

The next few hours he spent going back over the files again, trying to make head or tail of them, and by then the prof had sent over the full forensics report too. He was poring through that when his phone rang.

It was Christina, the girl he'd been seeing. Sort of. Seamus still wasn't sure if they were an item or not, but he took the fact she was calling him as a positive sign.

'I was just thinking about you,' she said as an opener, which he took as good too.

'Were you now? And why's that?'

'My mother has offered to take Steffie for the night, and I need someone to take me out for something nice to eat. I thought you might be interested in taking up the challenge.'

Seamus was about to tell her he would love to but that he had to work when he stopped himself. He hadn't eaten yet, and he did have to go in to Temple Bar, which is where the art shop and gallery were situated. He'd been working non-stop, pausing only for a couple of hours to sleep, for two days now. And there was actually nothing he could do until he had the list from the art dealer. Once he had it, he would have to return to the office and continue working – every second wasted was a second Rosie was closer to death – but for the next couple of hours, he was at an (admittedly frustrating) loose end. Maybe it was time to take a short respite, and to see this woman he was hoping to get to know better.

'I can do that. I need to pick up something for work at nine, but it won't take more than a second.'

'That's no problem. I rang you out of the blue. Text me where you want to meet and I'll see you in a couple of hours?'

'I'll do that. Thanks, Christina. See you soon.'

The date, he decided, would be a welcome distraction, even if it turned out to be an unmitigated disaster.

That said, he sincerely hoped it wouldn't be.

Seamus spent the next forty minutes agonising over the location – he didn't want to look cheap, but he didn't want her to think he was showing off either, so he finally settled on a small Italian place, one of those joints that had a charcoal oven and made a big deal out of their pizzas. He'd read some glowing reviews online, and it was the kind of place where you should probably wear a jacket but wouldn't look out of place without a tie.

That, he felt, sent the right message.

Seamus was what Terri laughingly referred to as a 'serial

monogamist'. He was not, by any definition, a lady's man, but he'd had a few long-term relationships and was certainly not awkward around members of the opposite sex. What he struggled with was the fact that the vast majority of relationships these days seemed to begin online, and this was a complete anathema to him.

He had no time or tolerance for social media. Seamus was one of that rare breed who had never had a Facebook page, had no real concept about what purpose Twitter served and had for a long time thought Instagram was a brand of disposable camera. He was convinced that dating apps were a total waste of time and would always lead to, at best, disappointment, and, at worst, utter humiliation.

This somewhat limited his dating options. Most women of his age, it seemed to him, did not see the physical world as a proper place to look for a mate and perceived uninitiated overtures to conversation, or even the making of eye contact, as a bit strange. Which was, he believed, somewhat tragic. So when Christina actually came up to him in the laundrette one evening and started to chat, he'd been more pleased than he could say.

He got to the restaurant early and was shown to a table. He was about to order a beer but then thought that his date may want wine when she arrived – he wasn't much of a drinker and figured he'd wait to see what she would opt for then follow her lead.

Seven o'clock, which was the time they'd agreed, came and went. Being a cop had taught Seamus that nineteen hundred hours meant just that: being early was okay, but being even sixty seconds late was unacceptable. He had to constantly remind himself that civilians weren't slaves to the clock in quite the same way and forced himself to be patient.

Five minutes ticked past. Then ten. He was beginning to believe he'd been stood up and was trying to work out if he should tell Jessie the relationship was actually not the big deal he'd hoped when the door opened and there, wearing a leather jacket belted at the waist, a paisley scarf about her neck, the outfit finished off with skinny jeans and ankle boots, was Christina.

'Seamus, I'm so sorry! My mother was late.'

Seamus grinned. 'I didn't notice.'

And in truth, he'd almost forgotten about it already.

Christina said she would love a glass of red wine, and they decided to throw caution to the wind and ordered a bottle. They had caprese salad, with delicious, ripe beef tomatoes and electric-green basil leaves, the buffalo mozzarella so creamy it was almost like a mousse, then had a mock disagreement when Seamus asked for anchovies on his pizza – though he got his own back when she ordered pineapple on hers.

They finished the meal by sharing a tiramisu.

And through it all, they talked.

Seamus didn't consider himself to be a particularly sparkling conversationalist. He usually had to get to know somebody very well before discourse really flowed, but with Christina, it wasn't like that. Somehow, they just seemed to 'get' one another right from the beginning. That night, the topics they covered weren't all deep and they weren't all profound: Seamus talked a little about being a cop and about his work with the NBCI – without mentioning any specific cases of course – but mostly, he told her about the traditional Irish musicians he liked, and about the movies he enjoyed, and why he wasn't embarrassed by the recent performance of the Kerry footballers even though everyone said he should be.

She talked about her experiences growing up in Dublin, about how Steffie was the most amazing little girl ever put on the face of the earth – although she admitted she was somewhat biased in her view. And she also talked a little about the death of her husband, though she said she didn't want to dwell on it.

Seamus had known Steffie had to have a dad, but he'd always assumed they'd just split up.

'I've spent a couple of years feeling like the sky fell in on top of me,' she said. 'But I'm finding my way back. He was a brilliant man, and I loved him, but I'm twenty-eight and I can't just stop living. He wouldn't want me to.'

When their meal was over, they walked up the road to the art shop, and Seamus popped in and got the list from the owner who, to Seamus's incredulity, was actually wearing a monocle.

As he waited with Christina for her taxi, he thought that maybe he was feeling truly happy for the first time in a while.

'Would it be out of line for me to ask if you'd consider going out with me again?' he asked.

'It would not,' she replied.

They were standing on the pavement just outside the art shop's door. It was just after ten o'clock – his date had told her tardy mother that she wouldn't be any later than ten thirty, although Seamus had suggested it would serve her right if her daughter's approach to getting home reflected her commitment to turning up on time, to which she'd told him not to be such a grump.

'Well, would you like to accompany me on another date?'

'That depends.'

'It does?'

'Absolutely.'

'On what?'

'On the quality of the goodnight kiss you're about to give me.'

Seamus pretended to look terrified. 'So there's no pressure then?'

'There is every pressure. I'm deadly serious. If you mess this up, it could be the end of a beautiful friendship. Get it right, and I can promise you the beginning of an adventure like no other.'

'Well it's a good thing I'm such an experienced combatant,' Seamus said.

'You'd better be able to back that up,' Christina said and leaned in to kiss him.

It was a long kiss, slow and sensual, and it took his breath away. As he came up for air, the cab pulled up to the kerb.

'Do I pass the audition?' he asked, although his voice sounded very small and not a little hoarse.

'Seamus Keneally,' she said, 'you may ask me out again.'

And giving him one more kiss, she ran to the cab.

'Call me,' she said as she got in.

It felt like he was walking on air as he strolled back to Harcourt Street.

37

'Richie was supposed to call us on Peter's work phone when he got to Galway,' Shauna said. 'But of course the call never came. I... I don't know what to do. This is like a nightmare that keeps getting worse and worse.'

'Did you speak to the man who was helping Richard? Did he have any idea who Richard might have met at the Hellfire Club?'

'He said he didn't know. He mentioned a rival gang, but he didn't seem to think that was very likely. He was as upset as me about it, I think. He seemed to hold Richie in quite high regard.'

Jessie nodded. 'I want you to think,' she said. 'Can you remember anything your husband said about the call he received that might be useful to me? Did he mention any noises in the background? Did they have a particular kind of accent? Did they ask him to do anything he thought was odd when he was delivering the cash? It might seem silly, but please, any information at all might make all the difference.'

'I don't know...'

At that moment Jessie's phone rang.

'Hey, Terri. I'm with someone – can I call you back?'

There was nothing for a moment except the sound of the wind in the phone's earpiece. Then, barely audible over the sound of the storm: 'Jessie, I think I'm in trouble. I... I found the place they've been keeping Rosie. But... but they found *me*.'

'Who found you, Terri? Are you still on Tory?'

'The Reavers. Jessie, Rosie was here. She... she might still be.'

'Terri, get somewhere safe and stay there. I'm on my way.'

'You won't get here in time. I... I think he's coming. I can hear him calling. And he's not alone.'

'Listen to me, Terri. Whatever happens, you stay safe. Get to the hotel and tell the staff that there's a credible threat and they are to lock the place up. I *will* get there. I promise you. I'm on my way and we'll get you out of there.'

'Jessie... he's here.'

And then the phone went dead.

38

It was Seamus who worked out what they'd been missing.

He sat in the conference room at Harcourt Street, the files and maps and other information spread out before him. An old sergeant of his had taught him to do a trick when working on a really tough case, where you emptied your conscious mind, all the stuff at the front, and let your unconscious mind do the work for you, joining up the dots.

What was rankling him was Jessie's theory about the bus route. It didn't fit.

Obviously, all the locations were on route fifteen, but the other information – the clay and the lamp oil and the stick figures – seemed counter-intuitive to the bus route being what linked the murders. A bus route suggested working class, commuter belt, low income. The oil and the clay and the pagan imagery all hinted at something else.

He'd been back from his date with Christina for an hour when he found it.

And once again it was the forensic work that pointed him in the direction. In fact, it was the pine-cone head that did it.

Forensic Science Ireland had just forwarded their findings

on the cone, and these suggested it came from a very particular type of fir tree – something called the *Taxodium distichum*, otherwise known as the swamp cypress. It was, apparently, quite rare and only grew in a few places in Ireland. Seamus, once again wishing Terri wasn't off doing fieldwork, pulled out his phone and googled.

Of the three places where swamp cypress could be found, one was in Dublin. The grounds of the estate of the Aldridge family, according to the *Interesting Trees and Plants* Facebook page, had an admirable collection of rare species, among which was a fine specimen of swamp cypress.

A bit more googling told Seamus the house held traditional, lamp-lit dinners in their dining room, and the lady of the house, Daisy Aldridge, gave pottery classes during the winter months.

Seamus didn't care about the hour. He pulled on his coat and went to get a car.

GARTH CALHOUN

He was seventy-five years old and felt every day of it.

Most men in his profession didn't live to see so many winters, but he had always been careful. He looked after his men, treated them with kindness where he could and only chastised (in a life of crime, a chastisement could often be a terminal experience) where it was absolutely necessary, and when he did, he made sure it was a public thing, and terrifying enough so that his men would see and remember he wasn't a man to be crossed lightly.

He hadn't been forced to act like that in many years. And he was glad of it.

He no longer had the stomach for violence.

He was, in fact, building a nest egg, a retirement fund so that he and his wife could spend the remainder of their days somewhere warm and peaceful. A place with a beach and drinks with umbrellas. AJ could take care of things. He'd been slowly training him up, and he thought he was ready. He was tough and fair and he had a good head on his shoulders. The other men liked and respected him and feared him just enough.

And at the end of the day, that was what it was all about.

Garth turned in his chair and stared at the photos of horses and jockeys on the walls of his office. When he was younger, that was what he had dreamed of being – the idea of sitting astride an animal so magnificent, pounding down the track, leaping fences and walls at breakneck speed, urged on by the cheers of the spectators... that had been what he really wanted for his life.

He thought he might have been really good at it too. His mother had got him riding lessons when he was younger, and he'd had an affinity for it. His instructors told him he had what it took to be not just good but great. He'd taken it seriously too. Garth was slim but not skinny, and he'd had to focus strongly on diet and a strict exercise regimen to keep his weight down, and while others might have found this miserable, he embraced it. The rewards of having the career he loved more than compensated.

Yet that was not to be. Garth's father had built this empire, and it was decreed from the moment he had come screaming into the world that it would be up to him to keep the ship afloat after his old man passed on. And the Calhouns understood duty. Garth had had it rammed down his throat from as soon as he could understand the concept.

So, at the tender age of thirteen, he had shelved his dreams of Cheltenham and Leopardstown and beating the odds and bringing home winners. And instead he'd resigned himself that his life would be one of service. Service to someone else's dream.

And he believed he had done right by his father.

The businesses had grown. The empire had expanded, both on the legal and illegal side of operations. Not only that, Garth tried to put something back into the communities where he operated. Kids got a chance, a leg up in a world where your postal address could be a handicap and a barrier to progression. He turned no one away, tried to utilise the talents he saw in front of him and help each kid make something of themselves.

It was a business model that had served him. The Calhoun gang made money, but it also made a difference. Did it cause

harm too? Of course it did – drugs were an evil, the cars he reno-
vated and sold on were stolen, and he ran gambling operations
and a money-lending service too. But if he didn't do it, someone
else would, and he made sure the drugs he put out on the street
didn't contain rat poison.

Garth slept reasonably well at night. He felt he had taken
what could have been a poisoned chalice and made something
tolerably good out of it.

The one regret he had was Dawn Wilson.

He'd been married for more than twenty years when she
came to 'work' for him, ostensibly as a barmaid in the pub which
was the front for his operations. He was in his fifties, she in her
twenties, but the attraction had, he believed, been immediate.
He'd never had his head turned by anyone so young before (he
wasn't faithful to his wife, not by a long shot, but he prided
himself on being interested in women rather than girls), but
Dawn was different. She was funny and brash and while not
beautiful, there was strength and character in her face. Very tall
for a woman, Dawn towered over him, but Garth found he didn't
mind, and though he rarely imbibed spirits, found himself
looking for excuses to stay back in the bar in the evenings to sip a
glass of Scotch and talk to her while she cleaned up.

Initially these conversations were light, about nothing in
particular, just sharing the general ins and outs of each other's
days. He'd had to deal with a late shipment, she a rude customer.
But soon they were sharing more personal details: she told him
about her physically abusive father; he told her how he'd been
forced to abandon his personal goals to achieve his father's
instead.

The first time they kissed, he couldn't believe it was happening. When she took his hand and placed it gently on her breast, he
felt an immediate stirring, and they barely made it to the couch
in his office.

It wasn't long before he let his guard down and began to tell *her more and more about the specifics of his various businesses. He asked her opinion on things, looked for advice and guidance. He even considered taking her from the bar, which by now she was managing, to give her a job with wider-ranging responsibilities.*

This was to be his real downfall.

Because he decided she was going to take over the distribution of his drugs business. By doing this, he handed her the keys to his entire empire, his biggest earner. As soon as she had that and knew where the bodies were buried, so to speak, she pulled the plug and Garth's businesses, spread across a dozen properties throughout Dublin, were raided, and he was arrested.

Dawn gave evidence at his trial. He couldn't bring himself to look at her.

While he languished in Portlaoise Prison, Garth had sworn he would never allow himself to be so duped again. He would trust only those who'd earned that trust, and he would be certain before giving access to his secrets.

Yet, he knew he'd loved her. And part of him still did.

They had only been together for six months, but it was a period he still remembered with a thrill. Despite the prison sentence and the financial losses he'd accrued, he couldn't bring himself to regret being with her.

Maybe, he thought, it was a price he was happy to pay to have had those brief moments of happiness in a life that was so often grey and drab and an existence he knew he'd settled for. Dawn had elevated him from that, just for a short time.

Had she done so as part of her job?

He didn't believe so. She no longer had to say she'd loved him. There was no onus on her to do that. He knew it was true.

And it gladdened him to hear it.

Garth was still pondering the photograph of a chestnut mare leaping a fence when the door to his office opened and Eugene walked in, unannounced.

'Eugene, how can I help you? Is everything all right?'

'Everything is fine,' the lad said, and then Garth saw he had a gun in his hand, and Eugene shot the old man twice in the head and once in the chest for good measure.

'Everything is just fine,' he said, smiling contentedly.

Terri had been struggling through the driving rain for ten minutes and could see the lights of her hotel in the distance, when the sound of someone wailing was carried to her over the roar of the storm and the crashing of the waves. The cries were so chilling, they stopped her in her tracks, and she froze where she was, soaked to the skin, rainwater, salty mixed as it was with sea spray, running in rivulets down her face.

For a moment the crying tapered off, and she thought it might just be some kind of auditory illusion brought on by the ferocious gale, but then it sounded again. This time there could be no mistake: Terri was hearing the sound of a man in deep emotional anguish. And the crying seemed to be getting closer.

She turned for a moment, and as she did, there was a flash of lightning, which illuminated everything on the island, casting it in a glow as bright as a sunny day. In that instant, Terri saw a shambolic figure lurching up the path towards her. It was a tall, burly man in a woollen suit now heavy with rain. He was bald, his pink, glistening head uncovered, and in his arms he was carrying a bundle that the genealogist at first thought was a bag or maybe even a rolled-up rug or carpet. But then it moved weakly, and she realised it was the dog – the deerhound she had injured while making good her escape.

This man was carrying it like it was his child, tenderly cradling it as he walked through the howling wind and torrential rain.

'*You hurt my dog!*' he called after Terri. '*You blinded him! Now I'm going to hurt you.*'

In the few moments it had taken him to say those few words, the man had closed the gap between them so that, in the next flash of lightning, Terri could make out the buttons on his jacket, a lighter shade of brown than that of the rest of his garb.

And she turned and fled.

She thought she would never reach the front door of the hotel and would have rushed right in except for the fact that, leaning against the wall right beside the main entrance, not exactly barring the door but certainly standing guard over it, was a woman. She had long dark hair and was dressed in a shapeless duffel coat that was now sodden.

She turned a pallid, blue-veined face to Terri and said: 'You shouldn't ought to have hurt his dog, miss. He's awful fond of that dog. Had it all his life since it was a pup, and he loves it like it's his own kid. He's likely to get *real* mad. You'll be sorry you done it, I promise you that.'

Terri could hear the thudding footsteps of her pursuer now and made to step into the doorway, but the woman, in a rapid motion, was suddenly barring her way. Without even acknowledging the woman had spoken, Terri veered to the right, following the walls of the hotel and racing around the rear of the building, hoping to find a back entrance, perhaps to the staff kitchen. Back here, the structure of the hotel blocked out a lot of the air and the worst of the rain, and it seemed altogether calmer. Terri stopped to get her breath back and was sucking in huge gulps of the cold, wet air when someone grabbed her by the shoulder and spun her around. She squealed in spite of herself.

It was a young man clad in a similar style of suit to the brute carrying the dog. He looked at Terri with a strange, quizzical tilt of the head and said: 'You were in the house of the man that was crucified. Do you know that he roared and cried and begged for us to stop? He was the first one I'd initiated. He didn't last very long, but I was quite taken with him all the same. They let me hammer in the nail that killed him. They say you never forget your first. Do... do you think that's true?'

Terri pushed him away from her and ran to the closest door, banging and hammering on it, but to no avail. No one answered.

She stopped for a moment, frozen. There were a couple of houses nearby, but Terri was afraid that making for one of those would lead her right into the path of the man with the injured dog.

Crying with fear now, she ran away from the hotel and into the storm. Unwittingly, she charged into a drystone wall, knocking a chunk of it down as she tried to climb over it, and landing unceremoniously on top of the rubble, cutting one of her hands on a jagged shard of flint.

Dragging herself up, she staggered forward across a boggy, reed-choked field and looked around, only to be struck yet again by how little cover there was on Tory. With nothing else left to do, she threw herself on the sodden earth, hoping her dark clothes would camouflage her, and pulled out her phone.

Jessie picked up almost immediately. 'Hey, Terri. I'm with someone – can I call you back?'

Terri's heart fell, but, her teeth chattering against the cold she said:

'Jessie, I think I'm in trouble. I... I found the place they've been keeping Rosie. But... but they found *me*.'

'Who found you, Terri? Are you still on Tory?'

Somewhere very close by, the bald man shouted out: *'You cannot hide, Terri Kehoe. You can go to ground like the terrified mouse you are, but I will root you out.'*

Trying not to let the abject terror show in her voice, Terri said into the phone: 'The Reavers. Jessie, Rosie was here. She... she might still be.'

'Terri, get somewhere safe and stay there. I'm on my way.'

Terri wished those words could be a comfort. She understood on a visceral level that Jessie Boyle would be able to deal with these terrifying people, these Reavers. But that wasn't possible. That wasn't going to be a part of this story. For Terri, there could surely be no happy ending.

Terri heard a heavy thud, and she knew the bald man had jumped over the same wall she had and was now in the field. The sound was followed by two other impacts as his associates joined him.

'You won't get here in time. I... I think he's coming. I can hear him calling. And he's not alone.'

'Listen to me, Terri. Whatever happens, you stay safe. Get to the hotel and tell the staff that there's a credible threat and they are to lock the place up. I *will* get there. I promise you. I'm on my way and we'll get you out of there.'

A shadow fell across Terri, and hands reached down to grab her.

'Jessie... he's here.'

And the phone was dragged from her hand.

And then Terri knew no more for a time.

40

Jessie rang Dawn as she drove, helter-skelter, across the city.

'Terri's in trouble,' she said as soon as the commissioner answered. 'We need to get help to her on Tory immediately.'

'What you're asking is impossible,' Dawn retorted. 'The island is fourteen miles out in the fucking Atlantic. I'll call the Donegal office and see if they can't get someone out there as soon as. But that's as good as we can do.'

'Why the hell did I send her out there alone?' Jessie said, panic clear in her voice.

'I'm ringing them now,' Dawn said. 'Stay on the line.'

Jessie heard a muttered conversation, the only clear bit of which was Dawn shouting: *'Is that the best you can fucking do? Don't bother – I'll deal with it myself!'*

Five seconds later she was back on with Jessie.

'Apparently a storm has just hit the north-west coast. No boats can put out, so there's nothing they can do until it passes.'

'You're telling me she's on her own?' Jessie asked, horrified.

'I didn't say that,' Dawn said. 'I said there's nothing *they* can do.'

'Okay,' Jessie said. 'What's your plan?'

'Meet me at Casement Aerodrome,' Dawn said. 'What use is it being the commissioner if you can't take the toys out of the box every once in a while?'

Casement Aerodrome was home to the Garda Air Support Unit. The Irish police service utilised a Britten-Norman BN 2T-4S Defender 4000 aeroplane and four Airbus EC135 T2 helicopters. Dawn and Jessie were met in the hangar by the head of the unit, Chief Superintendent Charlie Byrne, a slim, gaunt-looking man wearing a grey uniform.

'Thanks for helping us out, Charlie,' Dawn said. 'I believe it's blowing up a storm out there. You're sure you can keep this thing in the air?'

'I wouldn't have okayed the flight if I didn't. The trip will take us about an hour but could be longer if the weather gets really rough. There's a helicopter landing pad on the island, more or less dead centre, so I'll put her down there. We won't be able to come back without refuelling, but we can do that in Donegal Airport. We'll take a detour there before making for Dublin.'

'Very good,' Dawn agreed. Then to Jessie: 'Did you call Seamus?'

'His phone rang out and I left two messages. I'm assuming something has come up. We'll have to go without him.'

'A pity for him to miss the party,' Dawn said. 'Okay, Super-intendent. Let's go.'

'I was awaiting your order, Commissioner.'

'May we board?'

'Please do.'

'Okay, Jessie,' Dawn said. 'Let's go and save the day.'

detective who's arrived at my door unannounced in the middle of the night?'

'I don't care if you feel like taking it or not,' Seamus said. 'I am an officer of the law and I am simply doing my duties.'

'Did I ask for your opinion, son?'

Seamus and Aldridge locked eyes. No one said anything for a moment. Tension was palpable in the room.

'With the greatest of respect, sir,' Seamus said, trying to keep his temper in check, 'I am a special investigator with the National Bureau of Criminal Investigation. A very sick little girl has been kidnapped, and three people connected with that kidnapping, one of whom is her father, are dead. If she's not found within the next four days, she will die, and the trail leads here, to your estate. You have a civic duty to furnish me with any information I require to solve this case, and you have a legal obligation to assist me. Now, you don't have to give me leave to search your house and the surrounding buildings, but if you don't, I will go away and come back with a warrant, and then things will all become much more uncomfortable and unpleasant for you. And who knows, with a bit of luck, maybe I'll be able to rule the estate out of our inquiries.'

Aldridge sighed a deep sigh and opened a laptop that had been sitting at his elbow. He tapped a couple of keys, jabbing at them with his two index fingers. A printer in the corner of the room whirred into life, and he said: 'That's a map of the estate. Take it and snoop wherever you want to. I do not wish to be bothered about this again.'

Seamus stood and retrieved the freshly created document 'I can't guarantee that you won't be,' he said.

'You are walking a fine line, Detective Keneally.'

Seamus shook his head. 'You have a good night, sir. If I need anything else, I'll come looking for you.' And he left the old man to glower at an empty room.

42

The helicopter cut through the night sky, slicing through the darkness on a course due north-east. Jessie sat strapped into a seat in the back, Dawn opposite her. In the movies, people on helicopters always had large, noise-cancelling headphones equipped with radio mikes so they could talk over the raucous sound of the rotors. On the Airbus, no such luxuries were provided, and the two old friends sat in the ear-shattering noise, unable to converse, waiting for their arrival.

Jessie closed her eyes and tried to fight the sense of fear and anxiety she was feeling. She should have realised they were under threat and that separating was going to leave them vulnerable. The fact that Seamus was off somewhere alone didn't make her feel good either, but she had to believe he could look after himself, and that in this instance, Terri's need was greater. She checked the clock on her phone: *11.32 p.m.* They should be landing in fifteen minutes.

It was pitch-black outside the windows of the helicopter, and the further north they travelled, the harder the rain lashed the safety glass. They were flying into a storm of epic proportions.

Suddenly, the world outside was lit up as a zigzagging line of lightning flashed across the sky. In the brief instance Jessie could see outside, all that was visible was a choppy sea.

Dawn shouted across at her, but the words were lost under the sound of the engines.

'*What?*' Jessie shouted back.

'*We're going to find her safe!*' Dawn repeated. '*You and me, we'll bring her home.*'

Jessie nodded.

She had to believe that was true. If it wasn't, she didn't know if she could live with herself.

And maybe by finding Terri, she'd find Rosie Blake too. After all, Terri said she had been on Tory and might still be there.

She had to hope.

As the Airbus powered its way towards the dark shape of Tory Island, Jessie Boyle closed her eyes and repeated the old Celtic mantra that she had written on her own skin in the form of a tattoo: *Is mise an stoirm.*

I am the storm.

43

The Aldridge estate was vast. It covered two hundred acres of mostly woodland and marsh, but the two-hundred-year-old house sat on five acres of tended garden, upon which were more than twenty structures, many of them barns, sheds, greenhouses and storage units.

Seamus knew that, even if she was there, he was never going to find Rosie that evening. What he was hoping for was to come across something that would be seen as evidence enough for him to bring to a judge so he could get a warrant. He felt Aldridge's response to his arrival might be enough in itself but had to admit that such attitudes weren't uncommon in people with a lot of money: having a bank balance that resembled the GNP of a small country tended to give the owner airs and graces they probably didn't merit.

When Seamus left the old man, a person he assumed was a butler had met him in what they referred to (with no sense of irony) as the drawing room, where he had given him a skeleton key that would open 'the majority of the outhouses'.

'What about the ones that are in the *minority* and won't open for me?' Seamus wanted to know.

'This was the only instruction I was given,' the servant said. 'I assure you, you will find nothing incriminating here. The Aldridges are a good family.'

'Are they related to the footballer?' Seamus asked, referring to John Aldridge, who had played for the Irish soccer squad that had made their country so proud in the world cup of Italia 1990.

'I very much doubt it, sir,' the butler said, looking horrified at the suggestion.

'My friend, Terri, is a genealogist,' Seamus went on. 'I'll bet she could find out for you.'

'That really won't be necessary.'

'It'd be no trouble,' Seamus said, enjoying the man's discomfort now. 'She loves doing that kind of thing. I bet you she'd find a link.'

'Aldridge is only one side of this family's proud heritage,' the butler said sniffily.

'Oh really?'

'Mr Aldridge married into a very esteemed and genteel family when he was a young man. Indeed, Lady Aldridge's family have lived in Dublin and been a part of its social circle for many hundreds of years. Some say they go back as far as the Norman landings and the visit of Henry II to Dublin in 1171.'

'Really?' Seamus said. 'Do you think she's related to any famous footballers? Or maybe her family are more artistic. Think about it: she could be a distant cousin of Jedward!'

The butler turned a violent shade of puce.

'I assure you, sir, that Lady Aldridge's family are celebrated in the most exalted of circles. They have been reformers and members of the House of Commons, the House of Lords and both Houses of the Oireachtas over the centuries.'

'Well isn't that wonderful?' Seamus said, getting bored now and anxious to begin poking around.

'Oh yes. The Parsons have a long and elevated history.'

Seamus had to stop himself doing a double-take. 'The Parsons? Lady Aldridge is a Parsons?'

'You've heard of them, I take it?'

'You could say that, yes,' Seamus said.

'I can show you a portrait of the lady's great-uncle on the way to the front door. He was something of an eccentric, but the painting itself brings a lot of visitors to the house. He seems to be a figure of fascination for many.'

The butler led Seamus to the entry hall. The place had been in darkness when he'd come in, so he hadn't paid heed to the art. His host hit a switch, and the overhead lights came on, revealing a huge portrait, done in what Seamus took to be oils. It was of a big man, with huge shovel-like hands and a square, blocky head, which was completely bald. He was wearing a brown suit made of rough material, and at his side stood an enormous dog, like an Irish wolfhound but more slender and graceful.

'According to those who were fortunate to know him, that dog never left his side,' the butler said.

'When was the portrait painted?' Seamus asked.

'I believe it was the 1920s,' the servant said. 'Impressive, isn't it?'

'That's one word for it.'

'Mr Aldridge's son is the very image of him,' the butler said proudly. 'He even has a dog just like that one. Setanta – a fine animal.'

Seamus made his excuses and went out into the night.

44

When Terri came around, she found she was lying in darkness.

She knew she'd been hit on the head with something, and was dizzy and nauseous. She fought the waves of giddy sickness for a time, but then rolled over and threw up what was left in her stomach. That made her feel a little better, and she remained where she was, attempting to get her heartbeat to level out. Finally she felt the anxiety subsiding somewhat, and she found she could think straight again.

Using her feet, she stretched out and felt for the extremities of the room she was in. It wasn't very large – little more than a cubbyhole really. The stench of her vomit hung heavy in the air now, but before that she'd thought the place smelled familiar. And then she understood why. She was back in Póilín's house, in the room she believed Rosie had been locked up in.

They'd brought her back here.

To the house they had butchered a man in.

She hoped they weren't planning the same fate for her.

She tested her bonds. They seemed to be cable ties, and there was no point in trying to slip those. They were so tight on her wrists the circulation was almost cut off, and she could feel them pressing into the tendons on her ankles. So she leaned in against the wall so her body heat would be reflected back at her and tried to sleep. She needed to conserve energy for whatever lay ahead.

She must have slept, because suddenly she was being bodily lifted and slung over someone's shoulder, and then she was being dumped on the ground. She understood she was in the living room, the one that had no door. She pulled herself into a sitting position and saw the bald man squatting on his haunches in front of her, the dog lying on its side in front of him, panting heavily.

She could see there were what she took to be compresses on the animal's eyes.

In the far corner, leaning against the wall just as she had outside the hotel, was the woman she'd seen earlier.

There was no sign of the young man. Terri assumed he was standing guard outside.

'Where's Rosie Blake?' she asked, dispensing with any niceties – they didn't seem appropriate under the circumstances.

'You hurt my dog,' the bald man said, ignoring her question.

'I didn't want to,' Terri said. 'It was him or me. I couldn't let it be me.'

'Deerhounds are hunters,' the bald man said. 'He was doing what nature made him to do. And you were getting close and you had to be stopped. Setanta here hasn't killed anything in three months. I thought he'd enjoy tearing you apart. It wasn't personal. It just... had to be.'

'Begging your pardon, but... but that sounds very personal to me,' Terri said, trying to keep the shake from her voice.

'It wasn't. I assure you.'

'We'll have to agree to disagree then.'

The man stroked the dog's shaggy side. The animal was panting very rapidly.

'I tried to clean out the poison you put into his eyes,' he said. 'But they're badly burned. He inhaled a lot of it too. He's having trouble breathing.'

'He needs a vet, I'd imagine,' Terri said.

'It's too late for that,' the man said and continued to stroke the beast's flanks.

No one spoke for a long time.

'Do you know who I am?' he asked at last.

'You're a Reaver,' Terri said. 'I don't know your name, but I know you've taken on the mantle Algernon Parsons left vacant.'

'That's good enough,' the man said. 'You can call me Cain.'

'I'd say it was nice to meet you,' Terri said. 'But it would be a lie.'

'I appreciate your honesty,' Cain said. 'Most people simply express the inanity, regardless of meaning it or not.'

His voice had a very subtle American aspect to it. It was slight, but it was there.

'I used to be an aid worker,' he continued. 'The organisation I worked for went into poor areas, where people were suffering and needed help. I travelled all over the world. Saw lots of places. Met lots of interesting people.'

'That's really cool,' Terri said. 'Where's Rosie? Is she still on the island? Is she all right?'

'I always thought when I came out that I'd have a trade or a skill,' Cain went on as if she hadn't spoken. 'But I was good for nothing. I made some good friends, though. I came to have lots of Russian pals. Russians and Irish people have a lot in common. Has anyone ever told you that?'

'Can't say they have,' Terri said. 'Do you know how sick Rosie is? If you let me take her back to her mum, she might still be able to recover.'

Cain waved off her comments with a disdainful shake of his head.

'I'm telling you something that you need to hear, Ms Kehoe.

Please listen. I'm imparting wisdom you're going to need in the trials to follow. The aid company I worked with, International Support Outreach, has its head office in Dallas, Texas. They've been in operation since 1991 – and one of the first projects they were involved in was to bring aid on the ground to civilians affected by the first Gulf War. I got sent there and I was happy to go.'

'I suppose you thought you could help alleviate the suffering your government was causing,' Terri said. 'That's admirable, I suppose. What trials are you talking about?'

'While I was out there, I met this Russian guy. Illya Semenovich his name was. He was an aid worker too. He'd grown up tough and had been in a Russian gang when he was younger. They were associated with the Red Mafiya. Very tough people.'

'He was a former gangster.'

'Correct,' Cain said, still petting the dog. Terri could see its breathing was getting less regular. More ragged. Which did not make her feel very comfortable.

'My friends are coming to get me,' Terri said. 'You do know that, don't you? They'll be here any moment now. If you let me go and tell me where Rosie is, you'd be doing yourself a favour.'

Cain acted as if she had not spoken.

'No one is coming to get you in that storm, Ms Kehoe,' he said. 'Now hush, and listen to my tale.

'I was having a beer with Illya one evening. I noticed he had this small spade hanging from his belt. It's called a *saperka*, and it's supposed to be used for digging trenches. But I'd spotted that a lot of the Russian guys used them for all sorts of stuff – I saw one guy frying an egg on his; another used his for cutting wood.'

'Why are you telling me this?'

'I'm getting to the point. Just listen, and all will become clear. Me and Illya had kind of hit it off, and I said to him:

"What's the story with the spade, man? How come you and your boys seem so attached to it?"'

'What did he say?'

'He told me that, during his initiation into the gang, youngsters are put through a lot: sleep deprivation, simulated torture, going for days without food – all the usual hazing. Illya had tolerated all of this and had passed with flying colours. He thought he'd made it to the final phase, which usually involves some sort of physical challenge – often a fight to the death with another contender. Illya was ready.'

'I've seen movies,' Terri said.

'It's pretty common. Well, Illya was expecting this would be his final test. He's preparing himself for it, getting into the mental headspace. And then, one night, he's woken up by someone shoving a bag over his head and he's dragged from his bed and thrown into the back of a car. He's driven to a location, hauled out, and when they take the bag off his head, he sees he's in a warehouse. There's a group of gangsters around him, and they have a dog that looks like it's half Rottweiler, half wolf. And there's a man beating it and goading the animal. As Illya watches, the dog is dragged by its leash to a door and pushed inside, and the door is closed. They can all hear the animal howling and throwing itself against the door to get out.'

'That sounds cruel,' Terri said.

The dog, Setanta, was barely breathing at all now. The man continued to stroke his animal, as if he didn't notice anything wrong with it.

'"That dog has not eaten in three days," one of the gang members tells Illya. "We have tormented it and tortured it, and now it is hungry and very, very angry."

'A man comes up and hands Illya a *saperka*, one of these little spades. Now remember, he's just been dragged out of bed. He's in his bare feet, he's wearing a T-shirt and boxer shorts.

'"You are going in there with the dog," Illya is told.

'"Give me a weapon!" he says.

'"You have one," he's told. "All a good Russian fighter needs is a *saperka*. Take it and kill or be killed."

'And then they brought him to that door and pushed him in.'

Terri swallowed, her heart beating a rapid rhythm in her chest. 'Did he kill the dog?'

'That's what I asked him. You know what he said?'

'What?'

'He said: "I would not be here if I had not."'

'So it was him or the dog,' Terri said.

'He killed the animal and he did it because he wanted to live and he wanted to pass the last stage of his training,' Cain said slowly. 'He felt bad about it, but it wasn't a matter of choice.'

'So you understand then,' Terri said. 'I didn't want to hurt your dog. And I thought he would recover. I certainly never thought he would die from being pepper sprayed.'

'Intellectually, I can understand,' Cain said. 'But in my heart I am furious.'

'I'm very sorry. I didn't mean to harm your pet.'

'He wasn't a pet. He remained with me because he chose to. He could have gone at any time. I wouldn't have begrudged him his freedom. I would have released him happily and without regret.'

'If it helps, I got no pleasure from doing what I did.'

'That does not help,' Cain said. 'It does not help at all.'

Terri felt a chill working its way up her spine. 'I don't know what you want me to say. I can't believe an animal of this size is dying from a blast of pepper spray anyway. I never dreamed it would hurt him so much.'

'He is suffering. I would never get him to the mainland in this weather to see a vet. I have given him something to speed his end. It is the only kind thing to do.'

'You've poisoned him? So *you've* killed him then, not me!'

'This is your doing, Ms Kehoe. Don't get confused.'

'Where is Rosie Blake?'

He simply shook his head this time.

'What do you want with her? Why do the Reavers want a little girl like Rosie?'

Terri saw in horror that the dog had stopped breathing. The man's hand was just resting on its pelt now. He looked across at Terri, and she saw fury and vengeance in his eyes.

'You were faced with a test today, Terri Kehoe. You came face to face with an enemy, and you emerged from the experience victorious. Setanta here gave you the chance to be *initiated*. You passed the test, and he gave his life so you might live with a new awareness.'

'Where is Rosie Blake, Mr Cain?' Terri said urgently. 'I'm truly sorry about your dog, but there's nothing I can do to make him better. There *is* something we can do about Rosie though.'

'There's nothing you can do for the child. Her fate is sealed. And so is Setanta's. And so, now, is yours.'

He placed a hand lovingly on the dog's huge head and then, reaching over, stroked Terri's hair. It was a gesture that was almost tender.

'What are you going to do?'

'I am going to kill you,' the man said and stood up, pulling Terri upright.

'You will know pain as Setanta did. At first.'

The woman strode forward all of a sudden, and Terri saw that she had her can of pepper spray in her hands.

'You don't need to do this,' Terri said, trying to think of something to say that might prevent what was about to happen.

'I know we don't,' Cain said, producing a penknife from his pocket and cutting her bonds. 'But we want to.'

He began to pull Terri towards the wall, and she saw that

there, on the floor, was a hammer and a collection of steel plaster pegs – large nails designed to be hammered into walls.

'Please don't!' Terri cried.

'Hold her hands,' he said to the woman, and she grabbed Terri's wrist and pressed it to the wall.

At that moment, the window of the room exploded inwards, and the sound of the wind rushed in, and Terri knew that, despite the odds, Jessie had made it.

45

Seamus had searched three outhouses (he found some ride-on lawnmowers, a collection of ancient-looking gardening tools and a few moss-covered statues of birds and animals) before he encountered the first shed that wouldn't open when he tried to turn the key in the lock.

This was a large, barn-like structure that looked like it had been built around the same time as the house. Seamus rattled at the door, fiddling with the key, turning it this way and that, and finally, frustrated, he stood back.

'What's that?' he said loudly, his voice echoing in the silent darkness. 'Can I hear someone in trouble in there? Somebody asking for help?'

He paused. If there was someone crying for help, they were doing so remarkably quietly.

'Hold on a moment – I'm coming!'

And he delivered a kick to the door, just beside the handle. It gave a bit but didn't budge, and he kicked it again. This time he heard something splinter, and with a third blow it burst open. Seamus switched on his torch and went inside.

A short hallway led him to the interior of the structure, a

vast open space that had once been used to store hay or grain. Someone had transformed it into what Seamus could only describe as a kind of church, though not like any he had ever seen before. An altar made from hewn logs and woven sticks stood atop a mound of earth in the centre of the room. All about the place were figures of various sizes, all made from sticks and twigs from different trees.

Seamus had always had an interest in nature, and he could identify the leaves and bark of oak, ash, rowan, spruce and willow. There were others though that he couldn't recognise. Obviously the gardens here yielded many other breeds that were rare and unusual.

He went to the altar and shone his torch on the flat surface, a hand-worked piece of oak that had been pocked with many holes where what looked like nails had been driven through it. In places, something black had dried in, and the earth below it was a different colour, as if whatever had seeped into it had changed its composition.

Taking a penknife from his pocket, Seamus scraped some of the black residue from the wood and put it in a plastic evidence bag he took from his jacket pocket.

That was when he heard something, the most subtle of movements, cloth rustling against skin. If his senses hadn't been so heightened, he wouldn't have noticed it.

Looking up, he saw that while he'd been focused on the altar, two men had silently come into the room. They were both dressed in old-fashioned suits of coarse material, one black, the other brown. The man closest to him looked to be about fifty and had long grey hair in a ponytail and a bushy beard. The other was probably Seamus's age and had close-cropped red hair and freckles. When he shone the torch on them, he was sure he could see the bulge of a weapon beneath Ponytail's jacket.

'Evening, lads,' Seamus said with a smile, tucking the

evidence bag back inside his jacket and slipping the knife up into his sleeve. 'Lovely night for a wander.'

'This is private property,' Ponytail said. 'Private property and sacred ground.'

'I'm a police detective,' Seamus said. 'If you keep your hands away from the piece you're carrying in the shoulder rig, I'll show you my ID.'

'It doesn't matter now,' Ponytail said and moved to draw his weapon.

Seamus had been expecting as much and didn't wait for the man to clear leather. He dropped to his knees behind the altar, pain flaring in his injured leg, and – cursing the fact that he was wilfully destroying what was probably a crime scene – put his shoulder against the underside and heaved, lifting it off the compacted earth and tipping it forward so that its heavy oaken top created a shield. He knew it wouldn't hold for long, but oak was a hardwood and would offer some cover at least.

The first shots thudded into the bloodied top of the edifice, and as he prepared to return fire, he heard a commotion from the other side of his foxhole.

'No! What have you done? You've defiled the sacred table!'

'I didn't mean to... how was I to know?'

'What are we to do now?'

Seamus took a deep breath and sprang up, his gun pointed at the two men.

'Lads, I don't want to have to hurt either of ye. I've no clue what's going on here, or what this whole setup is about, but I do know you've been carrying a concealed weapon which I'm damn sure you don't have a licence for, you've opened fire on a member of the Gardai, and I'm prepared to bet good cash money that when I have the sample of blood I took from your altar analysed, I'm going to find it belongs to a missing person.'

'You're a dead man,' Ponytail said, his entire body trembling with emotion. 'You don't know it yet, but you're finished. Cain is bringing about the moment that was prophesied, and no one can stop him.'

'That's great,' Seamus said. 'Something for us all to look forward to. Here's what we're going to do now though: you're going to put the gun down, and then we're going to walk out of here together, and you're going to accompany me to Harcourt Street where we'll have a little chat about things. How does that sound?'

With a howl of anger, Ponytail brought up the gun and fired. Seamus jumped sideways, firing his own weapon as he did so. He felt the heat of the bullet as it went past, millimetres from his ear, and landed on the earth and rolled, coming to a stop on his belly, gun held out in front of him.

Ponytail was now lying flat on his back, and the red-haired youngster was kneeling over him. The older man was trying to breathe, blood bubbling from a hole in his chest.

'Put your hand over the wound,' Seamus said, taking off his jacket and tearing off the sleeve, rolling it into a compress. 'Here, press this down on it. His lung has been punctured. He'll suffocate if you don't keep that hole covered.'

'Cain told us we were protected,' Red Hair said. 'That we couldn't be harmed by mortal weapons.'

'Everyone can be harmed by mortal weapons,' Seamus said, pulling out his phone.

He saw there were a couple of missed calls from Jessie but didn't have time to listen to the messages. He rang for an ambulance, noting as he did so that the gun Ponytail was carrying was a .22 gauge.

46

It was close to one in the morning when Seamus sat down opposite the red-haired youth in an interview room in Harcourt Street. He had refused to give them a name, or one for his fallen comrade, who was currently being operated on in St Vincent's Hospital, but his fingerprints had yielded results: he was Pavel Itrovich, of Russian birth, in Ireland a little over a year and supposedly employed as a gardener on the Aldridge estate, according to his work visa.

Which was odd, seeing as Aldridge, not to mention his butler, claimed they'd never seen him before.

Itrovich was a little over six feet in height and wiry. His close-cropped, copper-coloured hair came to a widow's peak just above his forehead. He was dressed in a black suit with a white shirt that was buttoned right up to the neck, and was tailored into a slightly odd box shape that was completely out of touch with modern fashion sensibilities.

'Where were you yesterday afternoon from 11 a.m. until about 3 p.m.?'

'I was working on the estate.'

'With whom? Your boss claims not to know who the hell you are.'

'I was working with David.'

He pronounced the first syllable with a broad vowel sound: *Dah-vid*. Seamus assumed this was a Russian thing. The young man didn't have an accent as such, but there was a very slight inflection to the way he talked that hinted at English not being his first language.

'Just him?' Seamus asked. 'No one else can vouch for you?'

'I usually work with just him. Why is this a problem?'

'Because you tried to shoot me.'

'Not me. David tried to shoot you. I tried to stop him.'

'No you didn't. I was there, remember? You tried to stop him shooting your precious *altar*. There's a not very subtle difference.'

'I have not committed any crime. I demand to be released.'

'You can't demand that. If I decide to release you, I'll be sure to let you know. Now, could you tell me who owns the gun your friend was carrying and which he chose to discharge in my general direction?'

'I never knew he had a gun. I was very surprised.'

'Interesting. I'm going to tell you right here and now, Pavel, that I think when forensics have had a look at that gun and run a few tests, we're going to find out it was used in a murder, probably more than one. What do you think of that?'

'I know nothing about any murders.'

'Well that's a pity, because you're now implicated in a couple, and your only alibi may well be dead by the time you get to court.'

'Okay. I was not working yesterday afternoon. I went for a drink with some friends.'

'Friends who will vouch for you?'

'Yes. Of course they will.'

'I thought you were supposed to be working. How come your story is suddenly changing?'

'I forgot – we had the afternoon off. We went drinking.'

'You went drinking all day?'

'You never done that?'

'Not in a while,' Seamus said.

'You should. You look like you could do with letting off some steam.'

'You have no idea. How long have you been working for the Aldridges?'

'I don't know.'

'According to the immigration people, you've been there for thirteen months. So you'd have started last December. Do these dates align with your recollection?'

Seamus pushed a sheet of paper across the table, but Itrovich barely looked at it.

'If you say it is correct, I am sure that it is.'

'You leave Ireland at all during that time? Go back to the old country?'

'No. I have no family here. My workplace is my family.'

'Do you mean the Aldridges?'

'Yes. They have been very good to me.'

'Where were you three nights ago? So we're talking about the eleventh of January. And I want to know about between the time of 11 p.m. until, we'll say, 3 a.m.?'

'I cannot remember. Probably at work.'

And so it went on. Itrovich laughed when Seamus mentioned the previous murders, the ones that had sent Terri to Tory.

'You want me to tell you what I had for lunch fifteen years ago? Give me a fucking break! Where were you on a Tuesday in March in 2004? Can you remember?'

'If I was being questioned by a police detective, I would make it my business to remember,' Seamus said.

'I work for a family, and my place of work is their home, but I am still an employee.'

'Me too,' Seamus said.

'Hmm. I think our lives are very different. When you are poor, your life is not your own. I work for a rich family, and I do what they tell me to do. I get up when they say for me to get out of bed. I eat what they give me when they give it to me. I have a beer when one is given and I shit during my allotted shit break. Where was I in 2004? I wasn't living in this shithole excuse for a country, but I can tell you, I was wherever whoever I worked for then told me to be.'

'What goes on in the barn where you people tried to shoot me?'

'I don't know. It looked like some crazy shit though.'

'What if I told you I could grant you immunity? Put you in witness protection?'

'I would tell you, with respect, to fuck off.'

Seamus let him go.

'What do you think?' Wally, the desk sergeant said as the young man signed out his few meagre belongings.

'I think he's one very scary chap,' Seamus said.

'But is he the Stick Man?'

'I don't know,' Seamus said. 'But I wouldn't be surprised if he was.'

47

Dawn Wilson came through the window, the rain and wind rushing in behind her, as if she was an elemental spirit bringing the fury of the night in with her. Crossing the room in two long strides, she struck the woman a blow to the throat with her left hand and pistol-whipped the bald man with her right. The woman went down, gagging, and the man (to his credit, for it was a blow that would have felled most people) staggered backwards.

'Terri, are you all right, love?' she asked as she cut her free.

'I'm okay,' the genealogist said.

She was still shaking and tears were streaming down her cheeks.

'They were going to... I mean... they wanted to...'

'I know, love. I know. But you're okay now.'

Jessie was in the room by then, her gun trained on the bald man, who was eyeing them both with unveiled hatred. Dawn's gun had opened a cut on his temple, and it was bleeding profusely. The behaviourist took in the body of the dog and the hammer and nails in the man's hands.

'Put down the carpentry gear,' she said.

The man didn't move.

'He says his name is Cain,' Terri told them.

'Put them down *now* or I will put a bullet in your knee,' Dawn said, idly pointing her Glock at him.

He looked at her, saw she meant it and tossed the nails onto the ground, though he kept the hammer in his hand, swinging it gently.

'Last chance,' Dawn said.

Cain gazed at her, meeting her barely contained rage with his own, and dropped the hammer onto the floor with a thud.

'Where is Rosie Blake?' Jessie demanded.

'I might tell you,' Cain said. 'But what would you give me if I did?'

The woman whom Dawn had punched was coming back to awareness on the floor, and she hissed like a cat.

'Don't tell them!' she said, her voice hoarse and rasping. 'Let the child die!'

'What the fuck is wrong with you?' Dawn asked.

The woman made to get up, and the commissioner placed her booted foot on her chest.

'Stay down. I don't want you roaming about causing mischief.'

Terri, who was still standing by the wall facing the window, suddenly gasped.

'What is it?'

'The other one,' Terri said. 'There's a third Reaver. He... he just went past the window.'

Jessie ran to the empty frame and peered out, but all she could see was the rain coming down ever harder, and a vague sense of the crashing waves beyond the cliffs nearby. Then she smelled it.

Smoke. It was faint at first, but it began to grow stronger, and when she looked up, she saw tiny billows of it creeping along the ceiling.

'Rosie Blake is in the attic of this house,' Cain said. 'Orson, my friend and associate, has just set alight a pile of tinder that we stacked near the opening to the roof space. Don't think because it's raining that the blaze will be extinguished – we haven't planned on burning the house to the ground. Our intention is to suffocate the child – the insulation in the roof will smoulder and create noxious fumes and she will choke to death.'

'You evil fuckers,' Dawn said.

'How do we get up to the attic?' Jessie asked urgently.

'I think I saw the trapdoor in the small room off the kitchen,' Terri said.

'Come on. Dawn, I'm going to need you.'

'You can come with us,' Dawn said to Cain.

'I respectfully decline,' the man said, his voice a purr.

'Come on!'

'I will not. Shoot me if you wish. But wounded or not, as soon as you're out of this room, my friends and I are leaving.'

'Dawn, we don't have time. Leave them!' Jessie said, and Dawn, the conflict writ large on her face, followed.

'Don't think Rosie Blake is safe,' Cain called after them. 'I'll find her, no matter where you hide her.'

48

Terri was right – the trapdoor leading to the attic was in the small room just off the kitchen, and smoke was pouring from the cracks between it and the ceiling.

'Is there a chair or something I can stand on?' Jessie asked.

They cast about quickly but there wasn't.

'Here, I'll hooch you up,' Dawn said and made a cup out of her hands. Jessie stepped into it and allowed herself to be lifted upwards.

The second she got within inches of the trapdoor, she knew it wasn't going to work. The paint on its wooden surface was already starting to blister. It was far too hot to touch.

'I can't get it open!' she called down.

'You have to!'

'It's scorching to the touch. If I pull that down we'll all be burned and we won't be able to get to her.'

'Hold on,' Terri said and ran back into the living room.

Cain and the woman were gone, but the hammer was still where he'd thrown it on the ground. She picked it up and jogged back to the others.

'Can you use this to smash through the ceiling at another point? Maybe get into her through there?'

'You're a fucking genius, Terri,' Dawn said.

Jessie took the hammer and Dawn lifted her again, but out in the kitchen this time. Jessie tapped the ceiling a couple of times to make sure she wasn't trying to knock through a joist, found a spot that sounded hollow and was through the plaster with a single blow. It was easy to widen the hole. Smoke poured down in a blinding cloud. Jessie pulled her T-shirt up over her mouth and switched on the torch on her phone.

'Can you push me up higher? I can't see.'

Dawn angled Jessie's knee onto her shoulder, and Jessie climbed upwards, using her friend as a ladder. She pushed her head and shoulder into the hole and shone the torch about. She'd expected the attic to be full of junk and the usual odds and ends people keep in such places, but this one was empty – of course, no one had lived in the house for fifteen years, and Jessie supposed Póilín's family had come and taken anything that was of value or interest.

She easily spied the pile of rags, papers, cardboard and wood that had been used to start the fire. It smelled as if it had been soaked in some form of accelerant, and she wondered if the same lamp oil had been used that had been found on Richard Roche's clothes.

She slowly scanned the area with the torch, and the circle of light fell on a bundle resting on a board that had been placed across the joists to create a kind of bed. A mattress had been placed on this, and there was what might have passed for a pile of old blankets on top of that. But was that a small head protruding from the top of those blankets. A head topped with a shock of dark hair.

'I've found her!' Jessie shouted down.

'Can you reach her?'

Jessie thought about how best to do that and realised in a

moment of panicked clarity that she couldn't. Jessie was a little over six feet in height. The space was too small for her to get in, crawl forward to get the girl, turn and come back safely.

'I'm too tall. I wouldn't fit.'

'Well if you're too tall, there's no point in my trying,' Dawn, who was an inch and a half taller than the behaviourist, said.

'I'll do it,' Terri said. 'Can you lift me up, Dawn?'

'You're so small, you're going to need both of us to climb up there,' Dawn said, grunting under the exertion of keeping Jessie aloft. 'Here, step into my other hand, and then sort of climb however you can. Jessie will grab you and haul you up too.'

This worked reasonably well – though Jessie probably hauled Terri more than the smaller girl really did much climbing – and within fifteen seconds of leaving the ground, she was in the attic and crawling over the boards towards the bundle they hoped was Rosie Blake. When she got there, she called back to the others to confirm it was indeed her – they had all studied the photos Shauna had given the police and committed her face to memory – and began to shake the little girl gently.

'Rosie?' she said. 'Rosie, are you okay?'

There was no reaction. Jessie watched as Terri – clearly terrified the girl might be dead – pressed her cheek to the child's nose and mouth and then sagged back in relief as she felt breath there. She was just unconscious, possibly drugged, as the email she had found on the deep web had suggested.

Terri pulled the child from the mattress, trying to keep her wrapped in the blankets for warmth (it was bitterly cold in the attic, despite the fire, which was simply smouldering and emitting smoke rather than heat) and kind of half dragged and half carried her back to the hole.

'I'll pass her down to you,' she said to Jessie.

'I'm ready. Lower her legs first.'

Terri did, and awkwardly (none of them had actually

thought through how they were going to do this) they got the child, and then Terri, back down to ground level.

They were just leaving the house with the little girl tightly wrapped in the blankets and Jessie's coat when a phone started ringing somewhere in the house.

'It's coming from back in the kitchen,' Dawn said.

Jessie went back in and hunted around, finally finding the object – a basic burner model – in a cupboard below the grime-encrusted sink. The number was withheld. She answered it and held it to her ear, moving quickly to get out of the burning house. She stopped in the front garden, the seascape spectacular and frightening, dark though it was.

'Hello, Jessie Boyle,' the voice at the other end said.

'Who is this?'

'An old and very, very dear friend. Have you been enjoying your games with the Reavers? They're an interesting little collective, aren't they?'

The voice spoke with an educated English accent, not quite aristocratic, but with a definite air of authority. Jessie had never heard Uruz's voice before. Funnily enough, this was just how she'd imagined it.

'They're no more interesting than any other murder case I've worked,' Jessie said. 'What do you want, Uruz?'

'To help you, Jessie Boyle.'

'Tell me where you are then, and you and I can sit down and have a proper conversation. Stop all of this messing about. I think you're a coward. You hide behind cryptic text messages and now calls to a conveniently abandoned burner. You believe you're so clever, but you're just the same as any other freak. Now why don't you fuck off and leave me alone?'

She was about to hang up when he said: 'Let me tell you this, Jessie. Trust *nobody*. You think that child is safe now? She's not. Richard Roche knew something you still have not uncovered, and he and the unfortunate Mr Lawler took it with them to their graves. Until you work out what that little nugget of truth is, you might as well have left her in the attic to suffocate.'

'What are you talking about?'

'Think about it, Jessie: why was the social worker killed? What could he possibly know that was a threat to the Reavers?'

'Roche went to his house – they had an argument. I'm assuming he told him something that implicated him in the abduction.'

'And who was planning to abduct Rosie Blake?'

'Garth Calhoun's organisation...'

'Exactly. So why would *the Reavers* kill both Roche and Rodney Lawler?'

'If you know something, tell me. Otherwise, crawl back under the stone you're hiding under and leave me to do my job.'

'All right then,' Uruz said. 'But remember, trust no one. Even those closest to you. That child's life depends on it.'

And the line went dead.

Uruz had disappeared again.

PART FIVE

THE DEVIL ON MY SHOULDER

'The devil doesn't come dressed in a red cape and pointy horns. He comes as everything you've ever wished for.'

Tucker Max

ARIZONA ROSE BLAKE

She woke up from a dream in which there had been a fire and smoke, and she had been trapped in a narrow space that smelled of damp and mould.

A woman was sitting beside her bed. Even though she was sitting down, Rosie could see she was tall. She had short dark hair that had a little grey in it, but the grey seemed to be at just the right places, and it actually looked nice. She was wearing blue jeans and boots with laces up the front, and a T-shirt that had a picture of an old man with a droopy moustache on it and the words: Guy Clark. A long grey coat hung on the back of the woman's chair.

'Who are you?' Rosie asked.

'My name is Jessie. I've been looking forward to meeting you, Rosie.'

'Where am I?'

'You're in a hospital in County Donegal. My friends and I found you in a little house on an island quite a few miles away from here.'

'Where's Richie?'

'Richard Roche?'

Rosie nodded.

The woman paused for a moment, and Rosie knew she was thinking about lying to her. But then she said: 'Richie died, Rosie. The people who took you shot him. I'm sorry.'

Rosie nodded. She'd been afraid that was what she was going to hear, but she tried to be brave about it.

'I think I remember that. There were lights – the people who came, they had lights on sticks, I think.'

'Lights on sticks? Do you mean like lanterns?'

'I don't know – they were carrying long sticks and there seemed to be lights on the end of them, but then it got very bright and I couldn't see and I heard bangs, but I didn't know what they were. I think that was... that was Richie being shot, wasn't it?'

'You know, we can talk about all of that when you're feeling a bit better. For now, I want you to rest. Your mam is on her way. She'll be here soon. So you don't need to worry.'

Rosie gave a kind of shrug. 'That's okay. I don't mind being on my own.'

The woman looked a little sad to hear that. 'You don't have to be on your own. I'll stay with you.'

'You can if you like.'

'Do you want me to read you a story? I'm sure I can get something on my phone. What would you like to hear?'

'I like the Harry Potter stories.'

'Any of them in particular?'

'The first one is good fun. Richie read it to me, but I wouldn't mind hearing it again.'

And then she couldn't be brave anymore, and the tears came, and Jessie sat on the bed and put her arm around her.

They stayed like that until Rosie's mum arrived an hour and a half later.

49

Jessie had dozed off and woke with a start to find Shauna Blake standing looking out the window at the grey early morning. Rosie was asleep, an expression of worry on her face, even in her unconsciousness.

'Are you all right, Mrs Blake?' Jessie asked, stretching in the chair and stifling a yawn.

The woman glanced over her shoulder and then returned her gaze to the patch of lawn Rosie's room looked out upon.

'Yes, I'm fine. Thank you.'

There was an off smell in the room, one that hadn't been there before. As she took a deep inhalation, Jessie realised she had been smelling it in her sleep. The scent had invaded her dreams.

'What am I smelling?' she asked Rosie's mother. 'Have they done something to the room? Used a cleaning product?'

'I burned sage,' Shauna said.

'Oh,' Jessie said. 'Were the hospital staff all right with that?'

'I didn't ask them. I felt it was needed. I didn't know what Rosie brought back in here with her after everything she's been through.'

Jessie nodded, even though Shauna still wasn't looking at her.

'I've read it's good for purifying the air,' she said. 'What's it called – *smudging*, isn't it?'

'Yes.'

'I know we didn't get a chance to talk on the phone earlier, but I can only imagine how upset you must be. I'm not going to lie, your daughter has been through quite an ordeal, but on the positive side, I think she was kept sedated for most of it. There will of course be psychological implications of that, but I'm hopeful they'll be minimal. With therapy, I think Rosie will be able to cleanse herself of what she's been through.'

'I wasn't talking about that,' Shauna said. 'I always feel these hospital rooms are full of bad energy. So many sick people passing through, being pumped with chemicals we can't be sure are beneficial. It has to leave its mark on the space, don't you think?'

'I suppose...' Jessie said uncertainly. 'I mean, hospitals can be stressful places, that's for sure. But without rooms like this one, Rosie would be dead by now.'

Shauna made a snorting sound. 'They can't give us any guarantees,' she said. 'I have my doubts they know what they're doing at all.'

Jessie wasn't sure what to say to that, so she followed what she often thought was the best course of action in situations like that and said nothing at all.

50

The following day, Jessie, Seamus, Terri, Donal Glynn and the commissioner met at eleven in Dawn's house in Clonsilla – Jessie insisted they not go to Harcourt Street, as she felt Uruz's comment about trusting no one seemed to hint there might be a spy in the ranks they weren't aware of. There was tea, coffee and croissants, and they were all tired and sore but also deeply relieved.

Jessie felt a bit uncomfortable including Glynn in their inner circle, but he'd been helping Seamus investigate the Aldridges while Jessie was busy with Rosie, so Dawn insisted he may have information that would be useful.

Rosie Blake was recovering from her ordeal in hospital and seemed none the worse for wear from the whole thing.

'She was knocked out for most of it,' Jessie said. 'They sedated her with mild opiates, kept her asleep. And – get this – they also gave her the chemo! Richard Roche had been stealing the drugs from the hospital a little at a time for a couple of weeks, and he had it on him in a bag when she was taken. Terri found one of the empty bags when she arrived, and the Donegal police searched the area around the house the next day and found the stash in a shed a field over. The whole thing was traumatic for her, and she wasn't exactly kept in clean environments, but the physical effects have been moderate.'

'If you discount trying to kill her,' Terri said. 'And I can't shake the idea they were keeping her alive *for* something.'

'What though?' Seamus asked. 'Getting the ransom?'

'They got that,' Jessie said. 'And killed Peter and kept Rosie.'

'Cain told me her fate was sealed,' Terri said. 'I think they had plans for her.'

'Some kind of ritual?' Dawn asked. 'I mean, what the fuck do these guys even do? What are they about? And don't tell me it's about bringing about hell on earth or any of that shite. There's something else happening. We just haven't been able to work it out yet.'

'How's Shauna doing?' Seamus asked. 'You were with her in the hospital, Jessie.'

'I have to keep reminding myself she's been through so much,' Jessie said. 'She seems really angry. At everything, including the medical establishment. We talked briefly just before she made the trip back to Dublin with Rosie. I... I'd classify her as confused right now.'

'In what way?' Dawn asked.

'She's become obsessed with alternative methods of medicine. Faith healing. Spiritualism. I know it's not unheard of for people with relatives with terminal illnesses to grasp at anything to help, but this strikes me as very entrenched. I get the feeling she's been going this way for a while. I wonder if it's one of the things that inspired Richard Roche to report her and Peter to social services.'

'Poor woman,' Seamus said.

'The fact Cain and his crew are still at large probably doesn't help her frame of mind,' Glynn said.

'Uruz said to trust no one,' Jessie said. 'I've been turning over what he meant, and the only thing I can come up with is that he's suggesting there are links and relationships here we're not seeing. But what?'

'He told you the key is in the murders of Roche and Rodney Lawler,' Dawn said. 'That's where we'll get the answer to all of this. I've been chewing that over too, and I'm none the wiser.'

'I know we'll come across it and it'll be blindingly obvious, but for now I just can't see it.'

'How have the investigations out at the Aldridge estate been going?' Terri asked.

'I took samples of blood from that altar, but it turned out not to be human after all,' Seamus said. 'Chicken blood, which I'm told is often used in black magic ceremonies, but that doesn't help us. The butler, who is a rude fecker and never deigned to introduce himself to me, is called Gus Thompson, and he just sings the same song every time I question him: the family is great and they're a shining example of all that's great about Irish society. I think he knows all the dirty secrets, but he's not telling. I did, however, find one member of staff at the house who *is* willing to talk. She's one of the kitchen staff, Gillian Quigley. She told me that over the past two years, Aldridge has been bringing in men to work on the estate. They seem to take on the role of security, but they rarely stay for very long. She thought they were being shipped out to work for other arms of Aldridge's business empire.'

'What does he do?' Terri asked.

'What doesn't he do?' Glynn replied. 'Mostly he buys and sells things. But there are stories that he's also involved in funding politicians, something he does under the table – in Ireland there are rules about how much can be given, and from what I've been learning, he's not playing by the rules at all. It looks like he's buying favours.'

'What kind of favours?' Jessie asked.

'Aldridge is as far right as you can go. He hates anyone who isn't white, Catholic and heterosexual and he wants to make sure that opinion is written into law so that anyone who doesn't fit the mould can either be driven out of the country or put in prison.'

'The men you encountered in that stick church,' Terri asked Seamus, 'they were Reavers?'

'Yes. The man I shot hasn't regained consciousness. He's still alive but on life support. I didn't have enough to hold the other guy, Itrovich, and he's vanished.'

'And Cain is Aldridge's son?' Jessie asked.

'He is but had his name changed to Parsons by deed poll when he was in his teens,' Glynn replied. 'From what the old man has told us, Charles became fascinated by his great-uncle Algernon and saw himself as part of that line of the family. Aldridge is a brute, but Lady Aldridge is his equal when it comes to unpleasantness. I wouldn't be surprised if she encouraged the hero worship.'

'Why does he call himself Cain?' Seamus asked.

'I've been looking into that,' Terri said. 'It's the name the High Priest of the Reavers has always taken. It's a reference to Adam's firstborn, the one who killed his brother and was cursed by God. The Reavers celebrate that banishment. They see themselves as throwbacks to Cain's tribe, left wandering the earth, cast out and forced to find solace in the spirits of the wastelands. There are also stories in the Jewish tradition that God sent a dog to shadow Cain, marking him out as a murderer and eternal nomad. It seems the Reavers have taken this on board. Their leaders seem to have adopted it as a tradition. They've always had a deerhound as a companion.'

'Isn't there something about a mark of Cain as well?' Seamus asked. 'Do I remember that correctly from my catechism?'

'Yes,' Glynn said. 'And that's an interesting one. The mark is never described in the Old Testament, but many scholars believe it was a visible physical sign. Possibly a letter. There's quite a bit of controversy about which letter it is, but there's a school of thought that says it's the Semitic letter *vav*. Which, when written in Syriac, looks like this.'

He held out his phone and showed them a symbol that looked like an upturned letter U.

∩

'It's more or less the Uruz rune,' Jessie said.

'It is,' Glynn agreed.

'The more we find out about all of this, the less I understand how it all joins up,' Jessie said.

'Well look, our task is very simple, as I see it,' Dawn said. 'We need to catch Cain or Parsons or whatever the fuck his name is and bring the rest of his crew to justice. And we need to keep Rosie Blake safe until then. I've put a couple of uniforms outside her room in the hospital. We can talk about the theology and philosophy of what those eejits believe about themselves until the cows come home, but ultimately it doesn't matter. So let's just focus on bringing them in.'

'You won't hear any arguments from me,' Seamus said. 'Where do we start?'

'We work with what we've got,' Dawn said. 'Which is the Aldridge/Parsons clan and wee Rosie Blake.'

'Rosie might have heard or seen something she doesn't even remember seeing,' Jessie agreed. 'We should take some time and see if we can tease it out of her. I'd say her mother might be a help with that too. I'll see if I can organise some play sessions at the hospital. Let's make it as gentle as we can for her.'

'I've sent a patrol car out to pick up the Aldridges,' Dawn said. 'So far, we've been very polite and understanding and only talked to them in the comfort of their own homes. I think it's time they experienced the luxury of our interview rooms. See how they enjoy them for a while.'

Seamus grinned. 'I'm liking this plan more and more all the time.'

51

Seamus was sitting at a desk in the bullpen in Harcourt Street, waiting to be informed the Aldridges had arrived for their interviews, when his phone rang. It was Christina.

'Hi. I'm just passing by outside your HQ, and I was thinking of you, so I thought I'd ring. I never expected you to answer. I thought you'd be off fighting crime.'

'Well, I'm waiting for crime to be brought in for questioning just at the moment. You're outside?'

'Just across the road.'

'I'll pop down. We could grab a coffee. I'm literally waiting for a phone call to tell me to go down to the interview rooms, so it'll take me as long to go there from outside as it would from where I'm sitting now.'

'Okay. See you in a second.'

They got coffees from a nearby pod and sat on the wall opposite Harcourt Street to drink them.

'Steffie is staying over at my friend Bea's house tonight,' Christina told him.

'She is?'

'Yeah. Which means if I went out, I don't need to get back early. I... I thought you might be interested in that information.'

'Well,' Seamus said carefully, not really sure how he should respond. 'I am a trained investigator. Information is my stock in trade.'

'I figured as much. So does anything occur to you now you've discovered this important clue?'

'I would say that a couple of options do present themselves.'

As he talked, she scooted over and snuggled into his arm. It was cold – there had been frost on the ground that morning, and while the day had heated up slightly, it was still bitter. Christina was wearing a black jacket that belted up about her slim waist, and she had a purple scarf knotted about her neck, but Seamus was still very pleased she felt the need to utilise his body heat too. He put his arm around her and continued to consider this new piece of intelligence she'd gifted him with.

'And would you care to share your thoughts on the possibilities these options present?'

Seamus began counting them off on his fingers. 'Well, first off, there's the obvious one.'

'What's that? I didn't think there was an obvious response to so interesting a dilemma.'

'Well you see, that's what separates the amateur sleuth from the professional detective. My laser-like mind can come up with options with the lightning speed of a computer.'

'Is that so?'

'Oh, it is.'

'Tell me your first, most obvious, choice then.'

'You'll kick yourself when you hear it. It's like *so* obvious.'

'You're killing me, Seamus Keneally!'

'We could find a bar that does late opening and get drunk.'

Christina looked at him in mock horror. 'That's not quite what I had in mind but go on.'

'Right, option two: I know a sushi place that stays open till late. I think they're trying to capitalise on late-night karaoke fans.'

'Really? Do you even like sushi?'

'No, but that's not important. We could go there, eat our fill of rice and raw fish, and then hit the local karaoke joint. I do a *mean* version of Bon Jovi's "Livin' On a Prayer" that has to be seen to be believed. Well, *heard* I suppose would be more accurate.'

Christina laughed. 'I'm almost tempted by that option,' she said, 'just to hear you butcher a rock classic!'

'Excuse me! I do a very accurate rendition! I'm offended.'

'Are those your ideas then?'

'I've one more.'

'Lay it on me.'

'Well if sushi isn't your thing, there's a cinema in Ballsbridge that shows a triple bill of Universal monster movies every weekend. I reckon that would bring us through until about six in the morning. After which I know a diner that does really, really good waffles.'

Christina shook her head in wonderment. 'Well, Seamus, you have it all worked out, don't you?'

'Yes, ma'am, I certainly do.'

'Can I counter by suggesting something you appear to have overlooked?'

'I'm open to suggestion.'

'Why don't we meet somewhere *really* nice for dinner, because I want an excuse to get dressed up really nice and put on some expensive perfume I've only just bought, and then you can take me back to my place. And perhaps you could come in for some... coffee?'

'Christina, you're on to a winner there, because I do really like coffee.'

And she leaned in and said: 'And drinking it so late, we'll not be able to sleep. So you'll have to think up something interesting for us to do instead.'

And the kiss that followed told him that the possibilities had just become infinite.

52

'You won't find him,' Aldridge said.

He seemed much smaller outside the safe haven of his mansion and its rambling grounds. The expensive tweed suit he was wearing was expertly tailored and somehow managed to hide a lot of his bulk.

'Your son, in his youth, tried to help people affected by poverty. By famine. It seems he was a good person. What went wrong? How did he become what he is now?' Seamus asked.

'He saw bad things,' Aldridge said. 'He went out to do good but found only horror.'

'I need to find him, Mr Aldridge. Bring him in before he hurts someone else.'

'You won't find him, Detective. I wish I could be of more help, but I'm afraid I can't. He will not break cover unless it suits him to do so.'

'Not good enough. He's killed – or ordered the deaths of – four people we know about for certain and probably lots more. He would have left that little girl to die to aid his own escape. He *has* to be stopped.'

'You're dealing with a man who's worked all over the world.

He can disappear in a city just as easily as he could in the mountains or the desert. He probably has a network of associates he's known of all nationalities he can turn to for support as well. I know the names of one or two of his former friends, people he's mentioned, but I don't know them all. How could I?'

'Help us,' Seamus said. 'Your son is a murderer. We can't just throw up our hands and let him go.'

'I don't expect you to. I have no doubt that a lot of time and resources will be spent trying to track him down. You'll all be able to say you did your best, and you'll rest a bit easier at night, and he'll still be just as missing.'

'Can you give me anything at all?' Seamus asked. 'There must be something you remember. Something to help me know how he ticks.'

Aldridge shook his head. 'I don't see how it will help.'

'Anything you can tell me will be better than nothing. It could give us the break we need. While he's at large, Rosie Blake's mother will never be able to rest easy.'

'Okay. This might be of some small use. Charles was captured by insurgents in the mountains in Afghanistan in 1999.'

'He was taken prisoner?'

'Yes. It happened a lot in those days: aid workers or foreign nationals being taken by terrorist organisations. Some were held for ransom or to raise political awareness. My son was taken because he was associating with men who had a reputation for... for cruelty.'

'Tell me what happened,' Seamus said.

'By the mid-1990s, the Mujahideen had split into several dozen splinter groups. Foreign powers, particularly the Russians, had committed so many atrocities right across the country – it was basically an attempt at genocide – that there were young men and women queuing up to join the various factions. Rape and mutilation, particularly of women and children, was a widespread tactic. In a place like that, there are many things a bad person could do if they had a mind to, and no one would ever know. Evil deeds could just be written off as acts of war.

'From what I can gather, my son's friend, Illya Semenovich, was a man like this. He took advantage of the environment he was in to perform his own atrocities. He posed as an aid worker, but he was quite the opposite. He was only there to do harm. Which made him and anyone he associated with prime targets. Charles and Semenovich were taken within days of each other. They probably thought Charles was like him – one of those sick people who travel to poor parts of the world to exploit the people and do awful things. Maybe they were right about that, in their way.'

Aldridge paused, seeming to shrink even lower in the uncomfortable metal chair.

'I wonder now if his propensity for violence might have already been starting to surface, even then. When he returned he became... he fully became Cain. But I suspect that personality was forged in Afghanistan. He may have engaged in some atrocities with Semenovich.'

'Did you know he was missing? That he'd been taken?'

'Yes. I was informed. I assumed he was dead. He was gone for almost a week, which usually meant a death sentence. But... he came back. Sort of.'

'You think he was tortured?'

'They probably intended to kill him, but it seems they wanted to take their time over it. He was held for about five days. I can't begin to imagine what his treatment during that time was, and he's never told me. But yes. I know he suffered. There's a part of me that wonders if he deserved it – some of it anyway. But I don't know the details.'

'Sometimes it's better not to know,' Seamus said.

'Indeed. Whatever the case, Charles did not die. His friend, Illya Semenovich, the man who was responsible for him being there, somehow escaped his captors and managed to make his way across more than thirty miles of hostile territory to the township where his team were entrenched. He then led a rescue attempt and got Charles out. But not before descending upon the rebel camp where they were held and butchering every soul in it.'

Aldridge reached into the inside pocket of his suit and took out a photograph.

'Charles was asked to see a psychiatrist when he went back to the States, and I was contacted to give some information about what he was like as a child to see if I might be able to help in his recovery. He was, as I'm sure you can imagine, deeply troubled. They sent me a photograph of the tent where he was held and tortured. The army took some shots of the place when they went in to clean up.'

He passed the photograph over to Seamus.

The image was a black-and-white shot of what looked to be a military-style tent. A chair, leather straps attached to the arms and legs, sat in the middle of the space, a black stain of some kind encrusted onto the seat. Painted on the wall of the tent in what Seamus took to be blood was a single symbol. Seamus no longer knew whether it was a Norse rune or a Semitic letter.

But there it was, in strokes that must have been three feet high:

∩

'Happy hunting,' Aldridge said.

And he would speak of his son no longer.

53

Jessie pulled the MG up outside the Blakes' residence in Clontarf. She had considered ringing ahead to let Shauna know she was coming, but lately the woman had been screening her calls and didn't always answer.

Jessie didn't blame her. She had her daughter back, and it was understandable she would want to try and put the whole thing behind her. So Jessie thought that arriving on spec might be a better idea. She would go in, have a cup of coffee and talk to the woman about helping her to get Rosie to open up about what she'd experienced.

The amount of sedative the child had been given would have kept her in a trance-like, semi-comatose state, but it was likely she'd been taken to locations before going to Tory Island and heard quite a bit of conversation, and that might be useful. She just needed a little help remembering.

Jessie got out of the car and was on her way to the door when her phone buzzed. She took it from her pocket and saw it was a text message from an unknown number.

Remember, Jessie: tread carefully. LOOK BEFORE YOU LEAP. *∩*

She remained where she was on the pathway to the house and reread the message. What was he trying to tell her?

Jessie was about to put the phone away and ring the front doorbell when something stopped her. Instead of going to the front, as she usually did, she scouted around the back and went to the glass patio doors that led into the kitchen.

What she saw when she looked through those glass doors stopped her in her tracks.

And changed everything.

54

Dawn Wilson was in her office in the Phoenix Park, her feet up on her desk, gazing out the window at the courtyard of the Garda complex. She had a mug emblazoned with the insignia of Aquaman in her hands, but the coffee it contained was long since cold.

Outside, the Garda Band were rehearsing, marching up and down the cobbled space, playing a march – 'Belphegor'. The commissioner, who had grown up in the North at the height of what was euphemistically known as the Troubles (it was, in much more accurate terms, a bloody guerrilla war fought along both nationalist and sectarian lines), had very mixed feelings about marching bands. The marching season in the North, when groups and factions from all sides felt it was important to get out on the streets to commemorate various events that had little or no real meaning anymore, and which stirred up animosity and ill-feeling on an annual basis, filled most people of her generation with dread.

She'd had to force herself to like the Garda Band. They were certainly talented musicians. And she had come to love some of the tunes. This one always made her smile – it was jaunty and had a nice swing. She liked 'Blaze Away' too. That one had words to it, something about making a bonfire of your troubles.

She was about to get up and make some fresh coffee when the phone on her desk rang.

'Boss, it's Shauna Blake,' her personal assistant informed her. 'She's pretty upset. And um... I've the CEO of Beaumont on the other line. He's upset too.'

'All right. Ask the CEO to hold and put Mrs Blake on first.'

'Will do.'

Dawn whistled along to 'Belphegor' while she waited.

'Commissioner!'

'Mrs Blake, what can I do for you?'

'Do you know where Jessie Boyle is?'

'I was under the impression she was going to speak to you about doing some work with your daughter to help her recall some of her experiences in captivity. We believe catching the people who held her hostage and murdered your husband is the best way to assure her safety. I hope you weren't offended by the idea. I promise it will be done with sensitivity.'

'I'm not offended by it because your employee was never here. But she *did* go to visit my daughter. Which is why I'm calling.'

Dawn felt a sinking sensation in the pit of her stomach. 'Could you hold for a moment please, Mrs Blake? I actually have a representative from Beaumont on the other line.'

'I would like to—'

Dawn cut her off.

'Bill, sorry for keeping you.'

'Commissioner, we have a problem.'

'What's happened?'

'Rosie Blake is gone again,' the CEO of Beaumont said. 'She's gone and this time Jessie Boyle took her.'

EUGENE DUNLIN

He sat on Garth's chair in the old man's dark office. The place smelled of leather and wood polish and dust. There was a vague scent of his former boss's aftershave too. It was something only an old bloke would wear: Old Spice or something of that nature.

Calhoun was gone. Of course, none of his crew knew that yet. Eugene had wrapped the body in clingfilm and put it in a freezer at the back of the beer cellar, a place he knew no one would ever look, because he'd had to unstack a load of dust and woodlouse-riddled crates to get in there, and he'd put them back when he was done.

He was waiting for the opportune moment to inform his associates there had been a change in leadership. Eugene had plans for Calhoun's empire. Plans for expansion. He just needed a capital investment, and he knew exactly where he could get it.

He'd even set it all up – but then everything had fallen apart. The carefully laid plans he'd set in motion had gone awry, and he was left momentarily stunned – and feeling completely helpless.

One thing his study of business had taught him, though, was that when one is faced with a seemingly impossible situation, the best approach is to try and turn the negative into a positive.

There were plenty of negatives.

His cash cow was gone. He had no allies. In fact, there was no one he could trust but himself. He therefore had no manpower to address the search he needed to find his missing asset.

But he knew there were other parties looking too.

All he needed to do was keep watch on them, and, hopefully, they would lead him to the prize.

And Eugene was nothing if not patient.

55

Dawn tried calling Jessie, but each time it went directly to voicemail.

Dawn's messages became progressively more and more panicked, and by the fifth one she was annoyed.

'For fuck's sake, Jessie, I don't know what you're playing at, but whatever it is, cop yourself on and come in right this minute!'

She hung up and sat staring at the handset.

What had happened? Had Jessie had a breakdown? They'd all been working so hard, and the case had been so stressful, was it possible her usually level-headed friend had simply had enough and gone off the deep end? It didn't seem like the Jessie she'd known for more than two decades, but Dawn was well aware that stress and trauma could change a person.

She sat for an hour, hoping against hope that Jessie would call her back. She didn't want to have to go the official route with this and call in a search team. If that happened, Jessie Boyle's career would be over.

Finally, not knowing what else to do, Dawn picked up her personal mobile phone.

'Seamus, I need to meet you and Terri. Now. There's a café near the O2. A wee small place – just called The Caff. ... Yeah. I'll see you both there in half an hour. And, Seamus – tell no one where you're going, okay?'

She hung up, hoping against hope that she could avert disaster before it overwhelmed them all.

56

They sat at the same table Dawn had sat at with Garth Calhoun two days ago, which felt like a lifetime ago now.

'Jessie has gone rogue,' Dawn said. 'She's taken Rosie and done a runner. Now, I don't know why, and I don't know where, but I've been thinking and thinking about this, and there's just no way she would do something like this for no reason. She has to be trying to tell us something.'

'What's she running from?' Seamus asked. 'Who? Does she think the Reavers are on her trail? Does she believe she can't trust us? I mean, I have to tell you, I'm pissed she's run off and not confided in me or Terri! We're her partners! Like, what the hell, boss?'

'We have to believe she knows what she's doing and this is her only choice,' Terri said. 'I can't be mad at Jessie. I just don't have it in me.'

'Well I do,' Seamus said sharply.

'I seem to remember you going off on a solo run when we were in Kerry,' Terri shot back. 'No one got mad at you. We just did what we had to do to bring you back.'

'That's not the same thing and you know it,' Seamus snapped. 'And I told you where I was going.'

'Lads, I appreciate this is a fraught moment, but I need ye both to shut the fuck up and listen,' Dawn said. 'I do not want to report this to anyone. It is to be kept strictly between us three, and no one else is to even get the slightest whiff that all is not rosy in our garden. Am I clear?'

'Yes, boss.'

'Yes, Commissioner.'

'I think I could get a slightly more enthusiastic response than that.'

'Yes, boss!'

'Yes, Commissioner. We won't utter a word.'

'Good. Now here's the situation. I want her and wee Rosie found, and I want it done fast. No mucking about, no sentimentality, just good, old-school police work. Seamus, this is your forte. You know Jessie Boyle as well as anyone alive. I know the two of you are thick as thieves. So tell me now, if you were her, where would you go to hole up?'

'Her primary concern is going to be Rosie,' Seamus said. 'So it'll be somewhere the child won't be put at any risk, somewhere that'll be accessible.'

'That doesn't narrow it down much.'

'She won't risk Rosie not getting her chemo,' Terri said. 'So she'll have had to get some of that.'

'We already know you can't get it on the street,' Dawn said. 'And she doesn't have access to a hospital supply store. So where would Jessie Boyle get chemotherapy medication?'

They thought about that for a while.

'Can you get it on prescription?' Terri asked.

'Hang on, I'll google,' Seamus said, and seconds later: 'Yes, you can.'

'Who would write her a script for that then?' Dawn asked.

They looked at each other, each thinking the same thing at the same time.

'I know someone who would,' Terri said.

57

Professor Julia Banks initially refused to see them.

'She's in the middle of an autopsy,' the receptionist at Forensic Science Ireland said. 'You'll have to come back later.'

'What's your name, son?' Dawn asked.

'It's Tony, Commissioner.'

'Tony, do you like your job?'

'I do. Very much.'

'I'm going to assume from that that you'd like to keep it?'

'I very much would.'

'Then press that button at your elbow so the door to the prof's inner sanctum opens and we can go in. If you don't, I'm going to come back with the riot squad and we'll smash the fucking thing down, which will cause all kinds of problems and probably end up on the six o'clock news. And, Tony?'

'Yes, Commissioner?'

'*That will all be your fucking fault!*'

Without another word, he pushed the door release button. As he did, he activated an intercom and said into it: 'Prof, they're coming through. I'm really sorry. I tried.'

Julia's voice could be heard responding: 'You did your best,

Tony. I know what the commissioner can be like when her dander is up.'

The prof was, in fact, performing an autopsy when they arrived in her lab, a fact which had little impact on Seamus and Dawn but which caused Terri to stop and put her hand to her mouth and then turn so her back was to the cadaver.

'You might have warned me,' she said.

'Hello, Commissioner Wilson, Detective Keneally and... do you have a title, Terri?'

'Terri will do fine,' the genealogist said, staring at the ceiling for all she was worth.

'How can I help you all this fine day?'

'You know damn fine and well how you can help us,' Dawn said.

'You'll have to pardon me, but I do not.'

'Do you know where she is?'

'To whom are you referring?'

'Where's Jessie Boyle?'

'Why do you think she'd tell me where she's going?'

'Because she may need more medicine,' Seamus jumped in. 'I'm guessing that if she's not back within a week, you'll deliver her the next dosage. Am I right?'

'I am not at liberty to divulge that information.'

'Prof, we want to help her,' Terri said. 'Please help *us* to do that. We're here because we love her.'

The pathologist sighed and put her scalpel down.

'Here's what I'm going to do,' she said, pulling off her surgical gloves and going to a drawer. 'Jessie left me this so I can contact her.' She produced what appeared to be a burner phone. 'Give her a ring and hear what she has to say. She suspected you'd find your way here through deductive reasoning and gave me permission to give you access to this phone if you became extremely belligerent.'

'Well how thoughtful of her,' Seamus said.

'Do you want it or not?'

'Give it to me,' Seamus sighed.

'She warned me you'd be the most annoyed,' Julia said. 'Sensitive sort, aren't you?'

'We're all feeling a bit tender at the moment,' Dawn said. 'Seamus, despite your obvious irritation, would you like to call your partner?'

'Try and stop me,' he replied.

He put the phone to his ear.

'Hello, Seamus.'

'Dawn and Terri are here too.'

'I thought they probably would be.'

'Jessie, I'm really pissed off. How could you run off like this and not tell us where you're going – or why? I thought we were a team.'

'I've got my reasons, Seamus. Surely after everything we've been through together, you believe that.'

'Tell me what they are, and I'll come and join you. We can sort out whatever's going on together.'

'Nothing would please me more. But I can't.'

'The prof knows your location. We could sweat it out of her.'

'Ha! I'd like to see you try!' Julia snorted.

'What are you going to do?' Jessie asked. 'You can lock her up, fire her from her job – she still won't tell. And when this is over, she'll be rehired again because she's the best.'

'You know we don't want to do that. But what choice are you giving us?'

'You've always got a choice. And if you threaten to follow her when she comes to bring Rosie's medication, then you'll be jeopardising the child's health as well as her safety. Seamus, if you're my friend, and I know you are, please leave this alone. Let me do what I need to to protect this little girl, and know that

I'll call you if I need you. For now though, I have to do this alone.'

'What you're asking is very hard.'

'I know. I do know that.'

'I don't know if I can do it.'

'Seamus, if you love me at all, you will.'

He suddenly realised tears were streaming down his cheeks.

'Jessie, it's because I love you that I can't. I won't. Come back in and we'll fight whatever comes together. You, me, Terri and the boss.'

'If I come back, Rosie will be handed back to her mother.'

Seamus paused. 'Yeah... and?'

'And she doesn't deserve to have her, Seamus. I can't tell you why and I can't go into any more detail, but believe me – that woman has no right to this little girl. Now for the love of God, Seamus, I am *begging* you. Please help me. *Please.*'

'All right, Jessie. For you. And for Rosie.'

'Thank you.' And he knew she was weeping too. 'One more thing.'

'What?'

'Promise me you won't let on to Donal Glynn that we've been talking or that Julia knows anything.'

'We worked out that she was in it with you. Don't you think he will too?'

'Just promise.'

'Okay.'

'Bye, Seamus. I don't know when we'll see each other again. But I hope it'll be soon.'

'Bye, Jessie,' he said, but she was already gone.

58

There was nothing to do but go back to work. Terri went to her desk and opened her emails to find a folder of photographs Aldridge had scanned and sent, at Seamus's request. The images had all been painstakingly labelled for her, showing the man now called Cain in a variety of locations with lots of different people. Terri was skimming through them when one caught her eye. She enlarged the image to get a closer look, then picked up her phone and called Aldridge.

'Mr Aldridge, could you help me out with something?'

'If I must.'

'One of the photographs you sent me is of your son with a man you've indicated in your caption is Illya Semenovich.'

'Yes. The two were friends. I've been quite consistent about it.'

'You're sure that's Illya Semenovich in the photo?'

'Second from the left, yes. He's wearing a black scarf around his neck.'

'Yes. Thank you. You've really helped me more than you know.'

When Aldridge hung up, Terri zoomed in on the figure of

Illya Semenovich. There could be no doubt about it – the man in the picture was younger and looked to be carrying an extra stone of muscle and sinew, but he was, unmistakably, Donal Glynn. In the photograph, he had his sleeves rolled up.

And on his right forearm was a tattoo:

 Π

Terri went straight to Dawn and told her what she'd just learned, and showed her the photograph. She listened intently, looked at the image and picked up the phone.

'Fancy that – his number's ringing out,' she said to Terri.

'So where does that leave us?'

'We go the official route. I want to know what the fuck is going on.'

She picked up the phone again and redialled.

'Hi, this is the police commissioner. I want someone picked up and brought in to me here directly. Consider this an all-points bulletin. I'm looking for one Donal Glynn. He's a special investigator with J2, but I want the army kept out of this for the moment. If you see him, I want him brought directly to me. Oh, and will you let everyone know to approach with caution please? He's to be considered armed and dangerous. Thanks, Ian. Keep me posted. I want to be called when he's picked up, no matter what time of the day or night.'

Terri sat opposite, looking distressed.

'It's not impossible he's a former US agent,' she said. 'He wouldn't be the first morally ambiguous person to have been recruited from another military superpower to work for the Americans.'

'I don't like it though,' Dawn said. 'He's too mixed up in it all. I mean, he's a friend of Parsons.'

'So who better to be sent to hunt him down?'

'And the tattoo? This is getting too messed up, Terri. I'm not liking it one bit.'

'Do you think he might actually *be* Uruz? Is that possible?'

'I don't have a clue. I wouldn't rule anything out at this stage.'

'So what do we do?'

'You keep working. I'm going to call the American ambassador's office to see if he'll put me in touch with someone who knows Glynn or can explain who the fuck he actually is.'

'Do you think anyone will do that?'

'Fuck no. I think I'll be stonewalled at every turn.'

'I'm glad you feel so confident,' Terri said. 'Right, I'll go and see what else I can dig up. It'll probably make us even more confused, but I don't know what else to do.'

59

Seamus gazed at the tracker app on his phone. It showed that Jessie's smartphone, which he knew she didn't have, was stationary in what was probably a field off the M50 motorway. Which led him to believe she'd dumped it on her way to wherever she was going. Of course the M50 ran in two directions, north and south, and it adjoined other routes going west, so the possibilities were almost endless.

Shauna Blake had been in, speaking with Dawn earlier that day, and she'd completely ignored Seamus when he'd offered her a greeting. The commissioner told him she'd been 'as happy as one would expect under the circumstances' and was considering suing the Department of Justice, which, the commissioner added, was no more than any of them deserved.

Seamus didn't much care.

He'd been up most of the night going over all the conversations he and Jessie had had over the months they'd worked together, trying to remember if she'd ever said anything that could offer even the slightest clue as to where she might be.

He'd drawn a blank, so now he'd pulled up a map of the

M50 and was slowly scrolling through it, running his eyes over the place names in case any of them rang a bell.

Nothing registered with him, and the map continued off the M50 and across into the Wicklow Mountains. His eyes fell on the trails and hiking paths that zigzagged this mountainous region, and suddenly he came upon something he did remember Jessie talking about once: Mucklagh Bothy.

She'd mentioned it about six months ago.

They'd been following up on a case that proved to be nothing, an alleged sighting of a known serial sex offender who'd been released from prison in the UK on a technicality and was said to be bound for Ireland. They'd only just arrived and had been interviewing the witness – who'd sworn up and down it was the dreaded sex offender – when they'd received a call from Terri informing them that news had just come through on Interpol's website that the predator had been picked up in Brussels.

So they'd been sent on a wild goose chase.

It was a beautiful day though, so they'd decided to make the most of the situation and stopped to have lunch in a nice pub in a little village called Schull, overlooking the ocean.

And it was there that Jessie had regaled him with the story of a recent date she'd been on with a guy from the armed response unit.

'Now don't get me wrong – before I tell you this story, I want to let you know he *is* a nice guy. Just not the guy for me. In fact, I feel a bit sorry for him.'

'I'm fascinated now,' Seamus had said. 'What did you do to the poor guy?'

'I didn't do a damn thing. Listen, here's what happened. I met him at the gym. He was lifting such heavy weights, I was sure he'd do himself an injury. He saw me watching, and I think he mistook my concern for approval, and we got to talking. He turned out to be an okay kind of a chap – I mean probably not the brightest, but I thought he might be fun to hang out with. I'm not really ready to start dating.'

'It's not like you to be drawn to someone who isn't razor sharp,' Seamus had replied. 'You're normally hot for the smarts.'

'He was pretty but also pretty thick, God bless him. He was so into his keep-fit regimen that I thought a good date might involve something physical, so I suggested we do a hike I'd done a couple of years back when I was on a holiday home from London. It was a full-day trek through the Wicklow Mountains which takes you to a newly constructed shelter, where you can spend the night, cook some food and sleep out under the stars if you so wish. The shelters are adaptable – you can have them open or closed, depending on the weather. I thought it might be nice. And he said he'd be well up for it.'

'Why do I suspect this didn't go well?' Seamus had asked, knowing she was building up to something.

'Put it this way,' Jessie had retorted. 'Gym fitness and mountain-trekking fitness are two very different things. It never occurred to me that carrying all that muscle over twenty-five kilometres of rough terrain mightn't be the easiest thing in the world. And it certainly never occurred to me that my date would start to get very red in the face, begin making a rasping sound and finally keel over from heat exhaustion.'

'He didn't!'

'He did. Ten kilometres in. I couldn't carry him home all by myself. I had to call in the Mountain Rescue service. He needed to be helicoptered out.'

'So did you ever get to the bothy?'

'Oh yeah. I said goodbye to him as they winched him up and went on alone. I had a great evening and hiked back to my rental car the next morning.'

'So not a successful date then?'

'Oh, I wouldn't say it was wasted.'

'No?'

'I know to steer clear of that level of muscles in the future.'

Mucklagh Bothy.

Seamus was convinced that was where she'd make for. In January it would almost certainly be deserted – a day's trek from anywhere. Jessie could hide out there comfortably for weeks, months even if necessary.

And he knew his partner was strong and physically fit enough to carry Rosie there on her back if necessary – he reckoned she wouldn't risk hiring a vehicle to make the journey.

Now he just needed to be sure.

And to know she was safe.

60

'You're asking me to hack into Met Eireann's weather satellite so you can get a look, in real time, at the location where you think Jessie and Rosie are hiding out?'

Seamus looked at Terri sheepishly. 'Yes, that's the shape of it.'

'You know that would involve breaking about fifteen different laws and statutes.'

'Like when you hacked into the Department of Defence's top-secret database?'

'Actually, this would probably not be as bad as that.'

'So you'll do it?'

'Of course I will. Give me five minutes and you can give me the coordinates.'

'You're a star, little sis.'

'I know. But then, I've only got one big brother, don't I?'

'One very proud big brother.'

Terri clattered the keys of her laptop, her fingers moving in a blur, the sound of the buttons clacking almost like the roll of a drum. After a few minutes of this and occasional clicks of the mouse she said: 'Okay. I'm in. What are the coordinates?'

'Right. So we've got +52° 54′ 55.08″, -6° 24′ 16.31″, T
074861. Did I read that right?'

'You did. Now as I understand it, it'll take a few moments
for the satellite to move into place so it can train its telescopic
lens on that location, but once it does, we can have a look at the
area and zoom in quite closely.'

'That's great. Even Jessie Boyle can't say I've broken my
promise to her by dropping in by satellite to make sure she and
Rosie are all right.'

'I would say not. Okay. We're almost ready. Here we go.'

The screen went black for a moment and was then filled
with the image of rolling moor and heath. The landscape was
mostly a yellow/green shade, with patches of red and purple,
and Seamus saw that they were looking at a kind of valley set in
a dip between four low peaks. Nestled against the slopes of one
was what looked to be a kind of barn.

'That must be it,' Seamus said. 'Can you zoom in?'

'I can,' Terri said. 'There. How's that?'

At first all they could see was the sloped roof of the structure, but then, as Terri fiddled with the direction of the camera,
a figure walked out from under the shelter of the bothy, and
Seamus let out a whoop. The long, rolling steps and the short
dark hair were unmistakable. It was Jessie Boyle.

'Found you!' Seamus said, high-fiving Terri joyfully.

'No sign of Rosie, but we have to assume she's inside,
bundled up,' the genealogist said.

'Of course she's there,' Seamus agreed. 'Right, let's just have
a quick snoop around to make sure the coast is clear on all sides.
Then all we need to do is continue to do this every day until she
feels safe enough to come home.'

'Yes, no one will notice us commandeering a satellite every
day,' Terri said ruefully.

They spent the next fifteen minutes doing long-range scans
of the region around the bothy, checking all routes and

approaches. They were almost finished when Seamus suddenly stiffened.

'Who's that?' he asked, pointing at a small group slowly making their way across the bleak tundra. There were three of them, and even at a distance, Seamus could see they were clad in drab colours, cut in an old-fashioned manner. And they had what appeared to be an enormous dog with them.

'Let's get a closer look,' Terri said. 'Though I think we both know who it is already.'

She zoomed in, and Seamus swore loudly.

'Cain,' he said. 'And a couple of pals. I see he's got himself a new pet too. How far out are they?'

'They're maybe three kilometres from the car park,' Terri said. 'So a good five or six hours from Jessie.'

'Which gives me time to narrow the gap,' Seamus said.

'How are you going to do that?'

'I'm damned if I know,' Seamus said. 'But I'm open to suggestions.'

PART SIX

THE BATTLE OF MUCKLAGH BOTHY

'Over every mountain there is a path, although it may not be seen from the valley.'

Theodore Roethke

61

Seamus Keneally and Dawn Wilson sped across the rough and uneven terrain of the Wicklow Gap on two camouflage-green quads, Polaris Sportsman models only recently purchased by the Gardai for actions that needed to be taken in mountainous regions.

'I think this fits the bill,' Dawn had said, before informing the detective that she would be joining him. 'If we're taking out the new toys, I'm sure as hell going to be the one playing with them.'

They had taken extra load for their handguns and a shotgun each, as well as several boxes of cartridges, and then loaded the quads into a truck, which Dawn drove to the car park just before the start of the Aughrim to Glenmalure trail. It was late afternoon when they got there, the sky growing darker with every passing minute as sunset approached.

'They've got about three hours on us now,' Seamus said. 'So we're going to have to go like hell.'

'Sure they'll love that,' the commissioner said, stowing her shotgun in a scabbard on the side of the quad and filling her pockets with shells. 'Isn't it hell they're looking for, these bastards?'

'Well let's make sure that's exactly what they get then,' Seamus said and turned the ignition on his quad, roaring away from the truck with Dawn close behind.

They made the trip in an hour, and nowhere along the route did they see a single soul. At one point, Dawn came to a stop atop a bluff and, taking a small pair of binoculars from a compartment on the quad, scanned the horizon.

'Over there,' she said, pointing west.

Seamus took the bins and looked. There, silhouetted against the sky, was what looked for all the world like a wolf.

'I'm guessing that isn't what it appears to be,' Seamus said.

'Well there aren't any wolves running wild in the Wicklow Mountains,' Dawn agreed. 'I think I'd have been told if there were. No, that's Cain's latest protégé. I'd say he didn't have time to get a deerhound, so this is the next best thing. And I'm not going to lie to you, it scares me more than a little.'

'I don't like it all that much myself,' Seamus said. 'But a dog is just a dog. If I have to shoot the damn thing, I will – though I won't like doing it.'

'That thing looks like it'd eat Grandma and come back for seconds,' Dawn said. 'I know you're an animal lover and into nature and all that. If Big Bad over there comes running at you, don't hesitate, are we agreed?'

'I hear you loud and clear, boss.'

'I just wanted to be sure.'

Twenty minutes later, the bothy came into sight, a black square on the horizon.

Seamus prayed his friend and the child she was trying so hard to protect would be okay when they got there.

They were moving down a goat path at a fair clip when something hit Dawn in the centre of the back, knocking her hard into the handlebars and causing the vehicle to swerve and then tip over, sending her tumbling into a bank of heather that scratched her face badly but prevented any broken bones. It was a second and a half before the gunshot itself was heard.

Seamus knew that meant the shooter was a good distance away, using a high-powered rifle.

'Boss, are you okay?'

'I'll live,' Dawn said, trying to suck in a breath. 'I'm just glad we both put on the Kevlar.'

As she spoke, a second round hit the upended quad.

'It got the fuel tank,' Seamus said and hauled the commissioner up as a third shot struck a rock, the spark from the impact causing the dripping petrol to catch fire. Dawn jumped onto the back of the other quad and they raced away just as the burning transport exploded.

'They'll have a bead on us now, so keep moving as erratically as you can,' Dawn shouted in Seamus's ear over the roar of the engine and the wind.

'How's this?' he bellowed back and swerved hard left as they both felt a round whizz past them, ricocheting off a rock face and causing sparks to fly.

'Where are they shooting from?' Seamus asked, navigating a wide zigzag through mounds of rock.

'An outcrop over to the right,' Dawn said. 'I just saw the muzzle flash.'

'I'm going to make a break for it,' Seamus said. 'We need to get to Jessie. That bollix is trying to slow us up, and I don't like it.'

'Go then!' Dawn said. 'Put your foot down.'

Seamus didn't need to be told twice. He revved the quad and exploded forward, and a volley of shots hit the earth where they had just been. Holding on to the detective's shirt with one hand, Dawn drew her handgun and fired in the direction the shots were coming from.

'It won't hit them,' she shouted at Seamus, 'but I defy

anyone not to cower down when they're being shot at, even if you know you're not in range.'

'Good thinking, boss,' Seamus said.

And then they were approaching the bothy and Jessie was standing outside waiting, a rifle held by her side.

'Nice of you to visit,' she said. 'I see you've brought some friends along.'

62

They huddled inside.

It was fully dark now, a gorgeous panoply of stars exploding across the vast sky. Inside the bothy, Jessie lit a fire. Rosie, bundled up in a thick sleeping bag, sat on the behaviourist's knee, seemingly quite content.

'Will we have some soup, Jessie?' she asked.

'We will as soon as I'm sure the bad people are gone away and it's safe again,' Jessie said.

'Is it the bad people who killed Richie and took me away?'

'It is, but we're not going to let that happen again,' Jessie said. 'Are you hungry? Would you eat a biscuit or something?'

'No. I'll wait, thanks.'

'Okay, sweetie. Why don't you read your book while I have a chat with Dawn and Seamus?'

'All right.'

The child took up a copy of *Gangsta Granny* by David Walliams and opened it at a marked page.

'She seems to be doing well,' Seamus said.

'Rosie is an amazing kid,' Jessie agreed.

'Are you ready to tell us what's going on?'

'I think I'd better.'

'Well we're all ears.'

'Keep it down,' Jessie said, dropping her voice to a whisper. 'I don't want Rosie hearing.'

'Why not?'

'Because what I'm about to tell you implicates Shauna Blake in everything.'

63

'Uruz messaged me just as I was approaching Shauna's front door,' Jessie began. 'It was one of those standard messages he loves to send, informing me that I should trust no one and all that jazz. Well, something in my head clicked, and I decided to go round the back of the Blake house rather than the front. I think my logic was that I was worried I was maybe being watched – I'm not really sure anymore. Anyway, I didn't knock or ring the bell – I just went around back. They have these big, glass patio doors that open right onto the kitchen, and up I walk, all prepared to knock and make my presence known, when there, standing only inches away from me on the other side of the glass, locked in a clinch, snogging the faces off each other, were Charles Parsons – Cain – and Shauna Blake.'

'What?' Dawn and Seamus said in unison.

'My thoughts exactly. Suddenly things started to fall into place for me. Now we had a motive for Peter Blake being killed. I think, somehow, Richard Roche suspected she was in league with the Reavers too, and that night when he went to Rodney Lawler's house, it was to tell him he believed her to be unfit, and he wouldn't accept it.'

'So that's why Lawler was killed?' Seamus asked. 'Because Roche told him that the Blakes were linked to the Reavers?'

'Yes.'

'Why did he agree to use Montpelier as a drop-off point when she suggested it then? Surely he knew he was walking into a trap.'

'At that stage, I don't think he expected them to take her. Maybe do some alternative healing or try to induce the family to change her course of medication, but I don't believe he thought the Reavers would take her. And he had arranged for Jamesie to meet him for the handover. I think he went up to Montpelier because Shauna told him to use it as a meeting place, and I'd guess she implied it was safe and he believed her.'

'Which was a mistake,' Dawn said.

'A bad one. She arranged for Cain to intercept him and take Rosie.'

'Do you think she knew Cain would kill Roche?'

'I have no idea,' Jessie said. 'If I'm honest, I don't think she'd have cared either way.'

'I can accept she's having a fling with Cain,' Dawn said, 'but why does she want the Reavers to have her daughter? That just seems too fucked up.'

'I've been thinking about that,' Jessie said. 'I can't believe she wants her harmed. Can she believe they've got some kind of mystical cure? That by giving herself and her child to them she's saving the kid's life?'

'Parents will grasp at any straw if their child is ill,' Seamus said. 'I suppose it makes a twisted kind of sense.'

'Richard Roche had quite a bit of medical training,' Jessie said. 'He loved Rosie, and he knew her best chance was to continue with her treatment. The medication was – *is* – working, and there's every hope they'll be able to operate in a year or two. But there's still a chance it might not work, and she'll not make it. I think that worry, the dread of that was too much for Shauna. So she went to Cain.'

'How'd she find him?' Dawn asked.

'Shauna is hugely into alternative lifestyles and New Age faiths. It stands to reason she could have encountered the Reavers on one of those websites or forums.'

'We've got company,' Dawn said as a light appeared in the darkness outside, followed by another and another.

They seemed to be bobbing and weaving, swinging and swaying, almost as if they were alive.

This was what Dave Gibb saw that night.

The lights drew closer, and as they did, the three watchers in the bothy could see they were lanterns attached to long posts by what looked to be bungee cord, carried by the three figures outside, causing the lights to create intricate patterns in the darkness. As the Reavers came near, Jessie realised they were singing.

It was an awful, guttural sound. The behaviourist had heard throat singing once, that odd, droning chant performed by Tibetan monks, but throat singing had a musicality to it, a certain rhythm and structure. This was discordant, cacophonous and disturbing.

'Make them stop,' Rosie said from behind them, covering her ears.

Jessie went to her and wrapped her arms around the child, whispering in her ear: 'Don't listen to them. You just listen to me, okay? I'm here and I've got you, and we are not going to allow any of the bad people in. I promise you, Rosie.'

Suddenly the singing did stop. There was a long, breathy moment of silence, before Cain's booming voice was heard: 'We've come for the child. Send her out and we will withdraw and leave you with your lives.'

Dawn shook her head in disbelief. 'These lads don't give up, do they?' she said to Seamus.

Then she called out: 'Cain, or Parsons or whatever the fuck you're calling yourself today, have you forgotten the last time we met? I drew first blood then and I surely will again. Now I'm giving *you* and *your people* to the count of five and then I'm coming out and I will not be responsible for what will go down. I've been in a *very* bad mood these past few days, and it's mostly been because of the pain in my fucking *arse* you and your pals have caused me. Believe me, Mr Cain, that I welcome the opportunity to take some of my annoyance out on you.'

This speech was met with silence.

'Right, I'm beginning my count,' Dawn shouted. 'One! Two! Three! You had better not still be there! Four!'

'Commissioner Wilson,' Cain called out. 'There is someone else here I would like you to meet. Take a look and see.'

Dawn and Seamus looked out the window.

There, standing in the light of the torches, was Cain. The wolf-like dog was beside him, its fur grey and luxuriant, its eyes flashing amber in the night. Pressed against Cain, who had his arm around her neck and a knife pressed against her cheek, was Shauna Blake.

'Send out the child or I will cut her throat,' Cain said.

'Fuck off,' Dawn called back. 'We know you two are an item. Don't treat us like fools.'

'Very well, have it your own way,' Cain said and, in a single sweeping motion, cut a deep gash into the woman's cheek, causing her to wail and thrash against him.

He held her firmly and pressed the knife to her other cheek.

'That will leave a scar,' he said. 'The next cut will remove a part of her which she will sorely miss. Now send out the child.'

'Rosie, it's Mammy!' the woman called out, and in the bothy Rosie sat up.

'Is that my mam out there?'

'It's okay, Rosie,' Jessie said. 'I'm going to go out there and have a talk with them, make them leave her alone.'

'You'll do no such thing,' Dawn said.

'I'm not going to sit in here while he cuts her to shreds,' Jessie hissed.

'Okay, well then you do this my way,' Dawn said.

'What's your way?' Jessie asked.

And Dawn told her.

When the commissioner finished, Jessie pushed open the door of the bothy and stepped out, her hands held aloft.

'Can we call a truce please?' she asked. 'There is a very frightened little girl in there, and I think she's been put through enough, don't you?'

'You don't know what's best for my daughter!' Shauna screamed, one side of her face a red mask. 'I know what she needs. Send her out here so I can have her healed!'

'You come back with me to Beaumont,' Jessie said. 'And you can even bring Cain with you, and he and the doctors can discuss her treatment, and who knows? Maybe they'll even reach some kind of agreement. Who says it all has to be one way? Cain's cure and the chemotherapy might work better alongside one another.'

'I'm growing tired of this,' Cain said. 'Give me the child or I'll gut her mother in front of her!'

'It doesn't sound like you're in the healing business,' Jessie said calmly. 'What do you really want her for?'

'She's the final piece of the dark trinity,' Cain said. 'Two parts were completed: I bled myself into the earth of Montpelier. We took a man's life – Richard Roche. Now we must sacrifice a virgin child. The cycle will be complete.'

A look of horror spread across Shauna's face.

'The sacrifice wasn't supposed to mean killing her,' she said, her voice trembling. 'You said you needed her blood, but I didn't think... I *never* thought you wanted to...'

'You're not a well man, Mr Cain,' Jessie said, and then two shots rang out in the darkness and the young man to his left and the woman to his right dropped, both shot neatly through the forehead, their lamps falling to the ground and shattering, the oil lighting small fires that burned with a blue flame.

The dog, clearly gun shy, let out a startled yelp and disappeared into the darkness.

'That's my friend Dawn on the roof of the bothy,' Jessie said. 'She's a crack shot, and her weapon is trained on you. Let Shauna go, and you might still survive this night.'

'You don't know what you're doing!' Cain growled. 'This is an event that has been in preparation for two hundred years!'

'I'm going to ask you one more time to let Mrs Blake go, and then I'm going to ask my friend to shoot you in the head,' Jessie said wearily.

Cain raised both his hands, and Shauna staggered away from him.

'Good choice,' Jessie said.

The door to the bothy opened, and Rosie came running out, her arms outstretched to greet her mother, when suddenly a shot rang from the darkness, and Shauna Blake dropped where she stood. Rosie screamed, and Jessie gasped in confusion, looking up at Dawn, who shook her head in complete bewilderment. That was when Eugene Dunlin – laughing as if at a wonderful joke – came strolling out of the night, carrying a rifle.

'Well I bet none of you expected to see me,' the young gangster said.

'I don't know who you are,' Jessie said, and with a vicious lunge, he struck her with the butt of the gun on the forehead, knocking her flat.

She fell beside Shauna, who she saw was alive and conscious, if in shock from a wound to her shoulder.

Dawn raised her weapon, but Eugene had his rifle trained on Rosie.

'My finger is on the trigger here, Commissioner, and if you hit me, the shock will cause me to fire and blow her head clean off. Do you want that on your conscience?'

'I've got him in my sights too,' Seamus called from the house.

'Keep him in them,' Dawn called down. 'What exactly *do* you want, Eugene?'

Jessie was still on the ground, shaking her head, trying to get her bearings.

'I want what everyone else here seems to want: Rosie Blake.'

'Cain there got the ransom,' Dawn said. 'Take it up with

him. You can't get blood out of a stone – Peter Blake is dead and Shauna doesn't have any more savings to give.'

'I don't want a fuckin' ransom,' Eugene sneered. 'I've gone one better – I've got a buyer for her. A very nice gentleman has offered me a tidy sum. I need the cash to get meself set up in business now that Garth Calhoun met an untimely end.'

'What happened to Garth?' Dawn asked, a note Jessie had never heard before in her voice.

'Someone went and shot him,' Eugene said. 'Which leaves a very convenient hole in the company, which I intend to fill. I just need a bit of a capital injection, and this little girl is going to get it for me. She fits a profile my buyer is very attached to and is quite hard to come by, so only she will do. Now kindly hand her over and I'll be on my way.'

'You might walk away from here,' Dawn said through gritted teeth, 'but I give you my word on this: I will hunt you down and I will see you spend the remainder of your days in a jail cell if it's the last thing I do.'

'Promises, promises,' he said. 'Now come on, Rosie. It's time to go.'

Rosie looked at Jessie, who was preparing to spring at the young man, when, with a roar, Cain launched himself at the gangster. Eugene spun and shot the Reaver twice in the gut, but Cain kept coming, wrapping his arms about the smaller man and hauling him to the ground. With a snarl, the dog suddenly launched itself from the darkness too and came to Cain's aid, catching Eugene by the throat and shaking him. The young man wailed, but the sound was cut off in a strangled gasp.

Seamus, gun in hand, walked out of the bothy, and with a look of horror on his face, trained his gun on the animal and shot it through the shoulder, hitting its heart and killing it instantly. It sagged and went over.

'Poor feckin' beast,' Seamus said, the pain of what he'd just had to do clear in his voice.

The detective prised the dead animal's jaws off Eugene, but it was too late: his neck was broken and there was no pulse. Seamus looked at the others and shook his head. Jessie checked Cain's carotid artery. It was still.

'He's dead too,' she said.

From where she sat on the roof, Dawn said: 'I reckon that's over then.'

Jessie went to Rosie, who was standing in the darkness gazing at her mother with a confused expression, and held the child closely.

EPILOGUE

'We are all born mad. Some remain so.'

Samuel Beckett

Rosie Blake was placed with a foster family, and Jessie visited most days. She and the child had bonded deeply during their time together, and while the behaviourist knew she couldn't foster her herself, she was determined to play as large a part in the child's life as she could.

Professor Cuddihy told Jessie he was hopeful he would be able to schedule an operation to resect the tumour within the next eighteen months. So while Rosie was destined to be in and out of hospital for another year and a half, there was a definite light at the end of the tunnel.

'Shauna Blake continues to protest her innocence about playing any part in her husband's death,' Dawn told Jessie, Seamus and Terri at a debriefing meeting later that week, 'but she's currently doing that from a cell in the women's wing of

Mountjoy Prison. And I doubt she'll be seeing the outside world for some time to come.'

'It'll give her space to think about the impact of her actions,' Jessie said. 'A lot of people are dead. I can't work out how many are directly because of what she did and how much of this was being manipulated by Cain and how much of it was Eugene making his power play...'

'It's a mess,' Dawn said.

'Is the Calhoun gang still active?' Seamus asked.

'They've gone to ground,' Dawn said. 'It's not unusual when there's been a blow-up like this. The Crossed Guns is boarded up, and I haven't been able to get hold of AJ or any of the other known members of their crew. The organised crime lads are on it, but I have a feeling nothing will be heard from them until they're good and ready.'

'You and Garth,' Seamus said, looking at Dawn with eyes that invited her to share if she wanted to.

'Were old adversaries,' Dawn said sadly. 'Let's leave it at that.'

'Right, boss, of course,' Seamus agreed.

'And the Reavers,' Terri said. 'Can we be sure they're gone from Ireland at least?'

'With Semenovich still missing, I don't think we can be sure of anything,' Dawn said. 'Except of course that the man we thought was an intelligence officer was not, in fact, Donal Glynn. He'd just assumed his identity.'

'Was he ever employed by the NSA?' Jessie asked.

'A man called Donal Glynn definitely was,' Dawn said. 'But his body was found in a dumpster in Chicago three days ago.'

'Semenovich killed him and stepped into his place,' Seamus said. 'He looked enough like him to get away with it, and as he was due to come to Ireland, he wasn't going to be meeting any officers who'd known him. No one really looks at the photos on

ID cards. They're usually not a good likeness, so he was able to pass himself off as Glynn without too much difficulty.'

'They must have done checks though,' Jessie said. 'This is the intelligence service after all.'

'Don't even get me started on that,' Dawn said. 'It looks like Semenovich managed to learn enough about Glynn's career to pull it off. I mean, Terri isn't the only hacker on the planet. And it's possible he kept journals or something in his house. The US side of things haven't been very forthcoming.'

'Surprise, surprise,' Terri said without much humour.

'Every Garda in the country is looking for Semenovich,' Dawn said. 'If he's still here, we'll find him.'

'There's no way he can get out, is there?' Jessie asked. 'I mean, the airports and the ports will have him red-flagged.'

'Everything we know about him tells us this man is incredibly resourceful and very, very dangerous,' Dawn said. 'So I'm not going to assume we've got him cornered just yet.'

'Is he Uruz?' asked Seamus.

'I have no idea,' Dawn said. 'Jessie?'

'Terri has the answer to that question,' the behaviourist said.

'Semenovich can't be Uruz,' Terri said. 'The only case we know Uruz was personally involved in was the one during which Jessie encountered him in London, but I've been able to place Semenovich in Beirut at that time. He was working for an NGO there. So we can say for certain he's not Uruz.'

'But he *is* working for him,' Jessie said. 'And has close affiliations. The tattoo, leaving the rune on the side of the prison van, the links to the Reavers – I'm guessing he's one of the network of killers Uruz has alluded to before.'

'His community of psychopaths,' Dawn said.

'I hate that idea,' Seamus said. 'That there's a group of them out there plotting and working together.'

'Me too,' Jessie said. 'But I think it's the truth.'

'There's no more to say here,' Dawn said. 'Take the rest of the day off and we'll talk tomorrow.

———

Seamus knew Christina was finished school for the day and got the bus to her house in a small housing estate in Ranelagh. He knew as soon as he opened the gate and began to walk up the short front drive that something was wrong: the front door was ajar, and Christina, who took security consciousness to the point of paranoia (Seamus had quoted statistics about break-ins in her area, which were quite low, to no avail) never left the door open and unattended.

He moved silently into the hallway but hadn't taken more than three steps when a voice from the living room called: 'Detective Keneally! Come and join us.'

He recognised the speaker immediately. It was Semenovich.

In the living room, he found the man the Irish police force were hunting sitting on the couch, with Christina on one side and Steffie on the other. He had a gun in his right hand, and in his left, the little girl's arm. Christina was very pale and was breathing rapidly. She looked at him with an imploring gaze.

'I'm taking the child,' he said. 'You thought you'd stopped us, but you didn't. Nothing can stop us.'

Seamus shifted position, moving his feet so he was comfortable and his weight was well balanced.

'Let them go right now,' he said. 'I'm giving you one chance. No countdowns or any of that silliness. One opportunity to live.'

He knew that somewhere, deep down inside, he was terrified. But he pushed the feeling away and concentrated on his breathing, and on the faces of the two people he cared for, people whose lives were now in his hands.

'He's coming for you,' Semenovich said. 'Uruz is coming for you and he will be here soon.'

The man made to stand, pulling Steffie, who seemed to be in a catatonic state from sheer terror, with him. Seamus, in a movement that would have looked slow and easy to an observer but was somehow too fast for his opponent to counter, drew his gun and shot Semenovich once in the forehead and three times in the chest. He fell back, releasing the child, who remained standing exactly where she was. Christina, with a wail of anguish, grabbed the little girl and held her.

Seamus, feeling a sense of other-worldliness, as if he was no longer really present, walked over and crouched down beside the fallen figure. There was no pulse.

He came around the side of the couch and went to sit beside the woman he thought he loved, but she pushed him away.

'Christina, I need to call this in,' he said with far more calm than he felt, 'and I need you and Steffie to stay right where you are. I know it's upsetting, but this is a crime scene now.'

'He told me he was here because of you!' Christina said through gritted teeth. 'To send you a message!'

'I'm sorry, love,' he said. 'I wish this hadn't happened.'

'I don't want you near me right now,' she said, and he nodded.

Straightening up, he went to the front door and sat on the step, where he pressed number one on his speed dial.

'Jessie, I'm at Christina's. I need you to come over here. Right away.'

She listened while he told her what had happened, told him to sit tight and that she'd take care of it, and then hung up.

He sat on the doorstep, and as he did, his phone buzzed. He thought it might be Jessie again, but it was a number he didn't know.

Consider this a gift from me to you. Now you and Jessie share a bond, an experience no one else would understand – she had a loved one killed, and you have killed for a loved one. Either way, you both loved and lost. I hope one day you and I can discuss how that feels in person. Until then, ttfn. Π

Seamus, a chasm opening inside him, remained sitting there, even after the patrol cars arrived.

A LETTER FROM S.A. DUNPHY

Dear reader,

I want to say a huge thank you for choosing to read *Her Child's Cry*. If you did enjoy it and want to keep up to date with my latest releases and all other news, just sign up at the following link. Your email address will never be shared and you can unsubscribe at any time.

www.bookouture.com/s-a-dunphy

I hope you loved *Her Child's Cry*, and if you did I would be extremely grateful if you could write a review. I'd love to hear what you think, and it makes such a difference helping new readers to discover one of my books for the first time.

I love hearing from my readers. I wouldn't be able to do what I do without you. If you'd like to, you can get in touch on my Facebook page, through Twitter, Instagram or through my website. I'm pretty active on social media, and value each and every interaction with my readers.

So thanks again, and I look forward to sharing more stories with you very soon.

Very best,

Shane (S.A. Dunphy)

KEEP IN TOUCH WITH S.A. DUNPHY

https://shanedunphyauthor.org

 facebook.com/shanewritesbooks

twitter.com/dunphyshane1

instagram.com/shanewritesbooks

ACKNOWLEDGEMENTS AND SOME COMMENTS FROM THE AUTHOR

This book would not have been possible without the help and support of a number of people.

I want to thank everyone at my amazing publisher, Bookouture, who as always made the experience of writing a novel as easy and collaborative as it could be. Sarah, Susannah, Rhianna and everyone else at this incredible, bookish place have helped to bring Jessie, Seamus, Dawn and the others to life. I am grateful to each of them.

I want to particularly mention Therese Keating, who has been my editor for these first three books in the Boyle and Keneally series but has now moved on to other adventures in publishing. I have rarely worked with someone more in tune with the genre, with such an acute sense of pacing or who possesses a finer ability to craft a story. Therese is also one of the wittiest and kindest editors I've ever encountered.

I vividly remember sending her the first draft of *Lost Graves*, book two in the series. She spent a good five minutes telling me how much she loved it, highlighting sections she particularly admired and pointing out sections she thought were well written.

'I'm so pleased you like it!' I gushed. 'That means a lot to me.'

'Brilliant,' Therese retorted. 'Now we can tear it to pieces and put it all back together again in the editing process!'

And we both laughed long and hard. Because that is exactly what we did, but it was okay, because the process began with a mutual love of the material. I knew Therese loved the characters and their world, and more importantly, she understood them.

Thanks so much, Therese. I really do hope we get to work together again.

My literary agent, Ivan Mulcahy, is a true friend and a huge support to me on both a personal and professional level. He has faith in me in ways I sometimes struggle to have for myself. Thanks, Ivan.

I want to thank two very special people who stepped in in the very early stage of this book and changed one important facet of its story: that of Rosie Blake.

Nola Clarke, my dear friend Emily's daughter, gave me the details of the types of things a nine-year-old would like and enjoy one afternoon in the late summer of 2021 (all the details of Rosie's favourite TV shows, books, games and sweets come from Nola). My daughter Marnie (who at twenty-three is a little out of touch with such things, which is why I turned to Nola in the first place), happened to be walking past as Nola and I were chatting over the phone, and asked me about the plot of book three. I explained to her that it involved the abduction of a little boy (yes, in the first draft, Rosie was male).

And, far more astute than her dad, Marnie suggested Rosie should be a girl – I'd had Nola on speakerphone so I could type her comments and ideas as she spoke, and Marnie commented on how full of fun and articulate she was, and how that energy would be great in the book.

So I went back to Nola, and she gave Rosie her name: Arizona Rose was Nola's suggestion. And it fit perfectly.

Rosie was born.

And once she took to the page, there really was no stopping her.

The Hellfire Club is a real place, sitting just as I describe atop Montpelier Hill, a short drive from Dublin city. I cannot recommend a visit highly enough. It's an easy hike from the car park, and on a sunny day, it offers an incredible, panoramic view of Dublin city and its environs. Of course, it's also the site of some very macabre activity, but one doesn't worry about such things when the sun is shining.

If you go there at night though... well, that's a different story.

If you'd like to learn more about the Hellfire Club, might I suggest you visit the Abarta Heritage website: www. abartaheritage.ie/hellfire-club. You'll find lots of information about the club, its members, Montpelier and the times which spawned such a nefarious organisation. The Reavers, however, are a group of my own creation. During my research I found that there are rumours that the Hellfire Club may have reformed, but to all indications they are quite harmless and more a kind of costumed recreationist group than a bunch of decadent devil worshippers determined to bring about a new world order. I didn't want to reflect badly on the modern version of the club so created the Reavers to fill the gap.

I think they work quite well, don't you?

Mucklagh Bothy is also a very real place. I visited it one windy afternoon during the writing of this book, as part of a birdwatching expedition, and was struck by the wildness of the location, and the sense of isolation it engendered in me. As I sat in its shelter, eating my sandwiches, I knew I had to bring Jessie and her friends there. And before long, I was choreographing the action in my head.

If you want to find the coordinates for this bothy, and others in the Wicklow Mountains – the ones Terri uses to direct the satellite to view the site are the real ones – you can learn more at:

http://microadventureireland.com/in-dex.php/2017/03/03/ireland-bothy-the-adirondack-shelters

Another real place that makes its way into *Her Child's Cry* is Tory Island. This beautiful, windswept community seemed the ideal location to send poor Terri into peril (I do put her through the wringer at times, I know), and I liked the fact the island is one of the locations the Celtic demon Balor is rumoured to have used as a stronghold – Terri of course had her own dealings with Balor in *Bring Her Home*, book one of the series, so I knew she'd already be a little on edge going there. I very much want these books to present a character arc for Terri. As each story concludes, we see that this amazing young woman is far tougher than she ever could have known and is incredibly resilient.

And of course, it gave Dawn and Jessie the opportunity to take a helicopter ride.

If you'd like to know more about Tory Island, this website is well worth a look: http://www.oileanthorai.com.

Finally, I'd like to thank you, dear reader. Without you, this series would not be the success it has been, and I hope will continue to be. Jessie, Seamus, Terri and Dawn have lots more adventures awaiting them. Uruz, as you can see, is escalating his activities and seems to have his sights set on Seamus now. Who knows what horrors he has planned for the future?

I promise that whatever happens, I'll bring the stories to you.

I can't wait to share them, in fact.